LOVE . . .

"DEATH OF A ~~ROMANCE WRITER~~"
by Joan Hess

The heroine of a bodice ripper decides to give a novel ending to a familiar tale ... and it's a real killer.

"A MAN AROUND THE HOUSE"
by Nancy Pickard

Even O. Henry couldn't have a more ironic ending than this short story of a jealous husband and one anonymous phone call too many.

"KILLING HOWARD"
by Ralph McInerny

A jilted suitor has thought up a dozen ways to kill his rival ... but someone else keeps beating him to it.

"BREAKFAST TELEVISION"
by Robert Barnard

What happens when a morning TV show host discovers his pretty wife is watching him on the telly while in bed with someone else? Tune in.

TALES OF OBSESSION

**Mystery Stories of Fatal Attractions
and Deadly Desires
from *Ellery Queen's Mystery
Magazine* and *Alfred Hitchcock's
Mystery Magazine***

TALES OF OBSESSION

Mystery Stories
of Fatal Attractions
and Deadly Desires
from *Ellery Queen's
Mystery Magazine*
and *Alfred Hitchcock
Mystery Magazine*

Edited by Cynthia Manson

A SIGNET BOOK

SIGNET
Published by the Penguin Group
Penguin Books USA Inc., 375 Hudson Street,
New York, New York 10014, U.S.A.
Penguin Books Ltd, 27 Wrights Lane,
London W8 5TZ, England
Penguin Books Australia Ltd, Ringwood,
Victoria, Australia
Penguin Books Canada Ltd, 10 Alcorn Avenue,
Toronto, Ontario, Canada M4V 3B2
Penguin Books (N.Z.) Ltd, 182-190 Wairau Road,
Auckland 10, New Zealand

Penguin Books Ltd, Registered Offices:
Harmondsworth, Middlesex, England

First published by Signet,
an imprint of Dutton Signet,
a division of Penguin Books USA Inc.

First Printing, February, 1994
10 9 8 7 6 5 4 3 2 1

REGISTERED TRADEMARK—MARCA REGISTRADA

Printed in the United States of America

Contents

Introduction

We are living in a society where the phrase "fatal attraction" conjures up a medley of terrifying images. For some it reminds us of the film of that name with Glenn Close and Michael Douglas; for others, it brings to mind the real events on which the film was based. Today's headlines are filled with "fatal attraction" stories. The "fatal attraction" syndrome as demonstrated in our everyday life is exploited as well in books and magazines, television and film. Stories of obsessive love, revenge, and murder are universally spellbinding. It is the essence of many great tragedies and is thus a theme that has intrigued writers for centuries.

To a certain extent one can argue that the very act of loving may cause a person to be slightly obsessive, fixed on the object of desire. The distinction, however, is a kind of desire that dominates one's existence and so blinds him that unnatural behavior results. In many cases relationships are only imagined. For instance, the object of this desire is often unaware that he or she has become the point of fixation, and that can lead to a whole host of frightening situations.

The majority of the authors in this collection explore the dark side of obsession that leads to revenge and ultimately murder. In Nancy Pickard's chilling story "A Man Around the House," for example, a possessive husband is convinced his wife is having an affair and plans to harm her and her supposed lover, only to make a ghastly discovery too late. In Ruth Rendell's "A Glowing Future," we find a jealous woman who seeks vengeance on her lover and his new wife in a unique and perverse way. Betrayal is inevitably linked to obsession

and revenge in two skillfully told tales by Patricia High-
smith and P.D. James. Three stories that will appeal to
the eternal romantic in all of us by Evan Hunter, Cor-
nell Woolrich, and Stanley Ellin, involve a protagonist
in search of a missing love. Finally, obsession is taken
a step further, carried beyond death, in Lawrence
Treat's "The Brothers."

The writers in this collection reveal different perspec-
tives on the nature of obsession. The actions of their
characters are determined by the intensity with which
their obsessive desires dominate their lives. Such obses-
sions will most often lead to heinous acts and impact
the final outcome of the story.

—Cynthia Manson

A Man
Around the House
by Nancy Pickard

"I didn't marry you to be alone," she complained. "If I wanted to be by myself all the time, I could have stayed single."

She tossed a rolled-up pair of black nylon socks at him. Resisting the temptation to throw them back at her, hard, he stuffed them in an empty corner of his suitcase.

"Alone?" He laughed without humor. "Since when were you ever alone, even when you were single? I thought you married me to get some privacy."

In spite of her anger she smiled. If his back had not been turned while he folded a shirt, he would have recognized the smile as one of her most charming—a little self-deprecating, but sexy, like a woman aware of herself.

"You don't mind the competition now that it's over, do you, darling?" she teased, her voice soft. "After all, you won the track meet."

He pressed the blue wash-and-wear shirt down on top of several days' supply of clean underwear, his wrists stiff, the tips of his fingers white.

"Well, I'll tell you, Arlene. It's like breaking the four-minute mile. You never know when somebody else is going to come along and beat your time."

"Oh, for God's sake." Her smile disappeared. "Don't start on me again. I've never given you any more reason for this jealousy and I never will. Besides, that other time I wasn't even married to you yet. You know perfectly well that I wasn't even sure I wanted to be married, and that's why I did it. But I promised to be faithful to you, and I am and I always will be."

She ran slim fingers through her long frosted hair, nervously pulling it back into a ponytail and tugging at it.

"Why don't you get a little less concerned about your silly fantasies," she said hotly, "and a little more concerned about my safety? I got another one of those phone calls while you were gone last week. They just scare me to death, Gene. The police say sometimes thieves call a house to find out if anybody's home before they rob it."

Releasing her hair so it curled over her shoulders, she leaned toward him. "And sometimes they call to find out if the woman is there by herself. I'm frightened when you're gone, darling. I hate to sleep alone."

He looked at her.

"Oh, Gene," she said, blinking back tears.

"I'll call home about eight o'clock," he'd told her, after they'd made up. "Just to tell you how much I love you."

But his first appointment kept him waiting an hour, and that put him behind schedule all day. Then he had to change hotels when the first one didn't hold his reservation. And then his dinner fish was undercooked, so back it went to the restaurant kitchen. By the time he dialed the area code it was nearly midnight.

"Hello?" She sounded sleepy and confused after the third ring. For some reason he didn't answer immediately. And then, suddenly, he knew he wasn't going to say a word. It was a rotten thing to do, but she'd never know it was he; she'd think it was one of those anonymous callers.

"Hello?" More alert this time, she spoke with a tremor in her light voice.

He pictured her on the left side of their bed, her side, her creamy skin pale with fear and sleep. Was she wearing the silky yellow nightgown with the low bodice? She always wore nightgowns when he was away, she'd told him, because she felt less vulnerable in some clothing. Straining to hear over his own breathing, he listened for a telltale slide of bedcovers, a murmur that was not her own.

"Listen, you scum," she said, her voice a shaky rasp. "I'm going to get my husband on the line."

Gene smiled and bowed his head in relief. She was trying to scare the caller by making him think her husband was at home. She really was alone.

From her end of the line a man's voice came at him.

"Who the hell is this?" the man said, and then the phone at his house clicked dead.

In his hotel room in Fort Lauderdale, Gene sat for a long time on the edge of the bed, the receiver in his hand.

He called her the next night, from Miami.

"Yes?" Her voice was mean, abrupt, not the loving tone with which she usually greeted him. "It's you again?"

He listened in agony to the shuffle of sheets and pillows.

"Don't call this house again," the man said. His voice was deep, harsh, almost absurdly masculine.

Only one more night on the road lay between him and home. He decided to call her earlier in the evening,

maybe while she and her lover were eating dinner together. Did they dine on the good china, he wondered,
the Wedgewood with the dainty pattern she had registered for their wedding six months ago? Did she trot
out the brass candlesticks and the incense? Did he stand
behind her at the stove, lifting her hair, kissing the back
of her neck?

"Hello?" Her voice was friendly, open. She wasn't
expecting a call so soon.

He put a hand to his chest, holding his heart in.

"You monster," she screamed. "Why don't you ever
say anything?" He heard her drop the phone and run
across the kitchen. Another receiver lifted, the one in
the bedroom.

"I have called the police," the man said. But Gene
knew he hadn't really; he wouldn't dare.

He parked three houses down the street and waited
for a few moments, sitting in his car, staring at his own
home. She'd switched on all the outside lights. In the
yard the gas light turned the lawn yellow; the front
stoop was bright as noon and the glow that rose over
the house told him the back porch light was also on.

But within, the house was dark, except for the light
on the stove. He let himself in as quietly as possible.
Thank God they didn't have a dog yet, though she'd
wanted one for protection. From the hallway he could
see the calendar she'd taped to the refrigerator door.
Before he'd left, she'd circled the 15th as the date of
his return.

In the dark he checked his digital luminescent watch.
It was two a.m., Thursday the 14th. Quickly he untied
his shoes and placed them neatly against the wall. Had
they heard anything yet? Were they beginning to be
afraid?

Then suddenly he was running, careening against the

walls, holding in front of him like a guiding light the pocket knife his father had given him years ago.

"Arlene," he yelled at the top of his voice. "Darling, I'm home!"

She had the light on by the time he reached their bedroom on the second floor. He wasn't even surprised to see her sitting up in bed, staring at him in terror, with no one at her side.

"Couldn't make it tonight, darling?" Gene purred as he lunged at her. "My poor baby, I know how you hate to sleep alone."

Perhaps because of the fear, perhaps because of the pain, she didn't even call his name. She just died.

He didn't want to use the same knife on himself, not the one his father had given him; he didn't want to stain himself inside the way he was stained outside with her dirty blood. But it wasn't necessary to use the knife, he knew. He walked around to his own side of the bed, pulled open the drawer of the night stand, and removed the gun, the one he'd been promising to teach her to use.

Taking it back to her side of the bed, he shoved her body to the middle and sat down in the blood. He checked the gun to be sure it was loaded. There's only one thing this kind of gun is good for, he could see the editorials saying, and that's to kill people. Right on, he thought, right on.

But he needed to explain to somebody, didn't he? He had to let his family and friends know it wasn't his fault, it was her fault.

He looked around for a pencil and paper, but could only find her notepad, blood splattered on her monogram. He opted for the little tape player, the one she kept by the bed to play music when they made love. A nice irony, he thought.

To record his message, he had to push PLAY and RECORD at the same time, but his hands were slippery. His third finger fell off the RECORD button.

"Who the hell is this?"

The man's voice came at him loud and life-like from the speaker. "Don't call this house again. I have called the police."

With hands that shook as badly as her voice had trembled on the phone, he picked up the little machine. On the cassette tape a blue label bore bold printing: *MAN IN THE HOUSE*, it said, like the informative brochure beside the phone. "Put a stop to anonymous, obscene, or frightening telephone calls. These twenty different messages will convince anyone there's a Man in the House."

He pulled the trigger before he thought to stop the tape. The deep, harsh, almost absurdly masculine voice kept up its warnings to the very end.

A Glowing Future
by Ruth Rendell

"Six should be enough," he said. "We'll say six tea chests, then, and one trunk. If you'll deliver them tomorrow, I'll get the stuff all packed and maybe your people could pick them up Wednesday." He made a note on a bit of paper. "Fine," he said. "Round about lunchtime tomorrow."

She hadn't moved. She was still sitting in the big oak-armed chair at the far end of the room. He made himself look at her and he managed a kind of grin, pretending all was well.

"No trouble," he said. "They're very efficient."

"I couldn't believe," she said, "that you'd really do it. Not until I heard you on the phone. I wouldn't have thought it possible. You'll really pack up those things and send them off to her."

They were going to have to go over it all again. Of course they were. It wouldn't stop until he'd got the things out and himself out, away from London and her for good. And he wasn't going to argue or make long defensive speeches. He lit a cigarette and waited for her to begin, thinking that the pubs would be opening in an hour's time and he could go out then and get a drink.

"I don't understand why you came here at all," she said.

He didn't answer. He was still holding the cigarette

box, and now he closed its lid, feeling the coolness of the onyx on his fingertips.

She had gone white. "Just to get your things? Maurice, did you come back just for *that*?"

"They are my things," he said evenly.

"You could have sent someone else. Even if you'd written to me and asked me to do it—"

"I never write letters," he said.

She moved then. She made a little fluttering movement with her hand in front of her mouth. "As if I didn't know!" She gasped, and making a great effort she steadied her voice. "You were in Australia for a year, a whole year, and you never wrote to me once."

"I phoned."

"Yes, twice. The first time to say you loved me and missed me and were longing to come back to me and would I wait for you, and there wasn't anyone else, was there? And the second time, a week ago, to say you'd be here by Saturday and could I—could I *put you up*. My God, I'd lived with you for two years, we were practically married, and then you phone and ask if I could put you up!"

"Words," he said. "How would you have put it?"

"For one thing, I'd have mentioned Patricia. Oh, yes, I'd have mentioned her. I'd have had the decency, the common humanity, for that. D'you know what I thought when you said you were coming? I ought to know by now how peculiar he is, I thought, how detached, not writing or phoning or anything. But that's Maurice, that's the man I love, and he's coming back to me and we'll get married and I'm so happy!"

"I did tell you about Patricia."

"Not until after you'd made love to me first."

He winced. It had been a mistake, that. Of course he hadn't meant to touch her beyond the requisite greeting kiss. But she was very attractive and he was used to her and she seemed to expect it—and oh, what the hell. Women never could understand about men and sex. And there was only one bed, wasn't there? A hell of a scene there'd have been that first night if he'd suggested sleeping on the sofa in here.

"You made love to me," she said. "You were so passionate, it was just like it used to be, and then the next morning you told me. You'd got a resident's permit to stay in Australia, you'd got a job all fixed up, you'd met a girl you wanted to marry. Just like that you told me, over breakfast. Have you ever been smashed in the face, Maurice? Have you ever had your dreams trodden on?"

"Would you rather I'd waited longer? As for being smashed in the face—" he rubbed his cheekbone "—that's quite a punch you pack."

She shuddered. She got up and began slowly and stiffly to pace the room. "I hardly touched you. I wish I'd killed you!" By a small table she stopped. There was a china figurine on it, a bronze paperknife, an onyx pen jar that matched the ashtray. "All those things," she said. "I looked after them for you. I treasured them. And now you're going to have them all shipped out to her. The things we lived with. I used to look at them and think, Maurice loves that, Maurice liked that placed just here, Maurice bought that when we went to—oh, God, I can't believe it. Sent to *her*!"

He nodded, staring at her. "You can keep the big stuff," he said. "You're specially welcome to the sofa. I've tried sleeping on it for two nights and I never want to see the bloody thing again."

She picked up the china figurine and hurled it at him. It didn't hit him because he ducked and let it smash against the wall, just missing a framed drawing. "Mind the Lowry," he said laconically. "I paid a lot of money for that."

She flung herself onto the sofa and burst into sobs.
She thrashed about, hammering the cushions with her
fist. He wasn't going to be moved by that—he wasn't
going to be moved at all. Once he'd packed those
things, he'd be off to spend the next three months tour-
ing Europe. A free man, free for the sights and the fun
and the girls, for a last fling of wild oats. After that,
back to Patricia and a home and a job and responsibility.
It was a glowing future which this hysterical woman
wasn't going to mess up.

"Shut up, Betsy, for God's sake," he said. He shook
her roughly by the shoulder, and then he went out because it was now eleven and he could get a drink.

Betsy made herself some coffee and washed her swollen eyes. She walked about, looking at the ornaments
and the books, the glasses and vases and lamps, which
he would take from her tomorrow. It wasn't that she
much minded losing them, the things themselves, but
the barrenness which would be left, and the knowing
that they would all be Patricia's.

In the night she had got up, found his wallet, taken
out the photographs of Patricia, and torn them up. But
she remembered the face, pretty and hard and greedy,
and she thought of those bright eyes widening as Patricia unpacked the tea chests, the predatory hands scrab-
bling for more treasures in the trunk. Doing it all
perhaps before Maurice himself got there, arranging the
lamps and the glasses and the ornaments in *their* home
for his delight when at last he came.

He would marry her, of course. I suppose she thinks
he's faithful to her, Betsy thought, the way I once
thought he was faithful to me. I know better now. Poor
stupid fool, she doesn't know what he did the first moment he was alone with her, or what he might get in
France and Italy. That would be a nice wedding present

to give her, wouldn't it, along with all the pretty bric-a-brac in the trunk?

Well, why not? Why not rock their marriage before it had even begun?

A letter. A letter to be concealed in, say, that blue-and-white ginger jar. She sat down to write. Dear Patricia—what a stupid way to begin, the way you had to begin a letter even to your enemy.

*Dear Patricia: I don't know what Maurice has told you about me, but we have been living here as lovers ever since he arrived. To be more explicit, I mean we have made love, have slept together. Maurice is incapable of being faithful to anyone. If you don't believe me, ask yourself why, if he didn't want me, he didn't stay in a hotel. That's all. Yours—*and she signed her name and felt a little better, well enough and steady enough to take a bath and get herself some lunch.

Six tea chests and a trunk arrived on the following day. The chests smelled of tea and had drifts of tea leaves lying in the bottom of them. The trunk was made of silver-colored metal and it had clasps of gold-colored metal. It was rather a beautiful object, five feet long, three feet high, two feet wide, and the lid fitted so securely that it seemed a hermetic sealing.

Maurice began to pack at two o'clock.

He used tissue paper and newspapers. He filled the tea chests with kitchen equipment and cups and plates and cutlery, with books, with those clothes of his he had left behind him a year before.

Studiously, and with a certain grim pleasure, he avoided everything Betsy might have insisted was hers—the poor cheap things, the stainless-steel spoons and forks, the Woolworth pottery, the awful colored sheets, red and orange and olive, that he had always loathed. He and Patricia would always sleep on white sheets.

Betsy didn't help him. She watched, chain-smoking. He nailed the lids on the chests, and on each lid he wrote in white paint his address in Australia. But he didn't paint the letters of his own name. He painted Patricia's. This wasn't done to needle Betsy, but he was glad to see it was needling her.

He hadn't come back to the flat till one that morning, and of course he didn't have a key. Betsy had refused to let him in, had left him down there in the street, and he had to sit in the car he'd hired till seven. She looked as if she hadn't slept either. *Miss Patricia Gordon*, he wrote, painting fast and skillfully.

"Don't forget your ginger jar," said Betsy. "I don't want it."

"That's for the trunk." *Miss Patricia Gordon, 23 Burwood Park Avenue, Kew, Victoria, Australia 3101.* "All the pretty things are going in the trunk. I intend it as a special present for Patricia."

The Lowry came down and was carefully padded and wrapped. He wrapped the onyx ashtray and the pen jar, the alabaster bowl, the bronze paperknife, the tiny Chinese cups, the tall hock glasses. The china figurine, alas . . . He opened the lid of the trunk.

"I hope the Customs open it!" Betsy shouted at him. "I hope they confiscate things and break things! I'll pray every night for it to go to the bottom of the sea before it gets there!"

"The sea," he said, "is a risk I must take. As for the Customs—" He smiled. "Patricia works for them, she's a Customs officer—didn't I tell you? I very much doubt if they'll even glance inside." He wrote a label and pasted it on the side of the trunk. *Miss Patricia Gordon, 23 Burwood Park Avenue, Kew* . . . "And now I'll have to go out and get a padlock. Keys, please. If you try to keep me out this time, I'll call the police. I'm still the legal tenant of this flat, remember."

She gave him the keys. When he had gone she put her letter in the ginger jar. She hoped he would close the trunk at once, but he didn't. He left it open, the lid thrown back, the new padlock dangling from the gold-colored clasp.

"Is there anything to eat?" he said.

"Go and find your own bloody food! Go and find some other woman to feed you!"

He liked her to be angry and fierce; it was her love he feared. He came back at midnight to find the flat in darkness, and he lay down on the sofa with the tea chests standing about him like defenses, like barricades, the white paint showing faintly in the dark. *Miss Patricia Gordon* . . .

Presently Betsy came in. She didn't put on the light. She wound her way between the chests, carrying a candle in a saucer which she set down on the trunk. In the candlelight, wearing a long white nightgown, she looked like a ghost, like some wandering madwoman, a Mrs. Rochester, a Woman in White.

"Maurice."

"Go away, Betsy, I'm tired."

"Maurice, *please*. I'm sorry I said all those things. I'm sorry I locked you out."

"Okay, I'm sorry too. It's a mess, and maybe I shouldn't have done it the way I did. But the best way is for me just to go and my things to go and make a clean split. Right? And now will you please be a good girl and go away and let me get some sleep?"

What happened next he hadn't bargained for. It hadn't crossed his mind. Men don't understand about women and sex. She threw herself on him, clumsily, hungrily. She pulled his shirt open and began kissing his neck and his chest, holding his head, crushing her mouth to his mouth, lying on top of him and gripping his legs with her knees.

He gave her a savage push. He kicked her away, and she fell and struck her head on the side of the trunk. The candle fell off, flared, and died in a pool of wax. In the darkness he cursed floridly. He put on the light and she got up, holding her head where there was a little blood.

"Oh, get out, for God's sake," he said, and he manhandled her out, slamming the door after her . . .

In the morning, when she came into the room, a blue bruise on her forehead, he was asleep, fully clothed, spreadeagled on his back. She shuddered at the sight of him. She began to get breakfast, but she couldn't eat anything. The coffee made her gag and a great nauseous shiver went through her. When she went back to him he was sitting on the sofa, looking at his plane ticket to Paris.

"The men are coming for the stuff at ten," he said as if nothing had happened, "and they'd better not be late. I have to be at the airport at noon."

She shrugged. She had been to the depths and she thought he couldn't hurt her any more.

"You'd better close the trunk," she said absentmindedly.

"All in good time." His eyes gleamed. "I've got a letter to put in yet."

Her head bowed—the place where it was bruised was sore and swollen—she looked loweringly at him. "You never write letters."

"Just a note. One can't send a present without a note to accompany it, can one?" He pulled the ginger jar out of the trunk, screwed up her letter without even glancing at it, and threw it on the floor. Rapidly, yet ostentatiously, and making sure that Betsy could see, he scrawled across a sheet of notepaper: *All this is for you, darling Patricia, forever and ever.*

"How I hate you," she said.

"You could have fooled me." He took a large angle lamp out of the trunk and set it on the floor. He slipped his note into the ginger jar, rewrapped it, tucked the jar in between the towels and cushions padding the fragile objects. "Hatred isn't the word I'd use to describe the way you came after me last night."

She made no answer. Perhaps he should have put a heavy object like that lamp in one of the chests, perhaps he should open up one of the chests now. He turned round for the lamp. It wasn't there. She was holding it in both hands.

"I want that, please."

"Have you ever been smashed in the face, Maurice?" she said breathlessly, and she raised the lamp and struck him with it full on the forehead. He staggered and she struck him again, and again and again like a madwoman, raining blows on his face, his head. He screamed. He sagged, covering his face with bloody hands. Then, with all her strength, she gave him a great swinging blow, and he fell to his knees, rolled over, and at last was stilled and silenced.

There was quite a lot of blood, though it quickly stopped flowing. She stood there looking at him, and she was sobbing. Had she been sobbing all the time? She was covered with blood. She tore off her clothes and dropped them in a heap around her. For a moment she knelt beside him, naked and weeping, rocking backward and forward, speaking his name, biting her fingers that were all sticky with his blood.

But self-preservation is the primal instinct. It is more powerful than love or sorrow, hatred or regret. The time was nine o'clock, and in an hour those men would come. Betsy fetched water in a bucket, detergent, cloths, and sponge. The hard work, the great cleansing, stopped her tears, quieted her heart, and dulled her thoughts. She thought of nothing, working frenziedly, her mind a blank.

When bucket after bucket of reddish water had been poured down the sink, and the carpet was soaked but clean, the lamp washed and dried and polished, she threw her clothes into the hamper in the bathroom and took a bath. She dressed carefully and brushed her hair. Eight minutes to ten. Everything was clean and she had opened the window, but the dead thing still lay there on a pile of reddened newspapers.

"I loved him," she said aloud, and she clenched her fists. "I hated him."

The men were punctual. They came at ten sharp. They carried the six tea chests and the silver-colored trunk with the gold-colored clasps downstairs.

When they had gone and their van had driven away, Betsy sat down on the sofa. She looked at the angle lamp, the onyx pen jar and ashtray, the ginger jar, the alabaster bowls, the hock glasses, the bronze paperknife, the little Chinese cups, and the Lowry that was back on the wall. She was quite calm now, and she didn't really need the brandy she had poured for herself.

Of the past she thought not at all, and the present seemed to exist only as a palpable nothingness, a thick silence that lay around her. She thought of the future, of three months hence, and into the silence she let forth a steady, rather toneless peal of laughter. *Miss Patricia Gordon, 23 Burwood Park Avenue, Kew, Victoria, Australia, 3101.* The pretty, greedy, hard face, the hands so eager to undo the padlock and prize open those golden clasps to find the treasure within . . .

And how interesting that the treasure would be found

in three months time, like nothing Miss Patricia Gordon had seen in all her life! It was as well, so that she would recognize it, that it carried on top of it a note in a familiar hand:

All this is for you, darling Patricia, forever and ever.

Catalyst
by Evan Hunter

In the dream, or in the reality, I was on the roof of the Duomo in Milan. Gingerbread statuary laced the sky—I was surrounded by a forest of intricately carved stone. A girl in a yellow dress was leaning over the parapet, her back to me. And suddenly she lost her balance. I reached out, grabbed for the yellow cotton of her dress, and in a dizzying blur she fell over the edge. The piazza below was tiled in black and white, a geometrically patterned mosaic. The girl's scream shattered the torpid summer stillness as her body struck the tiles with bone-crushing force.

And in the dream, or in the reality, I saw myself racing down the circular stairs from the roof of the cathedral to the piazza below. A crowd was gathering outside and there was the sound of either a siren or another scream. Blurred images passed in miragelike heat; faces were too close to be distinct, voices distorted. An odd buzz hovered on the stifling air. The girl's broken body lay face downward on the black and white tiles. I heard the agonizing rise and fall of the ambulance siren as it came closer, closer.

There was silence now. And into the silence a rasping sound. The dream ended abruptly. I opened my eyes. Yellow drapes were being drawn back—the sound I'd heard was the sound of the pulley. There was blue sky beyond the parting drapes. I could hear the shrieking of gulls, the tumbling of distant surf. There were mullioned terrace doors and a craggy sun-washed landscape. I closed my eyes again. And opened them at once when I realized someone was in the room with Annie and me.

The man was in his late thirties. He was tall and brawny, his hair was black. He was wearing black trousers and a white turtleneck shirt, and he stood beside the drapes, working the pulley, as sunlight splashed wider and wider into the room. I sat up. I was surprised to discover that I was fully clothed—trousers, jacket, shirt, tie, socks, shoes. I was not in a bed, but on a sofa. Annie was not beside me, nor was she anywhere in the room.

Obliviously, the man kept pulling open the drapes, his back to me. The room was Moorish in design, large, with white stuccoed walls and hanging tapestries, colorful tiles and dark extravagant furniture, numerous closed doors, arches and balconies, I realized now that I was in a suite of some sort, but I couldn't remember which hotel I was in, or in what part of Italy. Everywhere in the room, there was evidence of a wild party the night before—whiskey bottles, soiled glasses, plates of leftover food, brimming ashtrays, a woman's satin slipper on one of the coffee tables. The slipper was not Annie's.

The man had turned from the terrace doors. He smiled at me and said, *"Buon giorno, signore,"* and then started around the room, picking up glasses, carrying bottles back to the bar.

"Can't you do that later?" I said, annoyed. There was a sour taste in my mouth, my head was pounding. To one of the closed doors I called "Annie?" and got no answer. The man was still clearing away the debris.

"I don't suppose you've seen my wife," I said.

"Sir?"

"My wife. Has she gone down for breakfast already, would you know that? Where *are* we, anyway?"

"This is the Villa Piontelli, sir."

I got off the sofa, stretched, yawned, and looked up at one of the balconies. "Annie?" I called again, and again got no response. "The Villa Piontelli," I said. "I don't remember checking in."

"It is not a hotel, sir."

"Then what is it?"

"A private residence."

"Really? Whose?"

The man's eyebrows lifted in surprise. "Why, Signor Piontelli's," he said.

"This is his house?"

"His villa, yes."

"Is it on the road to Milan?"

"Milano? No, sir. Milano is a long way to the north."

"Then where are we?"

"This is a private island, sir. Near Sardegna."

"You mean Sardinia."

"*È la stessa cosa.* The same thing, sir."

"My geography may be off, but isn't Sardinia south-west of Rome? Out in the Tyrrhenian?"

"*Sì, signore.*"

"What was that name again?"

"Piontelli. Marco Piontelli. You do not know the name?"

"I do not know the name."

"It is one of the most well-known names in Italy. Signor Piontelli owns Sistemi Italiani, it is the largest producer of—*ma come si dice*?—electronics? They make computing machines. He is the I.B.M. of Italy."

"I thought I.B.M. was the I.B.M. of Italy."

"Ahhh, good morning, Thomas."

The faintly accented voice startled me. I hadn't heard anyone coming into the room, but I turned now to find a man standing just inside the entrance door. He was in his late fifties, suntanned and handsome, with dark hair, graying sideburns, and brown eyes.

"I'm sorry we had to wake you," he said. "I thought it might be pleasant, though, if we all took lunch on the terrace. And since everything is still in such disorder from last night—" A look of sympathetic concern came onto his face. "Are you all right?" he asked. "You were complaining of a headache last night. I was hoping—"

"Last night?" I said.

"Yes, at the party."

"What party?"

"Thomas, let me explain," he said. "You seem not to remember—"

"Tell me," I said. The last time I'd drawn a blank this way had been three years ago, when Annie and I had gone to a midnight party on Montauk, and I'd awakened in Easthampton the next morning without the slightest recollection of how I'd got there. But nowadays I was drinking less; I told myself I was drinking less.

"I am Marco Piontelli," he said. "Surely you remember this, Thomas?"

I stared at him and said nothing. I was no stranger to hangovers, but last night's drinking must have been monumental. I could not remember this man who was addressing me so familiarly, nor could I imagine how I'd awakened on an island in the middle of the Tyrrhenian Sea, when I'd been driving north toward Milan all day yesterday.

Patiently Piontelli said, "We met at Cala di Volpe yesterday afternoon. Cala di Volpe—a hotel in Sardegna. You were sitting on the terrace, the one in the old section of the hotel, where the long wooden dock leads out to the yacht basin. You were alone. And you were drinking."

"Alone?"

"Alone. And you drank at the party last night as well. You drank quite a lot, in fact."

"Where?"

"Here at the villa. We talked a while at Cala di Volpe. I invited you to come back with me on the launch. You accepted."

"And my wife?" I said.

"Your wife?" A quizzical look crossed his face. His eyes shifted to the man who was still cleaning up the room. "Bruno?" he said.

"*Sì signore,*" Bruno replied. "*Mi ha domandato la stessa cosa.*"

"I'm sorry," Piontelli said.

I looked at him. I wasn't alarmed, not yet I wasn't; I was simply confused. Like so many mornings after nights before, I was trying now to pick up the pieces and put them together, without revealing just how vast a gap there'd been. "I assume she's around somewhere," I said.

He was staring at me now. "Why, no," he said. "No, Thomas."

"She's not here?" I said.

"She's dead," he said. "Surely you know this, Thomas. You told me yourself—"

The pain struck as suddenly and as powerfully as a clenched fist. I put my hand to my eyes, covering my eyes, and in that instant—as though fragments of the dream were triggered by the aching needles of pain—I saw behind my closed eyes a stretcher being lifted into an ambulance. A woman's bare arm hung limply over the side of the stretcher and I saw a portion of her yellow dress beneath the blanket covering her.

"Are you all right?" I heard Piontelli ask.

I suddenly lost my balance, and reeled back against the wall, clutching it for support.

"Bruno!" Piontelli shouted. "*Aiutami! Prendi i piedi.*"

They were lifting me. Bruno had my legs, Piontelli was supporting the upper portion of my body. As they struggled to carry me across the room, there appeared behind my tightly closed eyes the image of the girl in the yellow dress being wheeled down a long white corridor, nuns in black walking swiftly by her side. "Annie," I said, "where are they—?" and did not know whether I'd said it aloud or said it in my mind.

They were carrying me up the steps to the balcony. I heard Bruno and Piontelli whispering urgently to each other in Italian, and suddenly there was the vision of an operating table surrounded by men in green gowns and green masks, and the distorted sounds of heavy breathing. One of the surgeons removed his mask. His face was beaded with sweat. Slowly, deliberately, the surgeon shook his head, and I screamed, "No! No, it isn't true, no!"

They dumped me onto the bed. Piontelli looked over his shoulder. I tried to rise, but the pain was excruciating. Standing in the open doorway, I saw a slender man in a white linen suit. The man opened a black bag. A hypodermic needle flashed. Someone was loosening my tie. Bruno was shoving back the sleeve of my shirt. I tried to get off the bed again, but the needle was descending swiftly. The needle punctured my arm and I screamed "Annie!" again, then fell back against the sheets.

"Thomas?"

The voice was Annie's, the voice was a whisper.

"Just a few more steps," she said, *"we're almost there. This way, Thomas, this way."*

The stark white wall opposite the bed seemed to dissolve in a swirl of color, geometric shapes reassembling themselves in sharper focus. I recognized the interior steps of the Duomo in Milan, and heard Annie's voice again, *"Follow me, Thomas, follow me."*

And again, in dream or in reality, I did not know which, I was on the roof in blinding sunlight, and the girl in the yellow dress was moving ahead of me, her back to me, and Annie's voice echoed in clumsy, ungrammatical Italian, *"Come tutta bellissimo. Guardo, Thomas, i belli statue."* Everything went out of focus again, and on the wall or in my mind, in memory or in fantasy, a tall man in yachting cap and jacket approached, seemed to move from out of the wall into the room—though the room was no longer a room, it was instead a terrace overlooking a yacht basin—and the man was Piontelli, and he extended his hand and said, *"Excuse me, sir, but I saw you drinking alone and wondered if I might join you."* And now there was the sound of music, party noises, the laughter of women, the low conversation of men, the tinkling of ice in glasses . . .

The images faded.

I drifted off into sleep.

It was morning again.

I sat on the terrace in brilliant sunshine. The Milan newspaper was on the glass-topped table. The newspaper was three weeks' old. I looked at it again now. The banner read:

Ultima Edizione
LA NOTTE
Corriere Lombardo

The date beneath it was July 26th, the day after Annie and I had left Rome together. The story said that an American tourist named Anne Barnes had fallen from the roof of the Duomo at eleven o'clock that morning.

She had been rushed to Ospedale Fatebenefratelli, where they had tried to save her, but she had died at 1:17 P.M. The newspaper reported that her husband, Thomas Barnes, had made arrangements for her to be buried the following day at Musocco Cemetery.

I had read the article over and again this morning, struggling with the Italian, had heard it translated aloud by Marco Piontelli; the truth was there in black and white as stark as the tiles in the piazza to which she'd fallen. And now I understood, or thought I understood, why I'd been drinking alone at a hotel I could not remember going to, three weeks after an accident I'd tried to forget. And could understand, too, why I'd accepted an invitation from a stranger, and had drunk myself into a stupor at his party that night.

I looked out over the water. A white motor launch was moving closer in to the dock. Bruno and several other servants were watching its approach. Piontelli, a tiny figure from this distance, was coming down the wooden steps, waving at the launch as it maneuvered in. Lines were being thrown ashore now, a gangplank was lowered to the dock.

I watched as a tall slender woman in a summer dress came down the gangplank onto the dock, carrying a flowered parasol to ward off the intense rays of the morning sun. She embraced Piontelli, then arm in arm, seeming like doll figures from where I sat on the terrace, they started up toward the villa, Bruno and the other servants following behind them with luggage.

I sat in the sunshine and stared out at the water.

In a little while—I did not know how long, time no longer seemed relevant—I heard voices in the main room of the villa. Piontelli and the woman were moving toward the terrace now, chattering in rapid Italian as they approached.

"*I Pucci vanno a tutta passata!*" the woman said, and

laughed. *"Un vero assedio! Sai che i prezzi risalgono in autunno, e così tutti li comprono adesso."*

"Thomas," Piontelli said behind me, "I would like you to meet my wife. Francesca."

I turned from the sea. The woman had auburn hair, cut close to the oval of her face; her eyes were blue, her mouth—

"Annie," I whispered.

"Mr. Barnes, how do you do?" she said, and extended her hand.

I was rising from the chair. "Annie," I said again.

"Madonna mia!" Piontelli said in alarm. "He thinks you are his dead wife."

I stared at them across the length of the terrace. The sun was merciless on my head. I could feel the pain starting all over again—I'd thought I was done with the pain last night when I'd learned my wife was dead. But this was Annie standing here beside Piontelli, her long auburn hair clipped short, yes, but the blue eyes unmistakable, the wide mouth, the tilted nose—*my* wife clinging to another man's arm and looking at me as though I were a total stranger.

I hesitated only an instant, gauging the distance to the beach and the dock. Then I took half a dozen long strides to where they were standing, shoved Piontelli aside, breaking her grip on his arm, and seized her wrist.

"Mi lasci!" she screamed. "Are you crazy?" but I would not let go of her wrist. I dragged her down the steps and onto the beach. She kept trying to pull herself free, turning to shout back to the terrace for help. On the dock far ahead I saw Bruno and several other men running toward us on the wooden planking.

I reversed direction abruptly. There was a pebble-strewn path ahead, leading up off the beach at a sharp angle to an overhanging rock ledge. She tried to free herself again as I pulled her up the path, pebbles scattering beneath our feet. She fell and scraped her knee, and I yanked her to her feet again, and we struggled to the top of the ledge. Exhausted, we crouched behind a boulder overlooking the beach.

In the distance I could see Piontelli and Bruno in agitated conversation with two other men. I had still not released her wrist. The fight seemed to have gone out of her, but her blue eyes were angry and ... frightened? Was that fear in her eyes? Was she afraid of *me*, her husband?

"Annie," I said, "I don't know what—"

"I am *not* Annie," she said, and pulled herself free of my grip. "Will you please take me back to my husband?"

"I *am* your husband."

"My husband is Marco Piontelli," she said, "I am Francesca Di Luca Piontelli."

"Listen—"

"I am listening, Mr. Barnes."

"Try to understand—"

"I am trying to understand."

"We came to Italy together—"

"I was *born* in Italy!"

"—at the beginning of July."

"This is pointless."

We fell silent. I kept studying her face. Overhead a gull shrieked.

"Who are you?" I said.

"I have already told you."

"Tell me again."

"Why?"

"Because ... if you're *not* my wife, then she's dead and buried in Milan. And I have to learn if ... if that's true, I ... I can't turn every corner in the world and expect to find her there each time."

We were silent again. She studied my face with genuine sympathy now, and when she spoke again, her voice was gentle. "I am Francesca Di Luca Piontelli," she said.

"Where do you live?"

"This winter I will live in Rome. With my husband."

"Where?"

"*A Via Gregoriana. Ma solo in inverno. In estate—*"

"Where'd you learn Italian?"

"In my cradle. I am Italian."

"And English?"

"In school. Also, I have been to America many times."

"When's your birthday?"

"March eleventh."

"Are you sure it isn't May sixth?"

"You wanted to know," she said, "and so I am telling you. Why do you persist—?"

"Where do I work?"

"I have no idea."

"What's your mother's name?"

"Bianca Di Luca."

"Wasn't your mother a woman named Beth McCauley?"

"Of course not."

"Where's your mother now?"

"Dead."

"When did she die, Annie?"

"She was killed in an American air raid on Rome. When I was still a child."

"And your father?"

"He was killed at the same time."

"Then you're alone."

"I am not alone," she said. "I have Marco."

"How long have you been married to him?"

"We were married last month."

"When last month?"

"On July twenty-seventh."

"Where?"

"In Rome."

I searched her face again, and suddenly I kissed her. She did not resist my kiss. Slowly we pulled apart. I looked into her eyes. They were vacant. I rose swiftly and walked down the rocky path to the beach, and did not look back even once at the woman I knew was my wife . . .

The plane for Milan left Olbia at 11:30. In the piazza outside the Duomo I stood in stifling heat and looked up at the cathedral. The piazza was nearly deserted. Scaffolding was in place along the buttressed walls where repairs were being made. I squinted up painfully at the spires on the roof, then walked toward the wide steps leading to the entrance doors. The interior of the church was cool and dim. The sexton who led me up to the roof was puffing hard as we made the long climb.

"I was not actually here on the day of the accident," he said over his shoulder, "but I am told the Americans went to the roof early in the morning."

Behind him I had begun to sweat. I had never been inside this church before, yet it seemed shockingly familiar to me.

"One hundred and fifty-eight steps to the first roof," the sexton said, "two hundred and sixty-one to the Tiburium, five hundred to the terrace of the highest spire—"

The memory was sharp. The sexton's broken English yielded to the lilt of Annie's voice and I could hear it clearly now as we continued to climb: *Just a few more steps, we're almost there. This way, Thomas.*

"There are a hundred and thirty-five arcs here," the sexton said, "all adorned with marble intaglios—"

Follow me, Thomas, she said, *follow me.*

"A strange and wondrous fairyland overlooking the city that Our Lady dominates—"

"Come tutte bellissimo. Guardo, Thomas, i belli statue."

And I remembered, I remembered saying, *"Be careful, Annie. You're getting too close to the edge there,"* and she said excitedly, *"Look, Thomas, look!"* and I shouted in alarm, *"Annie, be careful!"*

"This is the spot where the woman fell over," the sexton said.

"I know." I answered.

And at the Musocco Cemetery I found her grave, and I looked down at the inscription on the tombstone. ANNE McCAULEY BARNES, it read, and it gave the date of her birth, and it recorded the date of her death as July 26, the day after we left Rome.

I had never been here before, and yet as I stared at the chiseled letters I could hear a priest's voice intoning. *"Ut in te semper cum Sanctio tuis sine fine laetetur. Per Christum Dominum nostrum,"* and into my mind, unbidden, came a memory so vivid it could not be defined—a coffin poised on canvas straps, waiting to be lowered into the ground, five people standing around the open grave—the priest, an altar boy, two gravediggers, and me.

"Amen," the priest said.

"Amen," we responded.

The priest sprinkled the coffin and the grave with holy water. The altar boy handed him a thurible, and the priest incensed the grave and the coffin, and then chanted, *"Piae recrodationis affectu, fratres carissimi, commemorationem facimus sororis nostrae ..."*

I opened my eyes. It had happened, I could remember it happening. I walked swiftly from the grave.

At the hospital I felt I knew the man to whom I was speaking, felt I had seen him or someone very like him removing a green surgical mask from his beaded face and shaking his head in surrender to death. The man was seated behind a desk now, wearing a business suit, filling a pipe as he spoke. His name was Dr. Paolo Corrandino.

"There was, of course, nothing to be done," he said. "We tried, but—" He shook his head as he had done so often in my memory. "It was miraculous that she was still alive when they brought her here. She had fallen—how many meters from the roof? Impossible. But we tried." He shook his head again, "She was buried the next day at Musocco. Such a young woman." He started to light his pipe, then looked up at me. "What is your interest, *signore*?" he asked. "Are you another reporter?"

"I thought you knew," I said. "I'm her husband."

The hand holding the match hesitated. The doctor looked at me, then said, "*Signore*, there have been many reporters here since the accident. I have always told them the truth of what happened. There is no need for deception now." He lighted the pipe. Clouds of smoke enveloped his head.

"What do you mean?" I asked.

"I mean, *signore*, that I spent many hours with the husband of Anne Barnes." He paused. "And he was *not* you."

The plane from Milan did not arrive in Rome till almost four o'clock. At the Alitalia counter I asked an attendant where I might find information about a marriage that had taken place last month, and he advised me to ask any cab driver for the Anagrafe.

The building was ancient, the lobby thronged with people. There was no air conditioning. Instead, there was a mix of claustrophobic heat and voices raised in tedious inquiry. The room on the second floor of the building was cavernous and dusty. Rotating fans hung from the ceiling, attempting vainly to rearrange the contained heat of the day.

I followed a clerk between rows and rows of filing cabinets, each marked with an identifying cardboard placard on its top surface. "We have all records here of people living Rome," he explained. "Or people born somewhere Italy, then move to Rome. Everything here. Born, die, marry, everything."

He located the file cabinet he wanted, and began leafing through yellowed cards. "Piontelli, Piontelli," he intoned. "Piontelli, Carlo. Piontelli, Luigi. *Ah, finalmente.* Piontelli, Marco." He pulled out the card and translated it aloud for me. "Born Palermo, 1916. Marry Regian Forza, Switzerland, 1939. Second marry—" He raised his eyebrows. "Karin Wehler, Germany, 1943."

"And the third marriage?"

"Two is not enough? In Italy two is miracle. Must be important man, Piontelli." He shook his head. "There is no third marry."

"Are you sure?"

"*Certo, signore.*"

"He's supposed to have married a woman named Francesca Di Luca last month. On July twenty-seventh. Is there any way we can check further?"

"Francesca Di Luca," the clerk said, and sighed. "*Vieni.*"

I followed him down the aisle. He stopped at another cabinet, opened a drawer, and began scanning cards again. "Di Luca, Di Luca," he said. "*Ci sono molti Di Luca, signore,* many Di Luca, is common name Italy. *Ah, eccolà!*" he said, and pulled out a card. "Francesca Di Luca." He read the card silently, then translated it. "Born Palermo, 1918. Die Rome January second—"

"Died?"

"Die Rome, *si,*" he said. "January second." He looked

up from the card. *"Mille novecento trentasette."* He paused. In translation he said, "1937."

The fisherman's name was Giovanni Fabrizi. I found him in a bar in Santa Teresa and persuaded him to take me by boat to Piontelli's island. The island was still and dark except for some lights showing in the villa. Fabrizi dropped me off in a cove at the northern end, coming in as close as his draft allowed.

I paid him half of the agreed-upon price and told him I'd give him the rest when he picked me up again at midnight. I waded ashore then, my shoes in my hand, then sat on the sand and watched the boat as it moved out to sea. I put on my shoes and started for the villa.

There was the sound of explosions. Airplanes. Sirens.

A light was burning on the second floor of the villa, and the sounds were coming from behind a pair of partially opened balcony doors. I climbed a wooden trellis and silently moved closer to the doors. From where I crouched I could see only a portion of the room. The room was dark except for the luminous glow of the wall opposite the bed.

Annie was propped against the pillows, staring at the wall, her hands resting limply on the bedcovers, palms up. Projected onto the wall from somewhere behind it were motion picture images of bombs exploding and buildings crumbling. A title in white suddenly appeared on the wall screen—ROMA—a bomb exploded, shattering the script lettering. The noise in the room was deafening—the whistling of bombs, the cacophony of engines, explosions, sirens. A little auburn-haired girl in gray-striped smock and black stockings ran into the filmed street, screaming in panic as the bombs fell everywhere around her. "Mama!" she shrieked. "Papa!"

On the bed my wife backed away from the images in horror.

And suddenly the Allied warplanes on the screen dissolved to an idyllic view of waves rolling in gently against a seashore. The sound of the explosions segued to the music of violins, and another title appeared on the screen in white—ISCHIA—and on the bed the terror left my wife's eyes, and a faint smile formed on her mouth as she continued watching the screen.

The same little girl, now in a bathing suit, was running along the shore, a puppy following her. In the distance, off screen, a woman called "Francesca! Francesca!" and the child stopped and turned to smile at the camera. A man with a walrus mustache entered the shot and picked up the little girl, lifted her high over his head, his arms extended. A redheaded woman was laughing, the puppy dog was barking and nipping at the man's heels. The camera panned to the shorefront and lingered on the waves. Hypnotically the waves rolled in against the beach.

A man's voice whispered, "Francesca?"

Without turning her eyes from the screen she said, "Yes, Dr. Kleber?" Her voice was weak, without timbre or inflection.

"In Italian, Francesca," Kleber said. I did not know who he was. She had called him Doctor. Was he the man who had pushed a needle into my arm yesterday morning? "Italian is your language," he said now.

I tried to see into the portion of the room from which his voice was coming, but the drapes inside the mullioned doors cut the view.

"Francesca?" he said.

"*Sì, che vuole?*" she answered.

"Italian *is* your language, isn't it?"

"*Sì, certo.*"

"You were born in Italy, weren't you, Francesca?"

"*Sì.*"

"Where were you born?"

"*A Roma.*"

"Who is this man?" Kleber asked, and suddenly the screen opposite the bed flashed a still photograph of the man with the walrus mustache.

"*Il mio padre,*" she said.

"Yes, your father. What is his name?"

"Silvio Di Luca."

"And this woman?"

The screen flashed a still photograph of the red-headed woman who had earlier been laughing on the beach.

"*La mia madre.*"

"Yes, your dear mother. What is her name?"

"Bianca Di Luca."

"Where are they now, your mother and father?"

"*Sono morti, tutt'e due.*"

"How did they die?"

"There was an American bombing raid—"

I heard only a tiny click, almost like the sound of someone snapping his fingers—a harmless click, almost inaudible. And yet, as surely as though someone had thrown a switch, she winced at the sound of the click, and her features suddenly contorted in pain.

"In Italian, Francesca," Kleber said.

Trembling, she took a moment before answering, and when she did, she spoke very slowly and very carefully, in precise Italian.

"*Durante un'incursione americano a Roma quando ero bambina piccola,*" she said, "*tutt'e due i genitori furono uccisi.*"

"Yes," Kleber said. "And you were left an orphan."

"*Sì.*"

"Say it, please."

"*Fui lasciata*—I don't know how to say 'orphan'."

The click sounded again and her reaction to it seemed stronger this time. I almost rushed into the room in that instant. But even if she were alone in there, even if Kleber were not actually beside the bed where I couldn't see him, he was most certainly watching from somewhere—observing her reactions, listening to her, producing the clicking sound that triggered pain though no pain-inducing mechanism was anywhere in evidence. I wondered now how often in the past three weeks that tiny click had signaled *real* pain to come.

"You know how to say it in Italian," he said.

"No, please, I—" There was another click. *"Un'orfana,"* she shouted, *"un'orfana!"*

"Yes," Kleber said.

On the bed Annie began weeping.

"You are tired, Francesca," Kleber said. "I will let you sleep now."

"Yes. Thank you."

"In Italian."

"Grazie, dottore. Buona notte."

"Good night, Francesca. Sleep now. Sleep well."

On the wall opposite the bed the waves appeared again, rolling incessantly toward the shore. The weeping subsided. The only sound in the room now was the murmur of surf against sand. I waited. From the bed I could hear her gentle breathing. Was Kleber in the room with her? Or still watching from someplace other than the room?

I looked at my watch. It was close to eleven. I had told Fabrizi to pick me up in the cove at midnight. I waited now, uncertain of my next move. Surely they wouldn't continue to watch her all night long. Once they were certain she was asleep—

I listened to her breathing.

At ten minutes past eleven I went into the room. The motion-picture images of the lulling waves had faded three minutes before. The wall looked like nothing more than a wall now, a flat white surface. There was no one in the room with her, but I did not know if we were being watched by a camera eye. I went swiftly to the bed.

"Annie," I whispered, "wake up."

She mumbled in her sleep, and there was a faint medicinal scent clinging to her. I threw back the covers and was bending to lift her from the bed when a voice behind me said, "Good evening, Thomas."

I turned abruptly. The wall was covered now with a full-screen, black-and-white image of Piontelli. He was smiling.

"I see you are back," he said. "What do you want here, Thomas?"

"My wife."

"Your wife is dead. She fell from the roof of the Duomo—"

"*Someone* fell from the roof of the Duomo, but it wasn't Anne Barnes."

"She was identified as Anne Barnes," Piontelli said.

"Who identified her?"

"Her husband."

"Like hell! One of your stooges identified her, and buried her and—"

"What difference does it make? Who in Italy knows either of you? A girl, whoever she was, was buried in Milano, and a grieving husband was at her graveside. Whatever else—"

"Why are you doing this?"

"Because I want her."

"You *want* her? Who the hell do you think you are? You see someone you want, and you—"

"Exactly."

"—take her and change her to suit your—"

"She was *ready* to be changed," Piontelli said. "I only served as the catalyst."

"You haven't got Annie Barnes. All you've—"

"I have Francesca," he said. "From the moment I first saw you together in Rome—"

"When was that?"

"Last month. At the Hassler. I had gone there to dine with a friend. In Italy it is possible to make discreet inquiries. I found out who you were and where you were going from Rome. You see ... she was Francesca exactly. The resemblance was uncanny. I had to—"

"Francesca died in 1937!"

"Ah?" he said, surprised. "You know this?"

"When are *you* going to know it? Annie's *not* Francesca. Whatever your witch doctor's done to her—"

"Ah, but of course I know this," Piontelli said. "Annie is—" He hesitated a moment, searching for the appropriate English words. In Italian he said, *"Una immagine idealizzata, rifinita a perfezione.* The *ideal*, do you see? I have created the ideal. *My* Francesca was poor and ignorant. The one I've fashioned was educated in Florence, has traveled to London, Paris, and New York, a different person altogether. *My* Francesca died of influenza in Rome, where I took her with her parents thirty-eight years ago. The Francesca on the bed there is an orphan, the victim of an Allied air raid, but very much alive, *non è vero?"*

"You're deluding yourself," I said. "They may *look* alike, but—"

"Delusion? Perhaps," he said, and smiled. "But such a pleasant way to spend my waning years, don't you agree? I've brought Francesca back to life. I took Anne Barnes and changed her into a girl I once knew and loved. And no one can change her back again. Perhaps Dr. Kleber, yes. But certainly not you."

"I can try."

"You will fail."

"I'll take that chance. You can't keep her drugged and hypnotized forever."

"Is that all you think it is? Then you're the one who's deluded. Talk to her," he said. "You will find only *un'ombra istruita*—an educated ghost."

The screen blanked out.

The woman on the bed awakened at a little past 2:00 A.M. She did not see me at first. Her eyes fluttered open, and she took a deep breath and let it out, then yawned, then blinked into the room. Her face registered only mild surprise when she saw me sitting in the chair beside the bed.

"Did you sleep well?" I asked.

"Yes," she said. "Thank you."

"Do you know where you are?"

"Of course I know where I am."

"Do you know who I am?"

"Yes."

"Who am I?"

"Thomas Barnes."

"And who are *you*?" I asked.

"You know very well who I am," she said. "Francesca Piontelli." She got off the bed. She was wearing a long cotton nightgown, but she went immediately to a chair where a robe was draped. Putting on the robe, her back modestly turned to me, she said, "Where's my husband?"

"I'm your husband," I said.

She went to the door and reached for the bolt.

"Leave that locked," I said.

"Why?" she asked. "Am I a prisoner?"

"Yes. But not mine."

"In that case I am free to leave when I wish."

"No."

"Then I *am* your prisoner."

"My guest, let's say."

"Your prisoner, let's say. I thought you'd left the island."

"I did."

"And now you're back."

"Bad penny," I said, and smiled. She did not return that smile. "Annie," I said, "I haven't—"

"My name is Francesca," she said.

"I haven't had a drink since this started," I said. "Not a drop."

"That is of no interest to me," she said.

"It's why we came to Italy."

"I have been here in Italy since long before you arrived."

"Annie, I was drinking too much. We came here on vacation to try to save our marriage. We thought if we could only—"

"My name is Francesca Di Luca Piontelli," she said.

"Annie, I mean it this time. I swear to you I'll—"

"I was born in Rome on March eleventh—"

"Annie, for God's sake—"

"When I was a little girl I went to the Misericordia School. I wore long black stockings and a striped smock. The nuns sometimes beat us with birch rods. That's how I got the scar."

"What scar?" I said.

"On my arm. I raised my arm to defend myself."

"You . . . you don't have a scar, Annie."

"Oh, but I most certainly have. Would you like to see it?" She lifted her left arm in the position she would have used to ward off a blow. With her right hand she pulled back the sleeve of the robe. Just above the wrist there was a scar some two inches long.

"It's not very attractive," she said.

I stared at the scar. Annie did not have a scar on her arm. For an instant, just an instant, I doubted whether this woman pulling back the sleeve of her robe was really my wife. The instant was time enough. The doubt opened a channel through which all the false memories rushed. I heard Dr. Kleber's voice saying, *"You told her not to go too close,"* and saw again in vivid detail the girl in the yellow dress leaning over the parapet to look at the piazza below. I tried to reject the memory, but pain suddenly flashed inside my head, the punishment for refusing to believe.

"In sunshine—the cathedral in sunshine. The roof. A yellow dress. Don't you remember the yellow dress?"

"No," I said, and tried to conjure the *real* memory of what had happened—the road to Milan, the rented red Fiat speeding through the deepening dusk, the car radio up full. In the *real* memory, there were sudden headlights in the road ahead. I slowed the car, we rolled to a stop, and I saw three armed men standing in the road.

My first thought was that they were policemen—they were dressed in black, black trousers and jackets, black caps—and then Annie said only my name, "Thomas!" and my hands tightened on the steering wheel because I knew these were not policemen, I knew this was trouble.

They threw open the car doors. Two of them seized Annie—she was wearing a yellow cotton dress. I head her screaming, I tried to break away from the man who was pulling me out of the automobile. That was all I could remember, but I knew it was the *true* memory, knew that whatever else I *thought* had happened after that night was false—as false as Annie's death.

But I could not shake the image of the girl in the yellow dress. Whatever they had done to me, whatever memories they had implanted and repeated endlessly, whatever voices and images had been insistently forced on me, the results were effective and lasting. I found myself physically moving toward the non-existent girl as she leaned out over the parapet, heard myself shouting aloud, "Annie, don't—Annie, be careful!"

Suddenly she lost her balance. I reached out, grabbed for the yellow cotton of her dress, and in a dizzying blur she fell over the edge. The piazza below was tiled in black and white, a geometrically patterned mosaic. The girl's scream shattered the torpid summer stillness as her body struck the tiles with bone-crushing . . .

"No!" I shouted.

The pattern of the black and white tiles lingered, refused to fade, like neon that had died and left an afterglow. Slowly the room came into focus again, objects regained definite form and color. I found her, looked into her eyes, and realized in despair that Piontelli had been right—there was no bringing Annie back.

The indoctrination had been too strong, it could still overcome me with pain and false memory whenever I allowed the slightest doubt to intrude on reality. And Annie? What did she know of the truth, what did she even suspect of anything that had happened to her during these past several weeks? She had indeed become Francesca Piontelli, an educated ghost.

"Are you all right?" she asked.

"Yes, I'm—I'm all right now."

She was looking at me oddly. Her eyes were puzzled.

"Mr. Barnes?" she said, and hesitated. "Thomas?" she said. "Do I know you?"

I caught my breath.

"I thought I knew you," she said. "Just then." She paused. "And once before."

"When?" I asked.

She turned her head away abruptly. "I don't remember," she said.

"You *do* remember."

"Yes. I do remember."

"When was it?"

She would not look at me, she kept her head turned away. "This morning," she said. "When you kissed me."

I lifted my hand. I dared to take her chin in my cupped hand, risked turning her face toward mine, and gently, cautiously, I lowered my mouth to hers.

"No," she said. "Please don't."

"Why?"

"I'm married," she said. "I love my husband. I—"

My lips brushed hers. She moved her mouth from mine, and looked into my eyes, and I kissed her again, and again she pulled away, and shook her head, and said, "I shouldn't remember your mouth—but I do."

"Annie," I said, "Francesca, whoever you are ... I love you."

"No, please," she said. "You mustn't."

I took her in my arms, held her close, covered her lips with mine, and this time she responded, and when at last she pulled away, her voice was breathless. "And you," she said, "whoever *you* are—"

There was no warning. There was only the sudden sound of something heavy hitting the oak door, and then the bolt sprang free of the jamb. I leaped to my feet, but they were already in the room, Bruno following the door as it swung inward, Piontelli immediately behind him. Bruno had a pistol in his hand.

"We are finished here," Piontelli said to me. "Francesca!"

"Yes, Marco?" she said immediately, and one hand went to the collar of her robe and pulled it closer to her throat.

"We are leaving for Greece at sunrise," he said. "You must pack. I know you do not wish to appear rude to our American guest, but I think you should begin now. You will forgive her, Mr. Barnes? Bruno, take Francesca to her—"

I threw myself at Bruno and grabbed for his wrist, and the pistol went off twice as we struggled across the room. Both my hands were wrapped around his wrist. We smashed into the wall on which the motion picture images had flashed earlier, went into it and through it, glass splintering around us, and still I clung to his wrist. Piontelli was shouting.

We were on the floor now, Bruno and I, locked in sweaty struggle. I brought his forearm to my mouth, bit down hard, sank my teeth into the muscle, and he screamed in pain. He opened his fingers and the gun dropped to the floor. I hit him then. I had not had a fist fight since I was twelve years old, but I hit him with all the strength of my arm and shoulder, and I kept hitting him until he fell back to the floor unconscious. My hand hurt, I had hurt it on his jaw. I turned away from him. The gun—where was it?

Annie had picked up the gun. It looked ridiculously large in her delicate hand.

"Good girl," Piontelli said. "Give it to me."

"No," she said, and shook her head.

"Give me the gun, Francesca," he said.

"No."

"I told you to go pack," he said. "Now give—"

"Why are we going to Greece?" she asked.

"To be married," he said. "*Dammi la pistola.*"

"We are already married," she said.

"The church wedding, Francesca," he said quickly. "Because the other, when we were married in Rome—"

"You were never married in Rome," I said. "There's no record of a marriage in Rome."

"Francesca," he said, "I know you remember. It was a civil ceremony, do you remember? But you said you wanted to be married in church later on. So tomorrow . . . I'm sure you remember, darling. It was your express wish that we be married again in church. Don't you remember, Francesca?"

She hesitated a long time before answering. Then, slowly, precisely, and in English, she said, "No, Marco. I *don't* remember."

"*Maledetta, dammi quella pistola!*" he shouted, and reached for the gun. She thrust it forward sharply, threateningly, and he realized in that instant that she would shoot him if he took another step. His face fell, his shoulders slumped. He looked at her one last time before we rushed out of the room.

We ran down the steps and through the terrace doors. I did not know where to take her. The boat had surely left long ago. We kept running up the beach. They would come after us, I knew they would. Piontelli would send Bruno or some of the others.

The searchlight illuminated half of the beach. It burst into brilliance at our feet and stopped us dead in our tracks. I expected someone to shoot at us the next moment, then I realized the light was coming from the *sea*, and I heard a voice I hadn't expected to hear again tonight.

"*Signore!* It's me! Giovanni Fabrizi!"

We ran down to the water's edge and splashed into the sea. The villa was still, the island was still. She shucked her robe as we swam to the boat and when we climbed aboard, she was shivering. Fabrizi threw a blanket around her shoulders, and then gunned the boat out of the cove. I sat in the stern with her. She was trembling in my arms. I looked back toward the villa. Was that Piontelli standing on the terrace? I could not be certain.

Fabrizi turned from the wheel.

"I thought you'd be gone by now," I said.

"Why? You owe me money still. You are okay?" he asked.

"I am okay," I said.

"And you, lady?"

"*Anch'io, salva,*" she said.

"Ah?" he said, surprised. "*É italiana?* The lady is Italian?"

"*Sì,*" she said, and nodded.

I looked at her. I searched her face for the slightest trace of uncertainty or doubt, but none was there. I was sitting beside a strange and beautiful woman who now knew she wasn't married to Marco Piontelli, but who never in a million years would believe she was married to me. I was sitting beside Francesca Di Luca, 34 years old and single. And she had met an American who'd told her he loved her.

Now all I had to do was prove it.

"Yes," I said. "She's Italian."

Death of a Romance Writer

by Joan Hess

The young woman hesitated at the top of the curving staircase, grumbling rather rudely to herself as she gazed at the scene below. "Hell's bells!" she muttered under her breath. "Doesn't she like anything besides waltzes? A little new wave rock, or at least jazz?"

In the grand ballroom ladies dressed in pastel gowns swept across the floor under the benevolent eyes of elegant gentlemen in black waistcoats and ruffled shirts. A stringed orchestra labored its way through the familiar melodies with grim concentration. Servants moved inconspicuously along the walls of the vast room, their expressions studiously blank. The same old thing, down to the canapes and sweet sherry.

Gathering up her skirt with pale, delicately tapered fingers, the woman forced herself to move down the stairs. Her heart-shaped mouth was curled slightly, and her deep jade eyes flittered across the crowd without curiosity. He would make an appearance in a few minutes, she reminded herself glumly, but perhaps she could have a bit of fun in the meantime. The fun would certainly end when he appeared—whoever he was.

"Lady Althea!" gushed a shrill, nasal voice from the shadows behind her. "I was so hoping to see you this evening. The ball is absolutely delightful."

Lady Althea, the woman repeated to herself. A silly name, as usual, invoking images of moonlit gardens and scented breezes. Why not a simple "Kate" or "Jane"? Oh, no. It was always "Desiree" or "Bianca," as if her bland personality must be disguised by alluring nomenclature.

The dowager tottered out of the shadows on tiny feet. In her seventies (hundreds, Althea sniffed to herself), the woman's face was a mesh of tiny lines, and her faded blue eyes glittered with malevolence. Her thin white hair was decorated with a handful of dusty plumes, one of which threatened to sweep across her hawkish nose with every twitch of the woman's head.

"Who're you?" Althea demanded bluntly.

The dowager raised a painted eyebrow. "I am your mother-in-law's dearest friend, Lady Althea. You had tea only yesterday at my summer home. Your first introduction to society, I believe. I'm amazed that it has slipped your mind."

"Yeah, sorry." Althea moved away from the woman's rancid breath and fluttery hands. Surely these people could be induced to brush their teeth, she thought testily. They didn't, of course. As far as she could tell, they had no bodily functions whatsoever. A few bouts of the vapors, a shoulder slashed by a duelling sword, a mysterious scar across the cheek. But nothing mundane to interrupt the flow of their lives.

Ignoring the woman's frown, Althea stood on her toes to peer around the room. He wasn't here yet. Good. Now, if she could only liven up the music and get these nameless people to loosen up a little bit, the evening might provide some amusement. A ball could be a ball, but it seldom was.

The dowager was not ready to allow Althea to escape. "Your dear mother-in-law has told me of your tragic history, and I must tell you how much I admire your courage," she hissed. Little drops of spittle landed on Althea's cheek, like a fine mist of acid rain.

"Sure, thanks," Althea said. "I'm a plucky sort, I understand. Personally, I'd rather watch television or read a confession magazine, but I never get the chance."

"Television? What might that be, my dear girl?"

Althea shook her head. "Never mind. Hey, which one of these ladies" (dames, broads) "is my mother-in-law? The one with the chicken beak or that fat slug in the corner?"

"Lady Althea! I must tell you that I am somewhat shocked by your manner," the dowager gasped. Her hand fluttered to her mouth. "I was led to believe you had been raised most properly in a convent; that you were of gentle birth and delicate nature."

"Is that so? I guess I'd better behave," Althea said dryly. She tucked a stray curl of her raven black hair into place, and checked the row of tiny seed pearl buttons on her elbow-length gloves. Now that, she told herself sternly, was the accepted and expected behavior. She glanced at the dowager.

"So which one is my mother-in-law?"

"Your mother-in-law is there," the dowager said, gesturing with a molting fan toward a grim-visaged woman sitting on a straight-backed chair. "But where is your dear husband, Lady Althea? I had such hopes of speaking to him."

"Beats me," Althea said. So she was already married, she thought with a sigh. These rapid shifts were disconcerting. Dear husband, huh! Gawd, he was probably a bodice ripper like the rest of them. And she had decided to wear her new gown—genuine silk and just the right color for her eyes. Perhaps there was enough time to change into something more expendable.

Frowning, Althea glanced across the coiffed heads of the guests to study her mother-in-law. A real loser, with a profile that ought to be illegal. Translucent blue complexion, hooded eyes, mouth tighter than a miser's purse. But the woman did have a smidgen of charm—all found in the garish diamond brooch on her chest. From across the room, Althea could see the brilliance of the stone, and even the dull glow of the gold setting. Now *that* was charming.

Leaving the dowager puffing resentfully at the bottom of the staircase, Althea began to thread her way between the dancers. Despite her intention of finding the punchbowl, she found herself curtsying in front of her mother-in-law. Damn.

"Althea, dear child," the woman said frostily. She extended a limp white hand, as though she expected Althea to clasp it to her bosom—or kiss it, for God's sake!

Althea eyed it warily. At last she touched it timidly, then snatched her hand away and hid it behind her back. "Good evening," she said, swallowing a sour taste in the back of her throat. The diamond brooch. It would keep her in penthouses and champagne for the rest of her life, if only . . .

"Excrutia, this child is charming!" the dowager said, shoving Althea aside. "But where is your son? Dear Jared must be eager to present his charming bride to his friends . . ."

Jared, huh. Althea brushed a black curl off her eyebrow as she checked the crowd. She was destined to be stuck with an elegant moniker, and so was he. Once, she remembered with a faint sigh, she had particularly liked a chap named Sam—but of course he had become a Derek. Sam had had bulging biceps and a busted nose, but it hadn't kept him from stirring up a bit of inventiveness between the covers. Derek, on the other hand, had spent hours gazing into her eyes and murmuring (bleating) endearments that were supposed to sweep her off her feet. Sam's approach was brisker—and a hell of a lot more interesting.

The mother-in-law was snivelling down her nose. "Where is my son, Althea? Have you already managed to ... distract him from his duties as host?"

Althea thought of several snappy remarks but again found herself in an awkward curtsy. "No, ma'am. I haven't seen him since—"

Since what? It was impossible to keep track of the convoluted framework. Since he rescued her? Married her? Raped her? Jared would never do such a thing, she amended sourly. No doubt he had kept her from being raped by one of the marauding highwaymen that accosted virgins. Considering Jared, it might have been more fun to be accosted ...

"Well, Althea," the mother-in-law snorted in a well-bred voice, "you must feel most fortunate to have snared my son. He is, after all, the owner of this charming manor and of all the land from here to the cliffs. And you, a penniless orphan, destined to become a scullery maid—had not heaven intervened on your behalf."

Sam's mother was a cheery drunkard who was still producing babies on an annual basis. This one had probably produced Jared by virgin birth. Forget that; birth was messy. Jared had no doubt simply appeared one day, lisping French and nibbling cucumber sandwiches under his nanny's approving smile.

Althea swallowed an angry response. Fluttering her thick lashes, she murmured, "Yes, ma'am, I was most fortunate to have met your son. When my father died, leaving me a penniless orphan at the mercies of my unscrupulous uncle, I feared for my life." Melodrama, pure and nauseating. Why couldn't she have been a barmaid? A bit of slap and giggle in the shadows behind the stables, a feather bed to keep warm for a guy like

Sam. But instead she had to hang around with the aristocracy. Snivellers and snorters, bah!

But there was no point in worrying about this Jared fellow. Maybe he was a Sam in disguise. Maybe chickens had lips, and the moon was made of green cheese. Maybe it was time to start expecting the Easter bunny to show up with a bunch of purple eggs.

The mother-in-law person stood up imperiously and held a lace handkerchief to her nose. "I am going into the garden for a bit of fresh air," she announced. "Send Jared to me when he appears, Althea. I must speak to him; it is of the greatest importance."

Hmmm? Had the old bat noticed her repeated glances at the diamond brooch? If she were to tattle to this Jared person, Althea might find herself scrubbing pots after all. It seemed prudent to assume the dutiful role.

"Please don't take a chill, Lady Excrutia," Althea said in a solicitous whine. "Shall I fetch a shawl for you from your dressing room? Allow me to bring it to you in the garden."

The dowager with the plumes beamed approvingly at Althea's meek posture. "Charming child, just charming. But look, here's Jared!"

Oh, hell. Althea tried to forget about the promised encounter in the garden—for a few minutes anyway. Forcing herself into a semblance of pleased surprise, she lifted her eyes to meet those of the unknown Jared.

Oh, my God, she thought with a scowl. Another arrogant one. There went another bodice, ripped into shreds. Endless lovemaking, with nothing but simmering frustration as the result. And those granite gray eyes boring into her, for God's sake! It was more than anyone should have to bear . . . it really was.

"Damnedest thing I've ever seen!" The lieutenant leaned against the kitchen counter, watching the body being wheeled out of the tiny office. For the first time in his career even the paramedics were subdued.

The two men waited for the medical examiner to finish wiping the inky smudges off his hands, then crowded into the room. The desk was cluttered with notebooks, chewed pencil stubs, and an overflowing ashtray. A lipstick-stained coffee cup lay on the floor in a dried brown puddle. A typewriter hummed softly, and with a snort the second of the plainclothes detectives leaned over to switch it off.

"How'd you discover the body?" the medical examiner asked. Like Lady Macbeth, he seemed obsessed with the invisible marks on his hands, rubbing them against each other nervously.

"The woman in the next apartment called the super. It seems the woman who lived here was a writer, and the neighbor was used to the sound of the typewriter clattering all day long. She told the super the last couple of days there was no sound, and it was driving her crazy," the first detective said.

The second snorted again. "If I lived next door to one of these writers, and had to listen to that noise all day, I might have strangled the broad myself. As it is, I have to listen to my wife screaming at the kids every night and—"

"Damnedest thing," the first repeated, shaking his head. "In twenty-nine years on the force, I've seen a lot of weird things—but I've never seen anyone strangled with a typewriter ribbon."

The medical examiner laughed. "As good as a wire or a rope, but a hell of a lot messier. All you have to do now is find someone with ink-stained hands."

The second detective was reading the titles of the paperback books on a shelf above the desk. "Look at this, Carl. Do you know what the victim wrote? Romance novels, by damn! You know the things: *Sweet Moonlight, The Towering Passion of Lady Bianca*, etc., etc."

"My wife reads that stuff," the first admitted. He shook his head. "I dunno why, though. Gimme a good ball game on television and a six pack to keep me cool. That's my idea of romance—me, Budweiser, and the Yankees."

The medical examiner raised his hand in a farewell gesture. "I'll get back to you in a day or two, Carl. Don't waste your time reading the victim's books— unless you think the intellectuals of the world conspired to do her in!" Chuckling to himself, he left the two detectives exchanging glances.

"Naw, Carl," the second said, "don't get your hopes up. It was a prowler or something. Let's go talk to the doorman and the elevator operator."

The first sighed, thinking of the tedious interviews that would prove necessary, the trivial gossip that the neighbors would feel obliged to share, the dinner he would not have a chance to eat that night.

"Too bad it wasn't a suicide," he grumbled. "My wife always makes meatballs on Mondays and then goes bowling with a bunch of the girls. Good game on tonight."

"Then we'd have our note," the second added, pointing at a piece of paper sticking out of the typewriter. "But nobody, not even dippy romance writers, can strangle themselves. My money's on the neighbor; she's probably half-deaf from the noise. She just couldn't stand the sound of the typewriter any longer and went berserk. I would've."

"She's eighty-three," the first one said. He leaned over to read the manuscript page, then straightened up. "My wife will get a kick out of this, you know. Yours will, too. All women think this stuff is great—all the damned moonlight and wine and deep soulful stares! It spoils them for the real world, Marv."

"Yeah, my wife wanted me to take her out to dinner for her birthday. Hell, the babysitter drives a damn Mercedes! I can't see spending half a week's salary on fancy food."

"So what'd you do?" Carl asked as they went out the door of the office and started for the living room.

The one named Marv shrugged his shoulders. "I brought home a real nice pizza."

Lady Althea wrapped her arms around Sam's stocky waist and snuggled against him, ignoring the black smudges on his back from her previous caresses. For a long time, the horse's rhythmic clops were the only sound on the road. The moon illuminated the trees on either side of them with a silver haze, and the light breeze had an earthy redolence. At last the horse and its two riders were gone into the darkness, although a faint giggle seemed to linger in the air.

Back at the cold and lifeless manor house, the ball was over. The nameless gentility had disappeared, the orchestra vanished, the vast room as quiet as a tomb. In the center of the room lay a body. Two arrogant eyes stared at the darkened chandelier, unblinking and glazed with faint surprise. Blood had long since coagulated on the gash across his neck.

There was more blood in the garden. The figure there had the same surprised expression, and a similar slash across the neck. The bosom no longer heaved, although it had the appearance of a mountain range arising from the manicured lawn. The surface of this alpine region was smooth, except for a tiny rip in its surface where a broach had been removed hastily and without regard for the crinoline fabric.

His majesty's guards remained puzzled by the scene

for a few weeks, then dismissed it from their minds. One or two of the younger ones sometimes mentioned it over pints of ale in the new roadhouse, but the older officers usually ignored them. The barmaid, always full of throaty laughter and ready for a frolic, kept them more amused on the feather beds upstairs.

By the Time
You Read This

by Larry S. Hoke

Dear Dorothy,

By the time you read this I'll be dead.

That should be a "shocker" but of course it isn't as you couldn't care less whether I'm dead or alive. But, you see, the thing is that you will have killed me, and I mean that literally. How you are going to do it I'm leaving as a surprise at the end of this letter, but there's no way you can keep from doing it because by the time you read this it'll be too late.

I've given this a lot of time and thought, and I'm going to set everything down here just the way it happened because you're never going to be able to show this letter to anyone and I want you to know how it was and how it is.

It all started three years ago when you were getting bored with your husband and wanted some excitement. So you picked on me, not because I was anything special but because I was available and easy to get. I'm not fooling myself that I seduced you. We both know it was the other way around. But it was nice, it was beautiful, and I fell in love with you even knowing you were just amusing yourself.

And then when you started to break it off I couldn't take it. I became obsessed so that every hour of every day was spent in thinking of you and holding imaginary conversations with you and wondering what you were doing when I wasn't around.

I left my job, but you know that. What you don't know is that I left it so I could follow you. I'd call you at work and ask if I could see you and you'd say no, you had to work late. So I'd hide in my car in the parking lot across the street and watch your window, and I'd see you leave work and go down the street to have a drink with Morris. Good lord, Morris! You could do better than Morris. Fat, fifty, and bald. A joke on the human race. And after Morris it was George. And then Peter.

So I started writing you poems. Deep sensitive poems torn from the turmoil surging through my soul. But I had to let you know how I felt, you see. I had to be honest. If you were going to make a mockery of our friendship, of my love, you had to know what I really felt.

And I did more than just follow you everywhere. I spied on your window at work. I've already told you that. I also bugged your car and your living room. I wanted to bug your bedroom, but even I couldn't stoop that low. And I hated myself every minute. I hated what you were doing to me, and I was powerless to change it. And, after all, I'd been a private investigator for 20 years. People used to pay me for what I was doing to you. Paid good money, too. Enough to keep me going since I left my job.

I hated myself but I kept right on doing it. For six months now I can account for every minute of your day. It was about a month ago that I heard you reading my poems to Jim. And laughing at them! Remember the one I wrote that started out:

> You are a hidden part of me,
>   That goes where e'er I go,

A warm spot deep inside of me,
A happy little glow ...

I heard you read that to Jim and I heard him say, "What did the poor creep do—swallow a light bulb?" And you laughed. You both laughed.

That's when I started thinking about how to end it all.

I knew that just my dying wouldn't affect you. You've always had that ability (which I lack) of being able to think of yourself first. First and foremost there's Dorothy and to hell with what other people might feel, who might get hurt, who might even die because of you.

But there is one weakness in your character: you can't stand to kill anything. Remember that time in the park? You should, since it was part of that long poem I wrote you, the one that started:

I remember little things:
Like the sweater you used to wear,
Like the way you used to sing,
And the way you did your hair.

Like that noon at Echo Park
Where we walked and sat a while,
Like the way the day was dark
Till I saw your morning smile.

That day in the park you stepped on a beetle and it really broke you up. You just couldn't stand the idea that you had squashed something, that you had killed something. That's what gave me my great idea.

You see, dying isn't so terrible. Not for the person who dies. I'll be out of my misery then. I won't be following you around and spying on you and having my guts churn because you've made it plain you can't stand the sight of me.

The funny thing is that I still love you. That really is funny. Not "ha-ha funny" like you and Jim found my poems, but "sick funny" like laughing at someone as he breaks his leg. So if I love you, how can I give you this one final hurt? And it will hurt. Selfish as you are, it'll hurt you to know you killed me.

How can I do it? Because I won't be around to start feeling sorry about what I've done. And maybe I don't love you any more. Maybe I'm so sick I can't tell the difference. All I know is that I'm going to do it. Tonight.

You want to know how, don't you? Even now, as you read this letter, you have killed me but you don't know it. That's the beauty of the plan. You get this letter and then you find out that you've killed me and then you find out tomorrow that I'm really dead. Three little steps.

Tonight is Friday. On Fridays you always stay an hour late until everyone else in the office is gone and then you and Peter get in the elevator and ride it down to the basement floor and go out through the basement entrance to that little bar we used to go to.

But there's something you don't know about that elevator. In that old building you work in (remember how we used to brag that we worked in the oldest building in Los Angeles?) all the elevator machinery is on top of the elevator. The elevator itself comes within a half inch of resting on the cement floor of the basement. And I know how to open those basement elevator doors.

I'm going to watch your window until I see you and Peter turn out the lights. Then I'm going to run to the basement, open the doors, and lie down on the cement floor. You'll push the basement button (I remember that you always insisted on being the one to press the button), the elevator will come down, and I'll be dead.

My misery will be over and yours will start.

Goodbye, Dorothy

Harold

"Hey, Dorothy, did you see the item in the paper this morning about some guy getting crushed by the elevator in your building? Crushed so bad they can't even begin to make an identification. You do work in the Figueroa Building, don't you?"

"Yes, that's my building. I thought that elevator acted funny last night. It wouldn't go all the way down. Gee, that's weird. How would anyone get crushed by that elevator? Don't you think that's weird, Jim?"

"Yeah. Sure is. By the way, speaking of weird, you got a letter this morning from that weirdo, Harold. I recognized his writing on the envelope."

"Well, I don't want to read it. Throw it away."

"I already did."

"Good. Maybe he'll give up one of these days. Hey, how about going out for breakfast? There's a new Sambo's just opened down the street. Ought to have pretty good pancakes there."

All at Once,
No Alice

by Cornell Woolrich

It was over so quickly I almost thought something had been left out, but I guess he'd been doing it long enough to know his business. The only way I could tell for sure it was over was when I heard him say: "You may kiss the bride." But then, I'd never gone through it before.

We turned and pecked at each other, a little bashful because they were watching us.

He and the motherly-looking woman who had been a witness—I guess she was his housekeeper—stood there smiling benevolently, and also a little tiredly. The clock said one fifteen. Then he shook hands with the two of us and said, "Good luck to both of you," and she shook with us too and said, "I wish you a lot of happiness."

We shifted from the living room, where it had taken place, out into the front hall, a little awkwardly. Then he held the screen door open and we moved from there out onto the porch.

On the porch step Alice nudged me and whispered, "You forgot something."

I didn't even know how much I was supposed to give him. I took out two singles and held them in one hand, then I took out a five and held that in the other. Then I went back toward him all flustered and said, "I—I guess you thought I was going to leave without remembering this."

I reached my hand down to his and brought it back empty. He kept right on smiling, as if this happened nearly every time too, the bridegroom forgetting like that. It was only after I turned away and rejoined her that I glanced down at my other hand and saw which it was I'd given him. It was the five. That was all right; five thousand of them couldn't have paid him for what he'd done for me, the way I felt about it.

We went down their front walk and got into the car. The lighted doorway outlined them both for a minute. They raised their arms and said, "Good night."

"Good night, and much obliged," I called back. "Wait'll they go in," I said in an undertone to Alice, without starting the engine right away.

As soon as the doorway had blacked out, we turned and melted together on the front seat, and this time we made it a real kiss. "Any regrets?" I whispered to her very softly.

"It must have been awful before I was married to you," she whispered back. "How did I ever stand it so long?"

I don't think we said a word all the way in to Michianopolis. We were both too happy. Just the wind and the stars and us. And a couple of cigarettes.

We got to the outskirts around two thirty, and by three were all the way in downtown. We shopped around for a block or two. "This looks like a nice hotel," I said finally. I parked outside and we went in.

I think the first hotel was called the Commander. I noticed that the bellhops let us strictly alone; didn't bustle out to bring in our bags or anything.

I said to the desk man, "We'd like one of your best rooms and bath."

He gave me a sort of rueful smile, as if to say, "You

should know better than that." ... "I only wish I had something to give you," was the way he put it.

"All filled up?" I turned to her and murmured, "Well, we'll have to try some place else."

He overheard me. "Excuse me, but did you come in without making reservations ahead?"

"Yes, we just drove in now. Why?"

He shook his head compassionately at my ignorance. "I'm afraid you're going to have a hard time finding a room in any of the hotels tonight."

"Why? They can't all be filled up."

"There's a three-day convention of the Knights of Balboa being held here. All the others started sending their overflow to us as far back as Monday evening, and our own last vacancy went yesterday noon."

The second one was called the Stuyvesant, I think. "There must be something in a city this size," I said when we came out of there. "We'll keep looking until we find it."

I didn't bother noticing the names of the third and fourth. We couldn't turn around and go all the way back to our original point of departure—it would have been mid-morning before we reached it—and there was nothing that offered suitable accommodations between; just filling stations, roadside lunchrooms, and detached farmsteads.

Besides she was beginning to tire. She refused to admit it, but it was easy to tell. It worried me.

The fifth place was called the Royal. It was already slightly less first-class than the previous ones had been; we were running out of them now. Nothing wrong with it, but just a little seedier and older.

I got the same answer at the desk, but this time I wouldn't take it. The way her face drooped when she heard it was enough to make me persist. I took the night clerk aside out of her hearing.

"Listen, you've got to do something for me, I don't care what it is," I whispered fiercely. "We've just driven all the way from Lake City and my wife's all in. I'm not going to drag her around to another place tonight."

Then as his face continued impassive, "If you can't accommodate both of us, find some way of putting her up at least. I'm willing to take my own chances, go out and sleep in the car or walk around the streets for the night."

"Wait a minute," he said, hooking his chin, "I think I could work out something like that for you. I just thought of something. There's a little bit of a dinky room on the top floor. Ordinarily it's not used as a guest room at all, just as a sort of storeroom. You couldn't possibly both use it, because there's only a single-width cot in it; but if you don't think your wife would object, I'd be glad to let her have it, and I think you might still be able to find a room for yourself at the Y. They don't admit women, and most of these Knights have brought their wives with them."

I took a look at her pretty, drawn face. "Anything, anything," I said gratefully.

He still had his doubts. "You'd better take her up and let her see it first."

A colored boy came with us, with a passkey. On the way up I explained it to her. She gave me a rueful look, but I could see she was too tired even to object as much as she felt she should have. "Ah, that's mean," she murmured. "Our first night by ourselves."

"It's just for tonight. We'll drive on right after breakfast. It's important that you get some rest, hon. You can't fool me, you can hardly keep your eyes open any more."

She tucked her hand consolingly under my arm. "I don't mind if you don't. It'll give me something to look forward to, seeing you in the morning."

The bellboy led us along a quiet, green-carpeted hall, and around a turn, scanning numbers on the doors. He stopped three down from the turn, on the right-hand side, put his key in. "This is it here, sir." The number was 1006.

The man at the desk hadn't exaggerated. The room itself was little better than an alcove, long and narrow. I suppose two could have gotten into it; but it would have been a physical impossibility for two to sleep in it the way it was fitted up. It had a cot that was little wider than a shelf.

To give you an idea how narrow the room was, the window was narrower than average, and yet not more than a foot of wall-strip showed on either side of its frame. In other words it took up nearly the width of one entire side of the room.

I suppose I could have sat up in the single armchair all night and slept, or tried to, that way; but as long as there was a chance of getting a horizontal bed at the Y, why not be sensible about it? She agreed with me in this.

"Think you can go this, just until the morning?" I asked her, and the longing way she was eyeing that miserable cot gave me the answer. She was so tired, anything would have looked good to her right then.

We went down again and I told him I'd take it. I had the bellboy take her bag out of the car and bring it in, and the desk clerk turned the register around for her to sign.

She poised the inked pen and flashed me a tender look just as she was about to sign. "First time I've used it," she breathed. I looked over her shoulder and watched her trace *Mrs. James Cannon* along the lined space. The last entry above hers was *A. Krumbake, and wife.* I noticed it because it was such a funny name.

The desk clerk had evidently decided by now that we

were fairly desirable people. "I'm terrible sorry I couldn't do more for you," he said. "It's just for this one night. By tomorrow morning a lot of them'll be leaving."

I went up with her a second time, to see that she was made as comfortable as she could be under the circumstances. But then there was nothing definitely wrong with the room except its tininess, and the only real hardship was our temporary separation.

I tipped the boy for bringing up her bag, and then I tipped him a second time for going and digging up a nice, fluffy quilt for her at my request—not to spread over her but to spread on top of the mattress and soften it up a little. Those cots aren't as comfortable as regular beds by a darned sight. But she was so tired I was hoping she wouldn't notice the difference.

Then after he'd thanked me for the double-header he'd gotten out of it, and left the room, I helped her off with her coat and hung it up for her, and even got down on my heels and undid the straps of her little sandals, so she wouldn't have to bend over and go after them herself. Then we kissed a couple of times and told each other all about it, and I backed out the door.

The last I saw of her that night she was sitting on the edge of that cot in there, her shoeless feet raised to it and partly tucked under her, like a little girl. She raised one hand, wriggled the fingers at me in good-night as I reluctantly eased the door closed.

"Until tomorrow, sweetheart," she called gently, when there was a crack of opening left.

"Until tomorrow."

The night was as still around us as if it were holding its breath. The latch went *cluck*, and there we were on opposite sides of it.

The bellboy had taken the car down with him just now after he'd checked her in, and I had to wait out there a minute or two for him to bring it back up again at my ring. I stepped back to the turn in the hall while waiting, to look at the frosted glass transom over her door; and short as the time was, her light was already out. She must have just shrugged off her dress, fallen back flat, and pulled the coverings up over her.

Poor kid, I thought, with a commiserating shake of my head. The glass elevator panel flooded with light and I got in the car. The one bellhop doubled for lift-man after twelve.

"I guess she'll be comfortable," he said.

"She was asleep before I left the floor," I told him.

The desk man told me where the nearest branch of the Y was, and I took the car with me as the quickest way of getting over there at that hour. I had no trouble at all getting a room, and not a bad one at that for six bits.

I didn't phone her before going up, to tell her I'd gotten something for myself, because I knew by the way I'd seen that light go out she was fast asleep already, and it would have been unnecessarily cruel to wake her again.

I woke up at eight and again I didn't phone her, to find out how she was, because in the first place I was going right over there myself in a few more minutes, and in the second place I wanted her to get all the sleep she could before I got there.

I even took my time, showered and shaved up good, and drove over slowly, to make sure of not getting there any earlier than nine.

It was a beautiful day, with the sun as brand-new-looking as if it had never shone before; and I even stopped off and bought a gardenia for her to wear on the shoulder of her dress. I thought: I'll check her out of that depressing dump. We'll drive to the swellest restaurant in town, and she'll sit having orange juice and toast while I sit looking at her face.

I braked in front of the Royal, got out, and went in, lighting up the whole lobby the way I was beaming.

A different man was at the desk now, on the day shift, but I knew the number of her room so I rode right up without stopping. I got out at the tenth, went down the hall the way we'd been led last night—still green-carpeted but a little less quiet now—and around the turn.

When I came to the third door down, on the right-hand side—the door that had 1006 on it—I stopped and listened a minute to see if I could tell whether she was up yet or not. If she wasn't up yet, I was going back downstairs again, hang around in the lobby, and give her another half-hour of badly-needed sleep.

But she was up already. I could hear a sound in there as if she were brushing out her dress or coat with a stiff-bristled brush—*skish, skish, skish*—so I knocked, easy and loving, on the door with just three knuckles.

The *skish-skish-skish* broke off a minute, but then went right on again. But the door hadn't been tightly closed into the frame at all, and my knocking sent it drifting inward an inch or two. A whiff of turpentine or something like that nearly threw me over, but without stopping to distinguish what it was, I pushed the door the rest of the way in and walked in.

Then I pulled up short. I saw I had the wrong room.

There wasn't anything in it—no furniture, that is. Just bare floorboards, walls and ceiling. Even the light fixture had been taken down, and two black wires stuck out of a hole, like insect feelers, where it had been.

A man in spotted white overalls and peaked cap was standing on a step-ladder slapping a paint brush up and down the walls. *Skish-skish-splop!*

I grunted, "Guess I've got the wrong number," and backed out.

"Guess you must have, bud," he agreed, equally laconic, without even turning his head to see who I was.

I looked up at the door from the outside. Number 1006. But that was the number they'd given her, sure it was. I looked in a second time. Long and narrow, like an alcove. Not more than a foot of wall space on either side of the window frame.

Sure, this was the room, all right. They must have found out they had something better available after all, and changed her after I left last night. I said, "Where'd they put the lady that was in here, you got any idea?"

Skish-skish-skish. "I dunno, bud, you'll have to find out at the desk. It was empty when I come here to work at seven." *Skish-skish-splop!*

I went downstairs to the desk again, and I said, "Excuse me. What room have you got Mrs. Cannon in now?"

He looked up some chart or other they use, behind the scenes, then he came back and said, "We have no Mrs. Cannon here."

I pulled my face back. Then I thrust it forward again. "What's the matter with you?" I said curtly. "I came here with her myself last night. Better take another look."

He did. A longer one. Then he came back and said, "I'm sorry, there's no Mrs. Cannon registered here."

I knew there was nothing to get excited about; it would probably be straightened out in a minute or two; but it was a pain in the neck. I was very patient. After all, this was the first morning of my honeymoon. "Your night man was on duty at the time. It was about three this morning. He gave her 1006."

He looked that up too. "That's not in use," he said. "That's down for redecorating. It's been empty for—"

"I don't care what it is. I tell you they checked my wife in there at three this morning, I went up with her myself! Will you quit arguing and find out what room she's in, for me? I don't want to stand here talking to you all day; I want to be with her."

"But I'm telling you, mister, the chart shows no one by that name."

"Then look in the register if you don't believe me. I watched her sign it myself."

People were standing around the lobby looking at me now, but I didn't care.

"It would be on the chart," he insisted. "It would have been transferred—" He ran the pad of his finger up the register page from bottom to top. Too fast, I couldn't help noticing: without a hitch, as if there were nothing to impede it. Then he went back a page and ran it up that, in the same streamlined way.

"Give it to me," I said impatiently. "I'll find it for you in a minute." I flung it around my way.

A. Krumbake, and wife stared at me. And then under that just a blank space all the way down to the bottom of the page. No more check-ins.

I could feel the pores of my face sort of closing up. That was what it felt like, anyway. Maybe it was just the process of getting pale. "She signed right under that name. It's been rubbed out."

"Oh, no, it hasn't," he told me firmly. "No one tampers with the register like that. People may leave, but their names stay on it."

Dazedly, I traced the ball of my finger back and forth across the white paper under that name, *Krumbake*. Smooth and unrubbed, its semi-glossy finish unimpaired by erasure. I held the page up toward the light and tried to squint through it, to see whether it showed thinner there, either from rubbing or some other means of eradication. It was all of the same even opacity.

I spoke in a lower voice now; I wasn't being impatient any more. "There's something wrong. Something wrong about this. I can't understand it. I saw her write it. I saw her sign it with my own eyes. I've known it was the right hotel all along, but even if I wasn't sure, this other name, this name above, would prove it to me. Krumbake. I remember it from last night. Maybe they changed her without notifying you down here."

"That wouldn't be possible; it's through me, down here, that all changes are made. It isn't that I don't know what room she's in; it's that there's absolutely no record of any such person ever having been at the hotel, so you see you must be mis—"

"Call the manager for me," I said hoarsely.

I stood there waiting by the onyx-topped desk until he came. I stood there very straight, very impassive, not touching the edge of the counter with my hands in any way, about an inch clear of it.

People were bustling back and forth, casually, normally, cheerily, behind me; plinking their keys down on the onyx; saying, "Any mail for me?"; saying, "I'll be in the coffee shop if I'm called." And something was already trying to make me feel a little cut off from them, a little set apart. As if a shadowy finger had drawn a ring around me where I stood, and mystic vapors were already beginning to rise from it, walling me off from my fellowmen.

I wouldn't let the feeling take hold of me—yet—but it was already there, trying to. I'd give an imperceptible shake of my head every once in a while and say to myself, "Things like this don't happen in broad daylight. It's just some kind of misunderstanding; it'll be cleared up presently."

The entrance, the lobby, had seemed so bright when

I first came in, but I'd been mistaken. There were shadows lengthening in the far corners that only I could see. The gardenia I had for her was wilting.

The manager was no help at all. He tried to be, listened attentively, but then the most he could do was have the clerk repeat what he'd already done for me, look on the chart and look in the register. After all, details like that were in the hands of the staff. I simply got the same thing as before, only relayed through him now instead of direct from the desk man. "No, there hasn't been any Mrs. Cannon at any time."

"Your night man will tell you," I finally said in despair, "he'll tell you I brought her here. Get hold of him, ask him. He'll remember us."

"I'll call him down; he rooms right here in the house," he said. But then with his hand on the phone he stopped to ask again, "Are you quite sure it was this hotel, Mr. Cannon? He was on duty until six this morning, and I hate to wake him up unless you—"

"Bring him down," I said. "This is more important to me than his sleep. It's got to be cleared up." I wasn't frightened yet, out-and-out scared; just baffled, highly worried, and with a peculiar lost feeling.

He came down inside of five minutes. I knew him right away, the minute he stepped out of the car, in spite of the fact that other passengers had come down with him. I was so sure he'd be able to straighten it out that I took a step toward him without waiting for him to join us. If they noticed that, which was a point in favor of my credibility—my knowing him at sight like that—they gave no sign.

I said, "You remember me, don't you? You remember checking my wife into 1006 at three this morning, and telling me I'd have to go elsewhere?"

"No," he said with polite regret. "I'm afraid I don't."
I could feel my face go white as if a soundless bomb-

shell of flour or talcum had just burst all over it. I put
one foot behind me and set the heel down and stayed
that way.

The manager asked him, "Well, did the gentleman
stop at the desk perhaps, just to inquire, and then go
elsewhere? Do you remember him at all, Stevens?"

"No, I never saw him until now. It must have been
some other hotel."

"But look at me; look at my face," I tried to say. But
I guess I didn't put any voice into it, it was just lip-
motion, because he didn't seem to hear.

The manager shrugged amiably, as if to say, "Well,
that's all there is to it, as far as we're concerned."

I was breathing hard, fighting for self-control. "No.
No, you can't close this matter. I dem—I ask you to
give me one more chance to prove that I—that I—Call
the night porter, the night bellboy that carried up her
bag for her."

They were giving one another looks by now, as if I
were some sort of crank.

"Listen, I'm in the full possession of my faculties, I'm
not drunk, I wouldn't come in here like this if I weren't
positive—"

The manager was going to try to pacify me and ease
me out. "But don't you see you must be mistaken, old
man? There's absolutely no record of it. We're very
strict about those things. If any of my men checked a
guest in without entering it on the chart of available
rooms, and in the register, I'd fire him on the spot.
Was it the Palace? Was it the Commander, maybe? Try
to think now, you'll get it."

And with each soothing syllable, he led me a step
nearer the entrance.

I looked up suddenly, saw that the desk had already
receded a considerable distance behind us, and balked.
"No, don't do this. This is no way to—Will you get

that night-to-morning bellhop? Will you do that one
more thing for me?"

He sighed, as if I were trying his patience sorely.
"He's probably home sleeping. Just a minute; I'll find
out."

It turned out he wasn't. They were so overcrowded
and undermanned at the moment that instead of being
at home he was sleeping right down in the basement,
to save time coming and going. He came up in a couple
of minutes, still buttoning the collar of his uniform. I
knew him right away. He didn't look straight at me at
first, but at the manager.

"Do you remember seeing this gentleman come here
with a lady, at three this morning? Do you remember
carrying her bag up to 1006 for her?"

Then he did look straight at me—and didn't seem to
know me. "No, sir, Mr. DeGrasse."

The shock wasn't as great as the first time; it couldn't
have been, twice in succession.

"Don't you remember that quilt you got for her, to
spread over the mattress, and I gave you a second quarter for bringing it? You must remember that—dark
blue, with little white flowers all over it—"

"No, sir, boss."

"But I know your face! I remember that scar just over
your eyebrow. And—part your lips a little—that gold
cap in front that shows every time you grin."

"No, sir, not me."

My voice was curling up and dying inside my throat.
"Then when you took me down alone with you, the last
time, you even said, 'I guess she'll be comfortable'—" I
squeezed his upper arm pleadingly. "Don't you remember? Don't you remember?"

"No, sir." This time he said it so low you could
hardly hear it, as if his training wouldn't let him contra-

dict me too emphatically, but on the other hand he felt obliged to stick to the facts.

I grabbed at the hem of my coat, bunched it up to emphasize the pattern and the color of the material. "Don't you know me by this?" Then I let my fingers trail helplessly down the line of my jaw. "Don't you know my face?"

He didn't answer any more, just shook his head each time.

"What're you doing this for? What're you trying to do to me? All of you?" The invisible fumes from that necromancer's ring, that seemed to cut me off from all the world, came swirling up thicker and thicker about me. My voice was strident with a strange new kind of fear, a fear I hadn't known since I was ten.

"You've got me rocky now! You've got me down! Cut it out, I say!"

They were starting to draw back little by little away from me, prudently widen the tight knot they had formed around me. I turned from one to the other, from bellhop to night clerk, night clerk to day clerk, day clerk to manager, and each one as I turned to him retreated slightly.

There was a pause, while I fought against this other, lesser kind of death that was creeping over me—this death called *strangeness*, this snapping of all the customary little threads of cause and effect that are our moorings at other times. Slowly they all drew back from me step by step, until I was left there alone, cut off.

Then the tension exploded. My voice blasted the quiet of the lobby. "I want my wife!" I yelled shatteringly. "Tell me what's become of her. What've you done with her? I came in here with her last night; you can't tell me I didn't. . . ."

They circled, maneuvered around me. I heard the manager say in a harried undertone, "I knew this was going to happen. I could have told you he was going to end up like this. George! Archer! Get him out of here fast!"

My arms were suddenly seized from behind and held. I threshed against the constriction, so violently both my legs flung up clear of the floor at one time, dropped back again, but I couldn't break it. There must have been two of them behind me.

The manager had come in close again, now that I was safely pinioned, no doubt hoping that his nearness would succeed in soft-pedaling the disturbance, "Now will you leave here quietly, or do you want us to call the police and turn you over to them?"

"You'd better call them anyway, Mr. DeGrasse," the day clerk put in. "I've run into this mental type before. He'll only come back in again the very minute your back's turned."

"No, I'd rather not, unless he forces me to. It's bad for the hotel. Look at the crowd collecting down here on the main floor already. Tchk! Tchk!"

He tried to reason with me. "Now listen, give me a break, will you? You don't look like the kind of a man who—Won't you please go quietly? If I have you turned loose outside, will you go away and promise not to come in here again?"

"*Ali-i-i-ice!*" I sent it baying harrowingly down the long vista of lobby, lounges, foyers. I'd been gathering it in me the last few seconds while he was speaking to me. I put my heart and soul into it. It should have shaken down the big old-fashioned chandeliers by the vibration it caused alone. My voice broke under the strain. A woman onlooker somewhere in the background bleated at the very intensity of it.

The manager hit himself between the eyes in consternation. "Oh, this is fierce! Hurry up, call an officer quick, get him out of here."

"See, what did I tell you?" the clerk said knowingly.

I got another chestful of air in, tore loose with it. "Somebody help me! You people standing around looking, isn't there one of you will help me? I brought my wife here last night; now she's gone and they're trying to tell me I never—"

A brown hand suddenly sealed my mouth, was as quickly withdrawn again at the manager's panic-stricken admonition. "George! Archer! Don't lay a hand on him. No rough stuff. Make us liable for damages afterwards, y'know."

Then I heard him and the desk man both give a deep breath of relief. "At last!" And I knew a cop must have come in behind me.

The grip on my arms behind my back changed, became single instead of double, one arm instead of two. But I didn't fight against it.

Suddenly I was very passive, unresistant. Because suddenly I had a dread of arrest, confinement. I wanted to preserve my freedom of movement more than all else, to try to find her again. If they threw me in a cell, or put me in a straitjacket, how could I look for her, how could I ever hope to get at the bottom of this mystery?

The police would never believe me. If the very people who had seen her denied her existence, how could I expect those who hadn't to believe in it?

Docile, I let him lead me out to the sidewalk in front of the hotel. The manager came out after us, mopping his forehead, and the desk clerk, and a few of the bolder among the guests who had been watching.

They held a three-cornered consultation in which I took no part. I even let the manager's version of what the trouble was pass unchallenged. Not that he distorted what had actually happened just now, but he made it seem as if I were mistaken about having brought her there last night.

Finally the harness cop asked, "Well, do you want to press charges against him for creating a disturbance in your lobby?"

The manager held his hands palms out, horrified. "I should say not. We're having our biggest rush of the year right now; I can't take time off to run down there and go through all that tommyrot. Just see that he doesn't come in again and create any more scenes."

"I'll see to that all right," the cop promised truculently.

They went inside again, the manager and the clerk and the gallery that had watched us from the front steps. Inside to the hotel that had swallowed her alive.

The cop read me a lecture, to which I listened in stony silence. Then he gave me a shove that sent me floundering, said, "Keep moving now, hear me?"

I pointed, and said, "That's my car standing there. May I get in it?" He checked first to make sure it was, then he opened the door, said, "Yeah, get in it and get out of here."

He'd made no slightest attempt to find out what was behind the whole thing; whether there was some truth to my story or not, or whether it was drink, drugs, or mental aberration. But then he was only a harness cop. That's why I hadn't wanted to tangle with him.

This strangeness that had risen up around me was nothing to be fought by an ordinary patrolman. I was going to them—the police—but I was going of my own free will and in my own way, not to be dragged in by the scruff of the neck and then put under observation for the next twenty-four hours.

Ten minutes or so later I got in front of the first precinct house I came upon, and went in, and said to the desk sergeant, "I want to talk to the lieutenant in charge."

He stared at me coldly.

"What about?"

"About my wife."

I didn't talk to him alone. Three of his men were present. They were just shapes in the background as far as I was concerned, sitting there very quietly, listening.

I told it simply, hoping against hope I could get them to believe me, feeling somehow I couldn't even before I had started.

"I'm Jimmy Cannon, I'm twenty-five years old, and I'm from Lake City. Last evening after dark my girl and I—her name was Alice Brown—we left there in my car, and at 1:15 this morning we were married by a justice of the peace.

"I think his name was Hulskamp—anyway it's a white house with morning glories all over the porch, about fifty miles this side of Lake City.

"We got in here at three, and they gave her a little room at the Royal Hotel. They couldn't put me up, but they put her up alone. The number was 1006. I know that as well as I know I'm sitting here. This morning when I went over there, they were painting the room and I haven't been able to find a trace of her since.

"I saw her sign the register, but her name isn't on it any more. The bellboy says he never saw her. Now they've got me so I'm scared and shaky, like a little kid is of the dark. I want you men to help me. Won't you men help me?"

"We'll help you"—said the lieutenant in charge. Slowly, awfully slowly; I didn't like that slowness—"if we're able to." And I knew what he meant; if we find any evidence that your story is true.

He turned his head toward one of the three shadowy

listeners in the background, at random. The one nearest him. Then he changed his mind, shifted his gaze further along, to the one in the middle. "Ainslie, suppose you take a whack at this. Go over to this hotel and see what you can find out. Take him with you."

So, as he stood up, I separated him from the blurred background for the first time. I was disappointed. He was just another man like me, maybe five years older, maybe an inch or two shorter. He could feel cold and hungry and tired, just as I could. He could believe a lie, just as I could. He couldn't see around corners or through walls, or into hearts, any more than I could. What good was he going to be?

He looked as if he'd seen every rotten thing there was in the world. He looked as if he'd once expected to see other things beside that, but didn't any more. He said, "Yes, sir," and you couldn't tell whether he was bored or interested, or liked the detail or resented it, or gave a rap.

On the way over I said, "You've got to find out what became of her. You've got to make them—"

"I'll do what I can." He couldn't seem to get any emotion into his voice. After all, from his point of view, why should he?

"You'll do what you can!" I gasped. "Didn't you ever have a wife?"

He gave me a look, but you couldn't tell what was in it.

We went straight back to the Royal. He was very businesslike, did a streamlined, competent job. Didn't waste a question or a motion, but didn't leave out a single relevant thing either.

I took back what I'd been worried about at first; he was good.

But he wasn't good enough for this, whatever it was. It went like this: "Let me see your register." He took out a glass, went over the place I pointed out to him where she had signed. Evidently couldn't find any marks of erasure any more than I had with my naked eye.

Then we went up to the room, 1006. The painter was working on the wood trim by now, had all four walls and the ceiling done. It was such a small cubbyhole it wasn't even a half-day's work. He said, "Where was the furniture when you came in here to work this morning? Still in the room, or had the room been cleared?"

"Still in the room; I cleared it myself. There wasn't much; a chair, a scatter-rug, a cot."

"Was the cot made or unmade?"

"Made up."

"Was the window opened or closed when you came in?"

"Closed tight."

"Was the air in the room noticeably stale, as if it had been closed up that way all night, or not noticeably so, as if it had only been closed up shortly before?"

"Turrible, like it hadn't been aired for a week. And believe me, when I notice a place is stuffy, you can bet it's stuffy all right."

"Were there any marks on the walls or floor or anywhere around the room that didn't belong there?"

I knew he meant blood, and gnawed the lining of my cheek fearfully.

"Nothing except plain grime, that needed painting bad."

We visited the housekeeper next. She took us to the linen room and showed us. "If there're any dark blue quilts in use in this house, it's the first I know about it. The bellboy *could* have come in here at that hour—but all he would have gotten are maroon ones. And here's my supply list, every quilt accounted for. So it didn't come from here."

We visited the baggage room next. "Look around and see if there's anything in here that resembles that bag of your wife's." I did, and there wasn't. Wherever she had gone, whatever had become of her, her bag had gone with her.

About fifty minutes after we'd first gone in, we were back in my car outside the hotel again. He'd done a good, thorough job; and if I was willing to admit that, it must have been.

We sat there without moving a couple of minutes, me under the wheel. He kept looking at me steadily, sizing me up. I couldn't tell what he was thinking. I threw my head back and started to look up the face of the building, story by story. I counted as my eyes rose, and when they'd come to the tenth floor I stopped them there, swung them around the corner of the building to the third window from the end, stopped them there for good. It was a skinnier window than the others. So small, so high up, to hold so much mystery. "Alice," I whispered up to it, and it didn't answer, didn't hear.

His voice brought my gaze down from there again. "The burden of the proof has now fallen on you. It's up to you to give me some evidence that she actually went in there. That she actually was with you. That she actually *was*. I wasn't able to find a single person in that building who actually saw her."

I just looked at him, the kind of a look you get from someone right after you stick a knife in his heart. Finally I said with quiet bitterness. "So now I have to prove I had a wife."

The instant, remorseless way he answered that was brutal in itself. "Yes, you do. Can you?"

I pushed my hat off, raked my fingers through my hair, with one and the same gesture. "Could you, if someone asked you in the the middle of the street? Could you?"

He peeled out a wallet, flipped it open. A tiny snapshot of a woman's head and shoulders danced in front of my eyes for a split second. He folded it and put it away again. He briefly touched a gold band on his finger, token of that old custom that is starting to revive again, of husbands wearing marriage rings as well as wives.

"And a dozen other ways. You could call Tremont 4102. Or you could call the marriage clerk at the City Hall—"

"But we were just beginning," I said bleakly. "I have no pictures. She was wearing the only ring we had. The certificate was to be mailed to us at Lake City in a few days. You could call this justice of the peace, Hulskamp, out near U.S. 9; he'll tell you—"

"Okay, Cannon, I'll do that. We'll go back to the headquarters, I'll tell the lieutenant what I've gotten so far, and I'll do it from there."

Now at last it would be over, now at last it would be straightened out. He left me sitting in the room outside the lieutenant's office, while he was in there reporting to him. He seemed to take a long time, so I knew he must be doing more than just reporting; they must be talking it over.

Finally Ainslie looked at me, but only to say, "What was the name of that justice you say married you, again?"

"Hulskamp."

He closed the door again. I had another long wait. Finally it opened a second time, he hitched his head at me to come in. The atmosphere, when I got in there, was one of hard, brittle curiosity, without any feeling to it. As when you look at somebody afflicted in a way you never heard of before, and wonder how he got that way.

I got that distinctly. Even from Ainslie, and it was

fairly oozing from his lieutenant and the other men in the room. They looked and looked and looked at me.

The lieutenant did the talking. "You say a Justice Hulskamp married you. You still say that?"

"A white house sitting off the road, this side of Lake City, just before you get to U. S. 9—"

"Well, there is a Justice Hulskamp, and he does live out there. We just had him on the phone. He says he never married anyone named James Cannon to anyone named Alice Brown, last night or any other night. He hasn't married anyone who looks like you, recently, to anyone who looks as you say she did. He didn't marry anyone at all at any time last night—"

He was going off some place while he talked to me, and his voice was going away after him. Ainslie filled a paper cup with water at the cooler in the corner, strewed it deftly across my face, once each way, as if I were some kind of a potted plant, and one of the other guys picked me up from the floor and put me back on the chair again.

The lieutenant's voice came back again stronger, as if he hadn't gone away after all. "Who were her people in Lake City?"

"She was an orphan."

"Well, where did she work there?"

"At the house of a family named Beresford, at 20 New Hampshire Avenue. She was in service there, a maid; she lived with them—"

"Give me long distance. Give me Lake City. This is Michianopolis police headquarters. I want to talk to a party named Beresford, 20 New Hampshire Avenue."

The ring came back fast. "We're holding a man here who claims he married a maid working for you. A girl by the name of Alice Brown."

He'd hung up before I even knew it was over.

"There's no maid employed there. They don't know anything about any Alice Brown, never heard of her."

I stayed on the chair this time. I just didn't hear so clearly for a while, everything sort of fuzzy.

". . . Hallucinations . . . And he's in a semi-hysterical condition right now. Notice how jerky his reflexes are?" Someone was chopping the edge of his hand at my kneecaps. "Seems harmless. Let him go. It'll probably wear off. I'll give him a sedative." Someone snapped a bag shut, left the room.

The lieutenant's voice was as flat as it was deadly, and it brooked no argument. "You never had a wife, Cannon!"

I could see only Ainslie's face in the welter before me. "You have, though, haven't you?" I said, so low none of the others could catch it.

The lieutenant was still talking to me. "Now get out of here before we change our minds and call an ambulance to take you away. And don't go back into any more hotels raising a row."

I hung around outside; I wouldn't go away. Where was there to go? One of the others came out, looked at me fleetingly in passing, said with humorous tolerance, "You better get out of here before the lieutenant catches you," and went on about his business.

I waited until I saw Ainslie come out. Then I went up to him. "I've go to talk to you; you've got to listen to me—"

"Why? The matter's closed. You heard the lieutenant."

He went back to some sort of a locker room. I went after him.

"You're not supposed to come back here. Now look, Cannon, I'm telling you for your own good, you're looking for trouble if you keep this up."

"Don't turn me down," I said hoarsely, tugging away at the seam of his sleeve. "Can't you see the state I'm in? I'm like someone in a dark room, crying for a match. I'm like someone drowning, crying for a helping hand. I can't make it alone any more."

There wasn't anyone in the place but just the two of us. My pawing grip slipped down his sleeve to the hem of his coat, and I was looking up at him from my knees. What did I care? There was no such thing as pride or dignity any more. I would have crawled flat along the floor on my belly, just to get a word of relief out of anyone.

"Forget you're a detective, and I'm a case. I'm appealing to you as one human being to another. I'm appealing to you as one husband to another. Don't turn your back on me like that, don't pull my hands away from your coat. I don't ask you to do anything for me any more; you don't have to lift a finger. Just say, 'Yes, you had a wife, Cannon.' Just give me that one glimmer of light in the dark. say it even if you don't mean it, even if you don't believe it, say it anyway. Oh, say it, will you—"

He drew the back of his hand slowly across his mouth, either in disgust at my abasement or in a sudden access of pity. Maybe a little of both. His voice was hoarse, as if he were sore at the spot I was putting him on.

"Give me anything," he said, shaking me a little and jogging me to my feet, "the slightest thing, to show that she ever existed, to show that there ever was such a person outside of your own mind, and I'll be with you to the bitter end. Give me a pin that she used to fasten her dress with. Give me a grain of powder, a stray hair; but prove that it was hers. But I can't do it unless you do."

"And I have nothing to show you. Not a pin, not a grain of powder."

I took a few dragging steps toward the locker-room door. "You're doing something to me that I wouldn't do to a dog," I mumbled. "What you're doing to me is worse than if you were to kill me. You're locking me up in shadows for the rest of my life. You're taking my mind away from me. You're condemning me slowly but surely to madness, to being without a mind. It won't happen right away, but sooner or later, in six months or in a year—Well, I guess that's that."

I fumbled my way out of the locker room and down the passageway outside, guiding myself with one arm along the wall, and past the sergeant's desk and down the steps, and then I was out in the street.

I left my car there where it was. What did I want with it? I started to walk, without knowing where I was going. I walked a long time, and a good long distance.

Then all of a sudden I noticed a lighted drugstore—it was dark by now—across the way. I must have passed others before now, but this was the first one I noticed.

I crossed over and looked in the open doorway. It had telephone booths; I could see them at the back, to one side. I moved on a few steps, stopped, and felt in my pockets. I found a quill toothpick, and I dug the point of it good and hard down the back of my finger, ripped the skin open. Then I threw it away. I wrapped a handkerchief around the finger, and I turned around and went inside.

I said to the clerk, "Give me some iodine. My cat just scratched me and I don't want to take any chances."

He said, "Want me to put it on for you?"

I said, "No, gimme the whole bottle. I'll take it home; we're out of it."

I paid him for it and moved over to one side and started to thumb through one of the directories in the rack. Just as he went back inside the prescription room, I found my number. I went into the end booth and pulled the slide closed. I took off my hat and hung it over the phone mouthpiece, sort of making myself at home.

Then I sat down and started to undo the paper he'd just wrapped around the bottle. When I had it off, I pulled the knot of my tie out a little further to give myself lots of room. Then I took the stopper out of the bottle and tilted my head back and braced myself.

Something that felt like a baseball bat came chopping down on the arm I was bringing up, and nearly broke it in two, and the iodine sprayed all over the side of the booth. Ainslie was standing there in the half-opened slide.

He said, "Come on outta there!" and gave me a pull by the collar of my coat that did it for me. He didn't say anything more until we were out on the sidewalk in front of the place. Then he stopped and looked me over from head to foot as if I were some kind of a microbe. He said, "Well, it was worth coming all this way after you, at that!"

My car was standing there; I must have left the keys in it and he must have tailed me in that. He thumbed it, and I went over and climbed in and sat there limply. He stayed outside, with one foot on the running board.

I said, "I can't live with shadows, Ainslie. I'm frightened, too frightened to go on. You don't know what the nights'll be like from now on. And the days won't be much better. I'd rather go now, fast. Show her to me on a slab at the morgue and I won't whimper. Show her to me all cut up in small pieces and I won't bat an eyelash. But don't say she never was."

"I guessed what was coming from the minute I saw you jab yourself with that toothpick." He watched sardonically while I slowly unwound the handkerchief, that had stayed around my finger all this time. The scratch had hardly bled at all. Just a single hairline of red was on the handkerchief.

We both looked at that.

Then more of the handkerchief came open. We both looked at the initials in the corner. *A.B.* We both, most likely, smelled the faint sweetness that still came from it at the same time. Very faint, for it was such a small handkerchief.

We both looked at each other, and both our minds made the same discovery at the same time. I was the one who spoke it aloud. "It's hers," I said grimly; "the wife that didn't exist."

"This is a fine time to come out with it," he said quietly. "Move over, I'll drive." That was his way of saying, "I'm in."

I said, "I remember now. I got a cinder in my eye, during the drive in, and she lent me her handkerchief to take it out with; I didn't have one of my own on me. I guess I forgot to give it back to her. And this—is it." I looked at him rebukingly. "What a difference a few square inches of linen can make. Without it, I was a madman. With it, I'm a rational being who enlists your cooperation. I could have picked it up in any five-and-ten."

"No. You didn't turn it up when it would have done you the most good, back at the station house. You only turned it up several minutes after you were already supposed to have gulped a bottle of iodine. I could tell by your face you'd forgotten about it until then yourself. I think that does make a difference. To me it does, anyway." He meshed gears.

"And what're you going to do about it?"

"Since we don't believe in the supernatural, our only possible premise is that there's been some human agency at work."

I noticed the direction he was taking. "Aren't you going back to the Royal?"

"There's no use bothering with the hotel. D'you see what I mean?"

"No, I don't," I said bluntly. "That was where she disappeared."

"The focus for this wholesale case of astigmatism is elsewhere, outside the hotel. It's true we could try to break them down, there at the hotel. But what about the justice, what about the Beresford house in Lake City? I think it'll be simpler to try to find out the reason rather than the mechanics of the disappearance.

"And the reason lies elsewhere. Because you brought her to the hotel from the justice's. And to the justice's from Lake City. The hotel was the last stage. Find out why the justice denies he married you, and we don't have to find out why the hotel staff denies having seen her. Find out why the Beresford house denies she was a maid there, and we don't have to find out why the justice denies he married you.

"Find out, maybe, something else, and we don't have to find out why the Beresford house denies she was a maid there. The time element keeps moving backward through the whole thing. Now talk to me. How long did you know her? How well? How much did you know about her?"

"Not long. Not well. Practically nothing. It was one of those storybook things. I met her a week ago last night. She was sitting on a bench in the park, as if she were lonely, didn't have a friend in the world. I don't make a habit of accosting girls on park benches, but she looked so dejected it got to me.

"Well, that's how we met. I walked her home afterwards to where she said she lived. But when we got there—holy smoke, it was a mansion! I got nervous, said: 'Gee, this is a pretty swell place for a guy like me to be bringing anyone home to, just a clerk in a store.'

"She laughed and said, 'I'm only the maid. Disappointed?' I said, 'No, I would have been disappointed if you'd been anybody else, because then you wouldn't be in my class.' She seemed relieved after I said that. She said, 'Gee, I've waited so long to find someone who'd like me for myself.'

"Well, to make a long story short, we made an appointment to meet at that same bench the next night. I waited there for two hours and she never showed up. Luckily I went back there the next night again—and there she was. She explained she hadn't been able to get out the night before; the people where she worked were having company or something.

"When I took her home that night I asked her name, which I didn't know yet, and that seemed to scare her. She got sort of flustered, and I saw her look at her handbag. It had the initials *A.B.* on it; I'd already noticed that the first night I met her. She said, 'Alice Brown.'

"By the third time we met we were already nuts about each other. I asked her whether she'd take a chance and marry me. She said, 'Is it possible someone wants to marry little Alice Brown, who hasn't a friend in the world?' I said yes, and that was all there was to it.

"Only, when I left her that night, she seemed kind of scared. First I thought she was scared I'd change my mind, back out, but it wasn't that. She said, 'Jimmy, let's hurry up and do it, don't let's put it off. Let's do it while—while we have the chance'; and she hung onto my sleeve tight with both hands.

"So the next day I asked for a week off, which I had coming to me from last summer anyway, and I waited for her with the car on the corner three blocks away from the house where she was in service. She came running as if the devil were behind her, but I thought that was because she didn't want to keep me waiting. She just had that one little overnight bag with her.

"She jumped in, and her face looked kind of white, and she said, 'Hurry, Jimmy, hurry!' And away we went. And until we were outside of Lake City, she kept looking back every once in a while, as if she were afraid someone was coming after us."

Ainslie didn't say much after all that rigmarole I'd given him. Just five words, after we'd driven on for about ten minutes or so. "She was afraid of something." And then in another ten minutes, "And whatever it was, it's what's caught up with her now."

We stopped at the filling station where Alice and I had stopped for gas the night before. I looked over the attendants, said: "There's the one serviced us." Ainslie called him over, played a pocket light on my face.

"Do you remember servicing this man last night? This man, and a girl with him?"

"Nope, not me. Maybe one of the oth—"

Neither of us could see his hands at the moment; they were out of range below the car door. I said, "He's got a white scar across the back of his right hand. I saw it last night when he was wiping the windshield."

Ainslie said, "Hold it up."

He did, and there was a white cicatrix across it, where stitches had been taken or something. Ainslie said, "Now whaddye say?"

It didn't shake him in the least. "I still say no. Maybe he saw me at one time or another, but I've never seen him, to my knowledge, with or without a girl." He waited a minute, then added: "Why should I deny it, if it was so?"

"We'll be back, in a day or in a week or in a month," Ainslie let him know grimly, "but we'll be back—to find that out."

We drove on. "Those four square inches of linen handkerchief will be wearing pretty thin, if this keeps up," I muttered dejectedly after a while.

"Don't let that worry you," he said, looking straight ahead. "Once I'm sold, I don't unsell easily."

We crossed U. S. 9 a half-hour later. A little white house came skimming along out of the darkness. "This is where I was married to a ghost," I said.

He braked, twisted the grip of the door latch. My hand shot down, stopped his arm.

"Wait; before you go in, listen to this. It may help out that handkerchief. There'll be a round mirror in the hall, to the left of the door, with antlers over it for a hatrack. In their parlor, where he read the service, there'll be an upright piano, with brass candle holders sticking out of the front of it, above the keyboard. It's got a scarf on it that ends in a lot of little plush balls. And on the music rack, the top selection is a copy of *Kiss Me Again*. And on the wall there's a painting of a lot of fruit rolling out of a basket. And this housekeeper, he calls her Dora."

"That's enough," he said in that toneless voice of his. "I told you I was with you anyway, didn't I? " He got out and went over and rang the bell. I went with him, of course.

They must have been asleep; they didn't answer right away. Then the housekeeper opened the door and looked out at us. Before we could say anything, we heard the justice call down the stairs, "Who is it, Dora?"

Ainslie asked if we could come in and talk to him, and straightened his necktie in the round mirror to the left of the door, with antlers over it.

Hulskamp came down in a bathrobe, and Ainslie said: "You married this man to a girl named Alice Brown last night." It wasn't a question.

The justice said, "No. I've already been asked that once, over the phone, and I said I hadn't. I've never seen this young man before." He even put on his glasses to look at me better.

Ainslie didn't argue the matter, almost seemed to take him at his word. "I won't ask you to let me see your records," he said drily, "because they'll undoubtedly—bear out your word."

He strolled as far as the parlor entrance, glanced in idly. I peered over his shoulder. There was an upright piano with brass candle sconces. A copy of *Kiss Me Again* was topmost on its rack. A painting of fruit rolling out of a basket daubed the wall.

"They certainly will!" snapped the justice resentfully.

The housekeeper put her oar in. "I'm a witness at all the marriages the justice performs, and I'm sure the young man's mistaken. I don't ever recall—"

Ainslie steadied me with one hand clasping my arm, and led me out without another word. We got in the car again. Their door closed, somewhat forcefully.

I pounded the rim of the wheel helplessly with my fist. I said, "What is it? Some sort of wholesale conspiracy? But *why*? She's not important; I'm not important."

He threw in the clutch, the little white house ebbed away in the night-darkness behind us.

"It's some sort of conspiracy, all right," he said. "We've got to get the reason for it. That's the quickest, shortest way to clear it up. To take any of the weaker links, the bellboy at the hotel or that filling station attendant, and break them down, would not only take days, but in the end would only get us some anonymous individual who'd either threatened them or paid them to forget having seen your wife, and we wouldn't be much further than before. If we can get the reason behind it all, the source, we don't have to bother with any of these small fry. That's why we're heading back to Lake City instead of just concentrating on that hotel in Michianopolis."

We made Lake City by one A.M. and I showed him the way to New Hampshire Avenue. Number 20 was a massive corner house, and we glided up to it from the back, along the side street; braked across the way from the service entrance I'd always brought her back to. Not a light was showing.

"Don't get out yet," he said. "When you brought her home nights, you brought her to this back door, right?"

"Yes."

"Tell me, did you ever actually see her open it and go in, or did you just leave her here by it and walk off without waiting to see where she went?"

I felt myself get a little frightened again. This was something that hadn't occurred to me until now. "I didn't once actually see the door open and her go inside, now that I come to think of it. She seemed to—to want me to walk off without waiting. She didn't say so, but I could tell. I thought maybe it was because she didn't want her employers to catch on she was going around with anyone. I'd walk off, down that way—"

I pointed to the corner behind us, on the next avenue over. "Then when I got there, I'd look back from there each time. As anyone would. Each time I did, she wasn't there any more. I thought she'd gone in, but—it's funny, I never saw her go in."

He nodded gloomily. "Just about what I thought. For all you know, she didn't even belong in that house, never went in there at all. A quick little dash, while your back was turned, would have taken her around the corner of the house and out of sight. And the city would have swallowed her up."

"But why?" I said helplessly.

He didn't answer that. We hadn't had a good look

at the front of the house yet. As I have said, we had approached from the rear, along the side street. He got out of the car now, and I followed suit. We walked down the few remaining yards to the corner, and turned and looked all up and down the front of it.

It was an expensive limestone building; it spelt real dough, even looking at it in the dark as we were. There was a light showing from the front, through one of the tall ground-floor windows—but a very dim one, almost like a night light. It didn't send any shine outside; just peered wanly around the sides of the blind that had been drawn on the inside.

Something moved close up against the door-facing, stirred a little. If it hadn't been white limestone, it wouldn't have even been noticeable at all. We both saw it at once; I caught instinctively at Ainslie's arm, and a cold knife of dull fear went through me—though why I couldn't tell.

"Crepe on the front door," he whispered. "Somebody's dead in there. Whether she did go in here or didn't, just the same I think we'd better have a look at the inside of this place."

I took a step in the direction of the front door. He recalled me with a curt gesture. "And by that I don't mean march up the front steps, ring the doorbell, and flash my badge."

"Then how?"

Brakes ground somewhere along the side street behind us. We turned our heads and a lacquered sedan-truck had drawn up directly before the service door of 20 New Hampshire Avenue. "Just in time," Ainslie said. "This is how."

We started back toward it. The driver and a helper had gotten down, were unloading batches of camp chairs and stacking them up against the side of the truck, preparatory to taking them in.

"For the services tomorrow, I suppose," Ainslie grunted. He said to the driver: "Who is it that died, bud?"

"Mean to say you ain't heard? It's in alla papers."

"We're from out of town."

"Alma Beresford, the heiress. Richest gal in twenty-four states. She was an orphum, too. Pretty soft for her guardian; not another soul to get the cash but him."

"What was it?" For the first time since I'd known him, you couldn't have called Ainslie's voice toneless; it was sort of springy like a rubber band that's pulled too tight.

"Heart attack, I think." The truckman snapped his fingers. "Like that. Shows you that rich or poor, when you gotta go, you gotta go."

Ainslie asked only one more question. "Why you bringing these setups at an hour like this? They're not going to hold the services in the middle of the night, are they?"

"Hah, but first thing in the morning; so early there wouldn't be a chance to get 'em over here unless we delivered 'em ahead of time." He was suddenly staring fascinatedly at the silvery lining of Ainslie's hand.

Ainslie's voice was toneless again. "Tell you what you fellows are going to do. You're going to save yourselves the trouble of hauling all those camp chairs inside, and you're going to get paid for it in the bargain. Lend us those work aprons y'got on."

He slipped them something apiece; I couldn't see whether it was two dollars or five. "Gimme your delivery ticket; I'll get it receipted for you. You two get back in the truck and lie low."

We both doffed our hats and coats, put them in our own car, rolled our shirtsleeves, put on the work aprons, and rang the service bell. There was a short wait and then a wire-sheathed bulb over the entry glimmered pallidly as an indication someone was coming. The door opened and a gaunt-faced sandy-haired man looked out at us. It was hard to tell just how old he was. He looked like a butler, but he was dressed in a business suit.

"Camp chairs from the Thebes Funerary Chapel," Ainslie said, reading from the delivery ticket.

"Follow me and I'll show you where they're to go," he said in a hushed voice. "Be as quiet as you can. We've only jut succeeded in getting Mr. Hastings to lie down and try to rest a little." The guardian, I supposed. In which case this anemic-looking customer would be the guardian's Man Friday.

We each grabbed up a double armful of the camp chairs and went in after him. They were corded together in batches of half a dozen. We could have cleared up the whole consignment at once—they were lightweight—but Ainslie gave me the eye not to; I guess he wanted to have an excuse to prolong our presence as much as possible.

You went down a short delivery passageway, then up a few steps into a brightly lighted kitchen.

A hatchet-faced woman in maid's livery was sitting by a table crying away under one eye-shading hand, a teacup and a tumbler of gin before her. Judging by the redness of her nose, she'd been at if for hours. "My baby," she'd mew every once in a while.

We followed him out at the other side, through a pantry, a gloomy-looking dining room, and finally into a huge cavernous front room, eerily suffused with flickering candlelight that did no more than heighten the shadows in its far corners. It was this wavering pallor that we must have seen from outside of the house.

An open coffin rested on a flower-massed bier at the upper end of the place, a lighted taper glimmering at each corner of it. A violet velvet pall had been spread over the top of it, concealing what lay within.

But a tiny peaked outline, that could have been made by an uptilted nose, was visible in the plush at one extremity of its length. That knife of dread gave an excruciating little twist in me, and again I didn't know why—or refused to admit I did. It was as if I instinctively sensed the nearness of something familiar.

The rest of the room, before this monument to mortality, had been left clear, its original furniture moved aside or taken out. The man who had admitted us gave us our instructions.

"Arrange them in four rows, here in front of the bier. Leave an aisle through them. And be sure and leave enough space up ahead for the divine who will deliver the oration." Then he retreated to the door and stood watching us for a moment.

Ainslie produced a knife from the pocket of his borrowed apron, began severing the cording that bound the frames of the camp chairs together. I opened them one at a time as he freed them and began setting them up in quadruple rows, being as slow about it as I could.

There was a slight sound and the factotum had tiptoed back toward the kitchen for a moment, perhaps for a sip of the comforting gin. Ainslie raised his head, caught my eye, speared his thumb at the bier imperatively. I was the nearer of us to it at the moment. I knew what he meant: look and see who it was.

I went cold all over, but I put down the camp chair I was fiddling with and edged over toward it on arched feet. The taper-flames bent down flat as I approached them, and sort of hissed. Sweat needled out under the roots of my hair. I went around by the head, where that tiny little peak was, reached out, and gingerly took hold of the corners of the velvet pall, which fell loosely over the two sides of the coffin without quite meeting the headboard.

Just as my wrists flexed to tip it back, Ainslie coughed

warningly. There was a whispered returning tread from beyond the doorway. I let go, took a quick side-jump back toward where I'd been.

I glanced around and the secretary fellow had come back again, was standing there with his eyes fixed on me. I pretended to be measuring off the distance for the pulpit with my foot.

"You men are rather slow about it," he said, thin-lipped.

"You want 'em just so, don't you?" Ainslie answered. He went out to get the second batch. I pretended one of the stools had jammed and I was having trouble getting it open, as an excuse to linger behind. The secretary was on his guard. He lingered too.

The dick took care of that. He waited until he was halfway back with his load of camp chairs, then dropped them all over the pantry floor with a clatter, to draw the watchdog off.

It worked. He gave a huff of annoyance, turned, and went in to bawl Ainslie out for the noise he had made. The minute the doorway cleared, I gave a cat-like spring back toward the velvet mound. This time I made it. I flung the pall back—

Then I let go of it, and the lighted candles started spinning around my head, faster and faster, until they made a comet-like track of fire. The still face staring up at me from the coffin was Alice's.

I felt my knees hit something, and I was swaying back and forth on them there beside the bier. I could hear somebody coming back toward the room, but whether it was Ainslie or the other guy I didn't know and didn't care. Then an arm went around me and steadied me to my feet once more, so I knew it was Ainslie.

"It's her," I said brokenly. "Alice. I can't understand

it; she must—have—been this rich girl, Alma Beresford, all the time—"

He let go of me, took a quick step over to the coffin, flung the pall even further back than I had. He dipped his head, as if he were staring nearsightedly. Then he turned and I never felt my shoulder grabbed so hard before, or since. His fingers felt like steel claws that went in, and met in the middle. For a minute I didn't know whether he was attacking me or not; and I was too dazed to care.

He was pointing at the coffin. "Look at that!" he demanded. I didn't know what he meant. He shook me brutally, either to get me to understand or because he was so excited himself. "*She's not dead.* Watch her chest cavern."

I fixed my eyes on it. You could tell only by watching the line where the white satin of her burial gown met the violet quilting of the coffin lining. The white was faintly, but unmistakably and rhythmically, rising and falling.

"They've got her either drugged or in a coma—"

He broke off short, let go of me as if my shoulder were red-hot and burned his fingers. His hand flashed down and up again, and he'd drawn and sighted over my shoulder. "Put it down or I'll let you have it right where you are!" he said.

Something thudded to the carpet. I turned and the secretary was standing there in the doorway, palms out, a fallen revolver lying at his feet.

"Go over and get that, Cannon," Ainslie ordered. "This looks like the finale now. Let's see what we've got."

There was an arched opening behind him, leading out to the front entrance hall, I suppose, and the stairway to the upper floors. We'd come in from the rear, remember. Velvet drapes had been drawn closed over that arch, sealing it up, the whole time we'd been in there.

He must have come in through there. I bent down before the motionless secretary, and, with my fingers an inch away from the fallen gun at his feet, I heard the impact of a head blow and Ainslie gave the peculiar guttural groan of someone going down into unconsciousness.

The secretary's foot snaked out and sped the gun skidding far across to the other side of the room. Then he dropped on my curved back like a dead weight and I went down flat under him, pushing my face into the parquet flooring.

He kept aiming blows at the side of my head from above, but he had only his fists to work with at the moment, and even the ones that landed weren't as effective as whatever it was that had been used on Ainslie. I reached upward and over, caught the secretary by the shoulders of his coat, tugged and at the same time jerked my body out from under him in the opposite direction; and he came flying up in a backward somersault and landed sprawling a few feet away.

I got up and looked. Ainslie lay inert, face down on the floor to one side of the coffin, something gleaming wet down the part of his hair. There was a handsome but vicious-looking gray-haired man in a brocaded dressing gown standing, behind him holding a gun on me, trying to cow me with it.

"Get him, Mr. Hastings," panted the one I'd just flung off.

It would have taken more than a gun to hold me, after what I'd been through. I charged at him, around Ainslie's form. He evidently didn't want to fire, didn't want the noise of a shot to be heard there in the house. Instead, he reversed his gun, swung the butt high up over his shoulder; and my own head-first charge undid me. I couldn't swerve or brake in time, plunged right in under it. A hissing, spark-shedding skyrocket seemed to tear through the top of my head, and I went down into nothingness as Ainslie had.

For an hour after I recovered consciousness I was in complete darkness. Such utter darkness that I couldn't be sure the blow hadn't affected my optic nerve.

I was in a sitting position, on something cold—stone flooring probably—with my hands lashed behind me, around something equally cold and sweating moisture, most likely a water pipe. My feet were tied too, and there was a gag over my mouth. My head blazed with pain.

After what seemed like an age, a smoky gray light began to dilute the blackness; so at least my eyesight wasn't impaired. As the light strengthened it showed me first a barred grate high up on the wall through which the dawn was peering in. Next, a dingy basement around me, presumably that of the same New Hampshire Avenue house we had entered several hours ago.

And finally, if that was any consolation to me, Ainslie sitting facing me from across the way, in about the same fix I was. Hands and feet secured, sitting before another pipe, mouth also gagged. A dark stain down one side of his forehead, long since dried, marked the effect of the blow he had received.

We just stared at each other, unable to communicate. We could turn our heads. He shook his from side to side deprecatingly. I knew what he meant: "Fine spot we ended up in, didn't we?" I nodded, meaning, "You said it."

But we were enjoying perfect comfort and peace of mind, compared to what was to follow. It came within about half an hour at the most. Sounds of activity began to penetrate to where we were. First a desultory moving about sounded over our heads, as if someone were looking things over to make sure everything was in order. Then something heavy was set down: it might have been a table, a desk—or a pulpit.

This cellar compartment we were in seemed to be directly under that large front room where the coffin was and where the obsequies were to be held.

A dawning horror began to percolate through me. I looked at Ainslie and tried to make him understand what I was thinking. I didn't need to, he was thinking the same thing.

She'd been alive when we'd last seen her, last night. Early this same morning, rather. What were they going to do—go ahead with it anyway?

A car door clashed faintly, somewhere off in the distance outside. It must have been at the main entrance of this very house we were in, for within a moment or two new footsteps sounded overhead, picking their way along, as down an aisle under guidance. Then something scraped slightly, like the leg rests of a camp chair straining under the weight of a body.

It repeated itself eight or ten times after that. The impact of a car door outside in the open, then the sedate footsteps over us—some the flat dull ones of men, some the sharp brittle ones of women—then the slight shift and click of the camp chairs. I didn't have to be told its meaning; probably Ainslie didn't either. The mourners were arriving for the services.

It was probably unintentional, our having been placed directly below like this; but it was the most diabolic torture that could ever have been devised. Was she dead yet, or wasn't she? But she had to be before—

They couldn't be that low. Maybe the drug she'd been under last night was timed to take fatal effect between then and now. But suppose it hadn't?

The two of us were writhing there like maimed

snakes. Ainslie kept trying to bring his knees up and
meet them with his chin, and at first I couldn't understand what his idea was. It was to snag the gag in the
cleft between his two tightly pressed knees and pull it
down, or at least dislodge it sufficiently to get some
sound out. I immediately began trying the same thing
myself.

Meanwhile an ominous silence had descended above
us. No more car-door thuds, no more footsteps mincing
down the aisle to their seats. The services were being
held.

The lower half of my face was all numb by now from
hitting my bony up-ended knees so many times. And
still I couldn't work it. Neither could he. The rounded
structure of the kneecaps kept them from getting close
enough to our lips to act as pincers. If only one of us
could have made it. If we could hear them that clearly
down here, they would have been able to hear us yell
up there. And they couldn't all be in on the plot, all
those mourners, friends of the family or whoever they
were.

Bad as the preliminaries had been, they were as nothing compared to the concluding stages that we now had
to endure listening to. There was a sudden concerted
mass shifting and scraping above, as if everyone had
risen to his feet at one time.

Then a slow, single-file shuffling started in, going in
one direction, returning in another. The mourners were
filing around the coffin one by one for a last look at
the departed. The departed who was still living.

After the last of them had gone out, and while the
incessant cracking of car doors was still under way outside, marking the forming of the funeral cortege, there
was a quick, businesslike converging of not more than
two pairs of feet on one certain place—where the coffin
was. A hurried shifting about for a moment or two,

then a sharp hammering on wood penetrated to where we were, and nearly drove me crazy; they were fastening down the lid.

After a slight pause that might have been employed in reopening the closed-room doors, more feet came in, all male, and moving toward that one certain place where the first two had preceded them. These must be the pallbearers, four or six of them. There was a brief scraping and jockeying about while they lifted the casket to their shoulders, and then the slow, measured tread with which they carried it outside to the waiting hearse.

I let my head fall inertly downward as far over as I could bend it, so Ainslie wouldn't see the tears running out of my eyes.

Motion attracted me and I looked blurredly up again. He was shaking his head steadily back and forth. "Don't give up, keep trying," he meant to say. "It's not too late yet."

About five or ten minutes after the hearse had left, a door opened surreptitiously somewhere close at hand; and a stealthy, frightened tread began to descend toward us, evidently along some steps that were back of me.

Ainslie could see who it was—he was facing that way—but I couldn't until the hatchet-faced maid we had seen crying in the kitchen the night before suddenly sidled out between us. She kept looking back in the direction from which she'd just come, as if scared of her life. She had an ordinary kitchen bread knife in her hand. She wasn't in livery now, but black-hatted, coated and gloved, as if she had started out for the cemetery with the rest and then slipped back unnoticed.

She went for Ainslie's bonds first, cackling terrifiedly the whole time she was sawing away at them. "Oh, if they ever find out I did this, I don't know what they'll do to me! I didn't even know what they'll do to me! I didn't even know you were down here until I happened to overhear Mr. Hastings whisper to his secretary just now before they left, 'Leave the other two where they are, we can attend to them when we come back.' Which one of you is Jimmy? She confided in me; I knew about it; I helped her slip in and out of the house the whole week. I took her place under the bedcovers, so that when he'd look in he'd think she was asleep in her room.

"They had no right to do this to you and your friend, Jimmy, even though you were the cause of her death. The excitement was too much for her, she'd been so carefully brought up. She got this heart attack and died. She was already unconscious when they brought her back—from wherever it was you ran off with her to.

"I don't know why I'm helping you. You're a reckless, bad, fortune-hunting scoundrel; Mr. Hastings says so. The marriage wouldn't have been legal anyway; she didn't use her right name. It cost him all kinds of money to hush everyone up about it and destroy the documents, so it wouldn't be found out and you wouldn't have a chance to blackmail her later.

"You killed my baby! But still he should have turned you over to the police, not kept you tied up all ni—"

At this point she finally got through, and Ainslie's gag flew out of his mouth like one of those feathered darts kids shoot through a blow-tube. "I *am* the police!" he panted. "And your 'baby' has been murdered, or will be within the next few minutes, by Hastings himself, not this boy here! She was still alive in that coffin at two o'clock this morning."

She gave a scream like the noon whistle of a factory. He kept her from fainting, or at any rate falling in a heap, by pinning her to the wall, took the knife away from her. He freed me in one-tenth of the time it had taken her to rid him of his own bonds. "No," she was groaning hollowly through her hands, "her own family doctor, a lifelong friend of her father and mother, examined her after she was gone, made out the death certificate. He's an honest man, he wouldn't do that—"

"He's old, I take it. Did he see her face?" Ainslie interrupted.

A look of almost stupid consternation froze on her own face. "No. I was at the bedside with him; it was covered. But only a moment before she'd been lying there in full view. The doctor and I both saw her from the door. Then Mr. Hastings had a fainting spell in the other room, and we ran to help him. When the doctor came in again to proceed with his examination, Mr. Chivers had covered her face—to spare Mr. Hastings' feelings.

"Dr. Meade just examined her body. Mr. Hastings pleaded with him not to remove the covering, said he couldn't bear it. And my pet was still wearing the little wrist watch her mother gave her before she died—"

"They substituted another body for hers, that's all; I don't care how many wrist watches it had on it," Ainslie told her brutally. "Stole that of a young girl approximately her own age who had just died from heart failure or some other natural cause, most likely from one of the hospital morgues, and put it over on the doddering family doctor and you both.

"If you look, you'll probably find something in the papers about a vanished corpse. The main thing is to stop that burial; I'm not positive enough on it to take a chance. It may be she in the coffin after all, and not the substitute. Where was the interment to be?"

"In the family plot, at Cypress Hill."

"Come on, Cannon; got your circulation back yet?" He was at the top of the stairs already. "Get the local police and tell them to meet us out there."

*   *   *

Ainslie's badge was all that got us into the cemetery, which was private. The casket had already been lowered out of sight. They were throwing the first shovelsful of earth over it as we burst through the little ring of sedate, bowing mourners.

The last thing I saw was Ainslie snatching an implement from one of the cemetery workers and jumping down bodily into the opening, feet first.

The face of that silver-haired devil, her guardian Hastings, had focused in on my inflamed eyes.

A squad of Lake City police, arriving only minutes after us, were all that saved his life. It took three of them to pull me off him.

Ainslie's voice was what brought me to, more than anything else. "It's all right, Cannon," he was yelling over and over from somewhere behind me. "It's the substitute."

I stumbled over to the lip of the grave between two of the cops and took a look down. It was the face of a stranger that was peering up at me through the shattered coffin lid. I turned away, and they made the mistake of letting go of me.

I went at the secretary this time; Hastings was still stretched out more dead then alive. "Where've you got her?"

"That ain't the way to make him answer," Ainslie said, and for the second and last time throughout the whole affair his voice wasn't toneless. "*This* is!"

Wham! We had to take about six steps forward to catch up with the secretary where he was now.

Ainslie's method was all right at that. The secretary talked—fast.

Alice was safe; but she wouldn't have been, much longer. After the mourners had had a last look at her in the coffin, Hastings and the secretary had locked her up for safekeeping—stupefied, of course—and substituted the other body for burial.

And Alice's turn was to come later, when, under cover of night, she was to be spirited away to a hunting lodge in the hills—the lodge that had belonged to her father. There she could have been murdered at leisure.

When we'd flashed back to the New Hampshire Avenue house in a police car, and unlocked the door of the little den where she'd been secreted; and when the police physician who accompanied us brought her out of the opiate they'd kept her under—whose arms were the first to go around her?

"Jimmy"—She sighed a little, after we took time off from the clinches—"he showed up late that night with Chivers, in that dinky little room you left me in.

"They must have been right behind us all the way, paying all those people to say they'd never seen me.

"But he fooled me, pretended he wasn't angry, said he didn't mind if I married and left him. And I was so sleepy and off guard I believed him. Then he handed me a glass of salty-tasting water to drink, and said, 'Come on down to the car. Jimmy's down there waiting for you; we've got him with us.' I staggered down there between them, that's all I remember."

Then she remembered something else and looked at me with fright in her eyes. "Jimmy, you didn't mind marrying little Alice Brown, but I don't suppose Alma Beresford would stand a show with you—?"

"You don't suppose right," I told her gruffly, "because I'm marrying Alice Brown all over again—even if we've gotta change her name first.

"And this ugly-looking bloke standing up here, name of Ainslie, is going to be best man at our second wedding. Know why? Because he was the only one in the whole world believed there really was a you."

I Don't Do Divorce Cases

by David Justice

When he come through the door, I don't know is he on the level or out to lunch. He looks around, he looks around some more, then he looks straight at me. He says he wants me to locate this dame who's missing. Okay, fine, but then he gives me an address where I'll find her at ten o'clock that night. I say I don't do divorce cases—I say that just to have something to say while I'm figuring what his game is. He says he isn't married to her and he isn't related to her. He just wants me to find her and learn everything I can about her. I figure the guy's a fruitcake, but he flashes a roll of bills at me and I figure my diet can stand some fruit. He's on, at twice the going rate.

Does this dame have a name? I begin, smiling. She does, but you don't need to know it yet, he says. Wants my first impressions to be free of associations. Great. How will I recognize her? He gives me a photograph, says, Memorize it, then burn it. No kidding, that's what he says. And I must admit she is one good-looking dame. Early twenties, but not so early there's any problem with the law. Dark-haired. Eyes a little out of focus, or maybe it's the camera. Then he thinks better of it and snatches it back, says I've seen enough. He's right, I have. Maybe he figures I wouldn't burn it. He's right, I wouldn't.

* * *

The address turns out to be a loft in an artsy part of the city. I show up a little early. I figure it'll be a little strange, me just bursting in on her, but there's no problem. The room is huge, there's some sort of party going on. Already lots of bodies and I just walk in real confident and nobody challenges. The blonde who opened the door wasn't doing it for me, anyway—she was just leaving the party to shoot up or be sick.

I'm dressed like a P.I. It doesn't matter. I don't exactly fit right in, but in this zoo I don't stick out. You got people dressed like Philip Marlowe, you got people dressed like Tarzan—before the party's over, you got people that they're not dressed at all.

Lots of bodies and some not bad broads, some of what are probably really men. No sign of the little lady. I grab a drink and wait.

Ten o'clock comes on and in walks the hot property. Right, you couldn't mistake her, but even so that snapshot oughta be shot for treason. Good-looking and what she is are just different ballparks. It's like trying to photograph a waterfall, or a moving cloud. Murphy, you're getting sloppy, but I mean really. Less and less am I blaming the guy.

This first trip, he said, no specifics. Just a general idea of what she drinks and who she talks to. And I'm supposed to get a bead on what she's really like. I watch, she doesn't see me watching her. At eleven, she leaves alone.

I meet my party at midnight in the diner like he said. He is sitting at a table, smoking. Cup of coffee, untouched. He is, how do I say it, unsentimental. He gives me these narrow eyes.

"Well?"

I tell him all I know about her. "Drinks plain vermouth, not a whole lot of it. Seems to know everyone, but only talks to a few. One guy particular seemed interested but she wasn't interested back. She left alone."

"Did you follow her?"

"You didn't tell me to."

He relaxes a little. "Good, good. I like your action, Murphy. Here's for tonight."

He rounds it off, upwards. Then he give me another address for tomorrow, mid-afternoon . . .

He might've said what it was, save me going around peering at all these street numbers where half the joints don't have any. Turns out it's the public library, f'r cr'sakes. I go in, this time feeling really out of place. I start browsing, so-called. Then I notice what I'm browsing—Young Adult Romance—and move off in disgust. I grab a novel off the shelves and make like I'm reading it. In she comes.

Now she's dressed simple, but she's even more beautiful. Even better without makeup—anyhow, none I can detect. She moves easily through the rows of books. Her slender hand selects a volume. A sad smile plays on her lips and, oh, Murphy, now you're talking like one. Just stay *professional*, you're not hitched up with this girl.

She settles on something and goes to the circulation desk. I go up behind her with whatever it is I've got and I get a gander at what she's checking out. Something about a swan in love. Sounds kinky, but this isn't the kind of place for that. As she heads for the door, I hand the librarian my book and gaze after her. I'm not supposed to follow her, but I stand at the glass doors and watch her go tripping down the steps and out of my life forever. Oh, Murphy, you've got it bad. But I don't go anywhere because I don't have a card. I'm stuck at the counter, feeling like a fool, and the librarian is very nice and says it's all right, will I just give my name and address and they can let me have the book on a temporary card.

I meet him at a luncheonette. This time he pays me before I even report. When he hears about the swan book, he gets real excited and says, Yes, that's just exactly right, things are going perfectly. Then he gives me another address for that very night.

I say, You seem to know a lot about this dame, always knowing where she's going to be. Not always, he says sternly, and there's a lot he doesn't know.

That night turns out to be the theater. Maybe he saw her buy tickets, there's some good explanation. Anyhow, he has one for me in the row behind her. I watch the actors. The play is hard to follow, but I watch her responses. It goes on like this all evening. Lots and lots of reaction shots, only shot from behind.

I meet him at a deli near the theater. "What can I tell you? She liked the play."

He seemed pleased. "She has good taste." Then he surprises me and asks if I liked it.

"What play was it?" I ask him.

Again he seems pleased . . .

The next day I follow her shopping, writing down everything she buys. After that it's an art museum. I'm supposed to say how long she spends at each painting, does she talk to anyone, does she look at any of them twice.

He studies the purchase list, frowning, but clears up when I tell him she charged it. I'm guessing maybe she's getting in over her head and could use his dough. She spent different times at different paintings, and let me tell you it was a pain going back and getting all the names.

No, she didn't talk to anyone, just to ask the guard something, like maybe where's the bathroom. Yes, she

went back to one painting. What was it? Just a bunch
of nothing, the title claimed water lilies—his head tilts
back and he kisses his own fingers, blows a little air.

Somehow this gets to me and I say if he's so keen
on her why don't *he* follow her? Why don't he go *up*
to her?

He comes back to earth fast and starts frowning and
says, You don't ask the questions—but the way he says
it I can see he's shaken and I figure he's really just a
little afraid of her. If you weren't just paid to do it and
you really wanted her, I can see where a guy would
freeze up.

Only then I get another idea and I'm thinking how
he's maybe some kind of prevert and he really wants to
bump her off. Only why would he want to do that?
Anyhow, just keep your mitts off her, I almost say.

He glowers at me and I glower at him and he hands
me another address, but I say I'm busy that day. Oh,
you're busy that day, are you—real sarcastic, but he
doesn't press the point. Okay, meet me at such and
such a place at 10:00 PM., anyway, and he'll have a
different address. Okay.

I got back to my apartment and shower and have a
TV dinner and don't finish it. I can't get the address
out of my mind. I lay awake a while and then decide
I'm going there, anyway. I fall asleep eventually. Crazy
dreams.

It's a kind of stadium, next to the middle of nowhere.
Weeds are growing up through the marble and you can
tell it was really something once, but they must of
screwed up because it's coming apart now, in bits and
pieces, here and there. She walks slowly around the
high part of it and I stand watching her and not moving.
If she sees me, she doesn't show it. Then she leaves . . .

That night at the diner, he gives the narrow-eye

treatment and I'm gruff so as not to be nervous. He hands me an address and says, Don't try to pull anything. I tell him he minds his business and I mind mine. He says that's a laugh, and it is, because I'm minding her business and he's buying mine.

This time it's a restaurant. Fancy place, but she's dining alone. I take a table not far from her. Not professional, Murphy, you could of seen her just as good from across the room.

She has a glass of wine and a cheese plate—then some kind of mixed-up stuff I don't know its name. Bad luck—I already got my steak or I coulda said I'll have what she's having and found out. Anyway, she has water with it, then salad, then some green stuff in a little glass.

I go to my drop and just read out the menu in a bored voice like a sergeant who for some reason he's a short-order cook. Wine, cheese, whatever, water, salad. I stop. He waits. He looks at me. Well?

Well what? How about my dollars?

The man is not buying it. You're holding out on me, he says.

Like splat I'm holding out on you. Don't gimme that. She didn't see anyone. I didn't talk with her. Whachoo looking at me that way for?

You haven't told me everything.

Yes—I did everything. Just sat alone and ate, not much—and not much wine at all. One glass, plus a glass of some greenish stuff.

Some greenish stuff, he says, very polite. I'm ready to bust him if he's getting sarcastic, but now he relaxes. Absinthe, he murmurs like he's talking to himself. He gets this far-off look. I say, What gives? He comes back to our planet and he pays me, he actually smiles.

He gives me an address for eleven o'clock at night. It's just a sidewalk in front of a record store that's

closed. A traffic light, going through the motions—
hardly any traffic. An alleyway with garbage cans.

But she shows up, all right. She comes across the
street and mails a letter. I step out of the shadows. She
puts her hand to her mouth, stifles a scream. I put my
hands out, palms forward, like, Lady, don't blame me.
She speaks—for the first time I hear her really speak
clearly. "What are you following me for?"

And, damn, I just don't have an answer. I move
toward her. My head I think it's going from side to
side, the mouth is moving but isn't saying anything. She
steps backward, looking afraid.

And then the guy shows up, Mr. Mystery Employer.
She looks at him and my jaw drops, because she's only
a little bit surprised and now she's less scared. "Why,
Charles, what are you doing here?"

He smiles, really debonair, and takes her hand.

"This man has been following me," she says, and she
points at me. I'm a big guy but it stops me dead in my
tracks.

"Oh, he has, has he?"

He turns on me, and he's about six inches shorter
and has this topcoat on and he's not in condition like
I am, but he's got me where he wants me and he's a
lot better shaved.

"I catch you around this lady again and I'll clean the
pavement with you, you understand? Now beat it."

Now *I'm* walking backward and my mouth is moving,
but nothing's coming from the brain. Then I turn and
I start cursing myself under my breath and walk back
to the subway. The last thing I hear him say is: "Come
on, darling, I'll take you home."

The next day I get a check in the mail for my time
plus a goodbye sweetener. He signs off wishing me the
best of luck. That's the last I ever saw of him.

Killing Howard
by Ralph McInerny

Walter Map did not decide lightly to become a murderer. The idea was repulsive to him. The intended deed would be unlike any deed he had performed in the previous twenty-seven years of his existence. He was a gentle man. He was a man on whose escutcheon might have been emblazoned *Vivre et laissez vivre*. He was ambitious without being competitive. Indeed, his character had been called noble by none other than Lorraine Kelso in computing only months before. Walter had been flattered by the judgment, all the more so because his estimate of Lorraine ran to the wildest of superlatives, no matter the inadequacy of anything he had as yet managed to say to her. Their paths had converged, they got along splendidly, they had ignored several movies together, transported by the feel of the other's hand. Moreover, just twice, Walter had chastely pressed his lips to Lorraine's. There are moments when the thought of death is, if not welcome, nonetheless tolerable. What greater bliss could await him in this vale of tears than the kiss of Lorraine Kelso? See Naples and die. On the other hand, being separated from her was productive of an almost exquisite pain. In the offices of Cook, Baker and Wassermann, Walter would steal from his desk hourly to catch a glimpse of Lorraine at her terminal. And, oh, the languorous look in her eyes when they rose to meet his! The message was as plain as electronic mail. Walter had done some computing of his own. His calculations matched the impulse of his heart. He would most definitely propose marriage to Lorraine.

That is how things had been until five weeks ago when the ineffable Howard Cook, son of a senior partner, arrived fresh from college to be put on the fast track to promotion. Howard had surveyed the women in the office as if they represented a portion of his inheritance. He produced a flutter when he sauntered through the departments, somehow always more interested in the tasks of the female employees. He had, it seemed, a weakness for computing. It became his practice to query Lorraine Kelso on this and that.

"What a nuisance he must be to you," Walter opined while enjoying a midafternoon yogurt with Lorraine. Consuming this wholesome food had been postponed several times because of Howard Cook's importuning of Lorraine.

"He is determined to learn the business from the ground up."

"Then he should be in the basement talking with the head of maintenance."

"He certainly doesn't know much about computers." Lorraine's hair bounced as she shook her head, but there was a forgiving smile on her lips, all the redder now with raspberry yogurt.

"Does he know anything?"

"Walter, he is here to learn."

"That is why some of us went to school. If we hadn't, we would not have been hired."

"It's not Howie's fault his father is a senior partner."

"Howie?"

"Aren't we talking about him?"

Indeed, they were. Wasting the break talking about

something other than themselves. But it was too late to change gear. It was time to return to work.

"There is a great movie at the mall tonight."

"Walter, I can't!"

He was struck dumb. She had never turned him down before. He tried to take her hand, but she gripped her yogurt container with both hands and stepped back. Surely only a serious illness in her immediate family could explain her refusal. She turned and ran off to the computing department. Poor darling, she was obviously overcome with emotion. He would not phone her at her terminal. He would wait until five and ask if there was anything he might do for her during this trying period.

When he went to computing at five, he found Lorraine huddled with Howard Cook. The other employees of the department were gone or on their way, but Lorraine was clearly in mid-lesson with the son of a senior partner. Walter backed down the hall toward the elevators. To try to extricate her from the slow-learning heir apparent might only prolong her agony. He decided it was best that she give the young man a crash course and have done with him.

But days passed and the lessons continued. It became almost impossible for Walter to have a minute with Lorraine. An unwelcome thought occurred to him. Lorraine was *enjoying* acting as tutor. Dread precedents flew through his mind. Abelard and Heloise. Francesca and Paolo. He tried to scoff at the idea. What could be less romantic than computing? But Abelard had been teaching his soon-to-be-beloved logic.

Distraction from these melancholy thoughts came in the form of a summons from the senior Cook. He was a stumpy, red-faced man on the top of whose head twenty-seven hairs were carefully arranged. It had never before struck Walter how unattractive a man Cook was.

No doubt his son would end up with the same porcine appearance. Howard might be an Adonis now, but a life of ease and affluence lay ahead of him and he was almost certain to crumble under the strain.

"You are doing excellent work, Walter."

"Thank you, sir."

"You deserve a raise and you shall have a raise. You shall have a promotion, too. I am moving you to this floor, young man. I want you to head up a team studying ways in which the firm can expand. Are you married?"

"Not yet."

"That suggests you have plans."

"Well, I have hopes."

"Go for her, Walter. Faint heart never won fair lady."

Walter left Cook's office in a state of exhilaration. What news to share with Lorraine! He would propose to her at the very first opportunity. He went directly to the computing room. Lorraine was not there. She was in the employees' dining room, seated across the table from Howard Cook. They were holding hands. Her eyes looked into Howard's as they had often looked into his. The significance of the scene seemed unmistakable. Walter withdrew in confusion.

He sat at his desk and suddenly felt a great calm come over him. In the space of minutes, he had gone from the heights to the depths. Success was ashes in his mouth without Lorraine to share it with. Something had come between them. Someone. Howard Cook. Howard must be removed. Vying with Howard's charm would take time, winning Lorraine back from this wily seducer would not be easy. And what if he failed? The thought could not be borne. The idea of a universe minus Howard Cook exerted a strong attraction. He realized he meant to get rid of Howard. To kill him. Murder him.

Somehow the realization did not shock him. He must be simply catching up with a resolution already made unconsciously. In any case, the die was cast. The only question was how.

No need to review the care with which Walter considered the variety of means available to him. His research brought home to him how vulnerable humans are. All men are mortal. A necessary truth, but it can be verified in countless ways. Poison detained him for nearly twenty-four hours; it definitely had attractions. Walter smiled as he read descriptions of the agonized expiring of the poisoned. But finally he waved it all away. Simple violence would be best. Push Howard off a building, shove him in front of a train, hit him with a blow on the head. No firearms, no weapons in any usual sense.

A less determined man might have felt uneasy making such plans in an office next to the proposed victim's father. Walter had moved to the top floor, two doors down the hall from Cook senior. He had accepted with pain in his heart and a brave smile on his lips Lorraine's congratulations. She looked as if she had received a similar promotion. That night he watched her drive away with Howard in his obscenely ostentatious red sports car. Walter's smile returned. He had selected his weapon. The red sports car would be the instrument of Howard Cook's death.

A few hours spent in the library poring over Porsche manuals sufficed. A few minutes' work on the steering and the Porsche would become a time bomb, ready to render the racing wheel Howard gripped with leather driving gloves inoperative. In a moment of forgetfulness, he thought of telling Lorraine what he had learned. Among her many charms was an interest in and knowledge of the mechanical unusual in a woman. Again, Walter was struck by how easily and by how many ways death can come. The Cook mansion was in a mountainous area. A mile after leaving the house, the road became twisting and precipitous. A driver who could not control his car on that road was not long for this world.

That night clad all in black, his face wearing a layer of burnt cork, carrying only a wrench of the appropriate size, Walter approached the Cook property from above, having parked his car where lovers did what lovers do. Walter felt he was striking a blow for them all in ridding the world of his rival for the heart of Lorraine Kelso.

A half mile above the house, he was stopped by the sound of barking. Ferocious barking. What must have been an extended family of German shepherds set up a wall of terrifying noise. Walter had been frightened as a child by a neighborhood dog. He turned and crept back to his car. As he was leaving the area, a state police car drove in and Walter turned his blackened face away, apparently in time.

The following morning when he was shaving he heard on the news that a car belonging to Howard Cook, Jr., son of Howard Cook, Sr., had gone out of control on a mountain road. Young Cook had managed to get out of the vehicle before it plunged into a valley and burned.

Walter turned off his razor and reviewed the previous night. He had not gone through with his plan. He had not fixed the steering system of Howard's Porsche so it would fail. He sought and found another station and heard the story again. Howard Cook had said his brakes failed and he could not control the speed of the car. Puzzled, Walter went off to work.

Cook senior did not come in that morning. Lorraine

did not respond when he called her terminal. The head of her department said she had phoned in and taken a sick day. Needless to say, young Howard was not on the premises. At noon, Walter left the building for lunch and to buy an early edition of the paper. Munching a burger that tasted awful and would take a long-term toll on his health, he read that there was evidence of tampering with the hydraulic fluid lines of Howard's brakes.

"Someone tried to kill my son," Cook senior said that afternoon. He spoke in awed tones. The thought that the universe might be hostile to him or his loved ones seemed new to him.

"His brakes were tampered with?"

"There's no doubt about it. He's lucky to be alive."

Walter nodded in agreement, but Howard must now face another attempt, Walter's.

"I do not want to hire private detectives, Walter."

"Why should you?"

"To find out who tried to kill my son."

"That's what the police are paid for, sir. "

"I'm also paying you. Walter, I like your mind. I like its versatility. How long have you been up here? A few days, yet already you are generating results. Why should I pay some dolt of a detective when I have a mind like yours in my employ?"

"Any dolt of a detective would know more than I do."

"At the moment, yes. But I wager that in days you will know more than all of them put together."

"You want me to find the one who tried to kill Howard?"

"I'll put it in writing. I'll give you carte blanche. Spare no expense. I want that maniac behind bars."

Back at his desk, Walter reflected that there must be someone other than himself who wanted Howard dead.

This did not really surprise him. He could imagine battalions of people who despised Howard Cook. But only one of them had tampered with the brakes of the Porsche. Who might it be? Would the assassin give up after this failure, or could he be relied on to try again and next time do it right?

Walter did not intend to wait. Howard was still in the hospital, under observation. Lorraine was at his bedside. Cook senior had not mentioned her by name, only that she was a young woman in computing. He sounded as if her salary covered sitting by Howard's hospital bed.

At three in the afternoon, Walter went to the county building and studied the plans of the hospital. He telephoned and asked for the number of Howard Cook's room. It was with a calm and determined mind that he drove to the hospital, parked, went inside, and put through a call to Howard's room. The phone was answered by Lorraine. Muffling his voice with a handkerchief, he identified himself as Mr. Cook and instructed Lorraine to call him back from a pay phone in the main waiting room of the hospital. He hung up on her confused protest.

He stepped unseen into the elevator from which she emerged and rose to Howard's floor. His plan was simple. He would either strangle or smother the man. He came out of the elevator into pandemonium. White-clad figures were running down the hallway, pushing and pulling various pieces of equipment. They seemed to be converging on what, if his study of the floor plan was correct, would be Howard's room. Walter stepped to the nurses' station where one obese angel of mercy remained.

"What's going on?"

"A code blue."

"Is that unusual?"

She looked at him. "Who are you?"

"Maynard of the *Tribune*. How do you spell your name?"

She tilted her bosom so he could read her name tag. Buonaiuto. "A code blue is emergency. Danger of death."

"What patient?"

"The Cook boy."

Walter nodded. He was trying very hard, and not too successfully, to keep his mind devoid of thought. He sauntered away from the nurses' station, opened the stairway door, and a moment later was descending at a great echoing rate. He emerged on the second floor and took the elevator to the lobby. As he was crossing to the door, Lorraine stepped out of a phone booth.

"Walter! What are you doing here?"

"Looking for you."

A pained look came over her face. "Walter, some things can't be explained . . ."

He stopped her. "You misunderstand me. I went up to look in on Howard. Apparently something has happened to him."

"He was very nearly killed last night."

"Something else just happened upstairs. A code blue?"

He watched her run across the lobby toward the elevators, and it was like watching the departure of hope. Would she, after a sensible interval, come back to him once Howard was out of the way?

Walter Map was not a drinking man. He had bored many with his account of what alcohol does to the heart and brain. He had felt tipsy once in his life, and he had not found it in the least attractive. Nonetheless, he drove from the hospital to the Kitty Korner Inn and ordered a drink.

"What kind of a drink?" The girl behind the bar had

her head tilted so she could follow the drama on the television set suspended overhead.

"An alcoholic drink."

He had her attention. "You mean liquor?"

"Exactly."

She half turned, then faced him again. "Bourbon all right?"

"Do you make doubles?"

Others along the bar lost interest in the televised drama and followed the course of Walter's colloquy with the redheaded bartender. "A double bourbon," she said, as if she were talking to more than Walter.

"Can I take it to a booth?"

"I'll bring it to you."

"Thank you."

Left alone with his drink, he raised it and drank off half the contents. It did not stop the thought that had been pestering him all the way from the hospital. He turned away from the bar and mouthed the sentence soundlessly. *I have psychic powers.* What other explanation was there? He had set out to tamper with Howard's steering but had been prevented from getting to the car. Nonetheless, the brake lines were tampered with and Howard nearly had the accident Walter had intended for him. Just now he had gone to the hospital to kill Howard and before he could get to him something had gone wrong and he was in danger of death.

Sitting in the booth, Walter felt in possession of a strange and frightening power. He drained his glass. It was good. He would like some more.

"Another?"

He lurched. The redhead was standing beside him. He nodded. "Bring me two."

"You mean another double?"

"Two doubles. Do you make quadruples?"

She took it as a joke and returned laughing to her

post behind the bar. Every eye in the place, no matter how blurred, followed the girl when she brought him two more drinks on her little tray.

Walter scarcely dared to formulate a wish in his mind, for fear of what might happen. He drank off his second drink in two large swallows. There was a phone booth at the back of the room. From it he telephoned the hospital and asked for Howard Cook's room. Again Lorraine answered.

"How is he?"

"They stopped the bleeding."

"Good."

"Someone pushed an IV needle into his artery, and blood just gushed from him."

Walter was almost relieved that it had not been strangling or smothering. "Someone?"

"It must be the same person."

He said nothing. The phone went dead. It was just as well. Walter felt dizzy. How much bourbon did it take to make a man drunk? His mind had become a deadly weapon and he wanted to dull it with drink.

He must have made a wish that he would get home safely. He woke in his own bed, not knowing how he had got there, his head pounding. His first thought was of Lorraine, perhaps because there were five different photographs of her strategically placed around his bedroom. He began to weep helplessly. In one of the dreams that had troubled his sleep, he had been explaining to Cook senior that the more he tried to kill Howard the more Lorraine loved him. He did not remember Cook senior's reply.

In the bathroom after showering he willed a towel to come to him, but nothing happened. He nearly lost his balance reaching for the towel. Seated at the kitchen table, he commanded the coffee pot to fill itself with water and brew coffee, but nothing happened. He was almost disappointed. Relief followed. He did not have psychic power. But that meant someone else had twice made an attempt on Howard Cook's life. He had been commissioned by the intended victim's father to find the one trying to kill Howard. It seemed inescapable that such a person existed.

The phone rang. It was Cook senior.

"What are you doing home?"

Walter closed one eye and read the time on the clock. "It is six forty-five A.M."

"That's right. Howard is missing from the hospital. What am I paying you for?"

In his car, Walter realized he was not wearing shoes. He could not go back without wasting precious time. He was caught by every red light on the way to the hospital and understood why some men curse and swear. He hoped that Howard would not survive this third attempt, if that was what it was. How he wished his wishes were efficacious. Had he really believed he had psychic powers? He laughed a skeptical laugh, wondering to whom it was addressed.

A crowd had gathered near a Dumpster in the parking lot. Barefoot, Walter joined the crowd. He had recognized Lorraine in its midst. He pushed forward in time to see Howard Cook emerge from a large plastic trash bag.

"I thought I heard moaning," a man with a Jonathan-sized Adam's apple said.

"And in a hospital zone," the bony woman beside him said.

They had parked near the Dumpster and detected the sound of a human voice emanating from it. The wife had gone inside while the husband stood guard. A glum looking man in a dark blue work uniform had gone into the Dumpster to investigate. He had found the plastic bag full of Howard Cook.

Thrown out with the trash, Walter mused. Lorraine turned and saw him. She came and stood before him and asked impatiently how long he had been there.

"What happened?"

She tipped her head to one side. Her eyes fell to his feet.

"You're barefoot!"

He put one foot modestly over the other and nearly lost his balance. The drinking of the previous day still affected him. Lorraine made a noise and went up to the little man in the dark blue work uniform. He shook his head. She straightened and spoke to him once more. A moment later, the fellow disappeared into the Dumpster. Lorraine stood expectantly next to it.

The head looked over the rim of the Dumpster's opening. "What kind of shoes are they?"

Walter closed the distance between them and took her arm. "Lorraine . . ."

She shook free from his hand. Not looking him in the eye, she said in a fierce whisper, "The state police saw your car in a parking lot for lovers above the Cook property."

"I was alone. I swear it."

She looked piteously at him, seemed about to speak, then did not. Had she ever looked more beautiful? She was a shy flower in the morning dew.

"Lorraine, I love you."

She took his hand. "I know."

"But you love Howard . . ."

Before he could make a noble renunciation, she shook her head violently. "I can't talk to you now."

A stretcher on wheels arrived and Howard was put on it. Lorraine, casting a glance at Walter, joined the parade as Howard was pushed back to the hospital. Walter stood barefoot and open-mouthed. How strangely Lorraine had acted. And no wonder.

She suspected him. If anyone in the world knew he had a motive, it was Lorraine Kelso. Furthermore, she had a logical mind. The report of the state police put him in the neighborhood when Howard's car was tampered with. Yesterday he had been in the hospital when someone shoved an IV needle into Howard's artery. And here he was this morning when a third attempt had been made on Howard's life. What else could she think?

"These yours?"

The man in dark blue was displaying a beat up pair of white shoes.

"You can have them."

As he drove away, there was a thudding sound. In the rear view mirror he saw a white shoe lying on the asphalt. Strange.

If Lorraine had a logical mind, so did Walter. She might suspect him because he was in the vicinity each time someone had tried to do away with her odious beloved. He had the advantage of knowing he was innocent. Someone else had had an even better opportunity than he had. That was when the penny dropped. Good grief, of course. Lorraine.

She had been with Howard in his car the day before his accident. She was fully capable of starting a slow leak of brake fluid; perhaps had worked out on her computer how many miles he must drive before he would once more be coming down the mountain. She had just left the hospital room before Howard was found half bleeding to death. And now the plastic bag in a Dumpster.

It all fit. Except for one thing. She had no motive. Why would she kill the man she had learned to love? These thoughts puzzled Walter and made his driving erratic, but he was scarcely aware of the angry horns, of fists being shaken at him, of the empurpled faces of those with whom he had managed not to collide. He stopped at his apartment and put on some shoes and continued to the office. But he was stopped in the hallway by Cook senior, looking so angry he might have been one of Walter's fellow motorists.

"Well, Mr. Smartypants?" Cook senior said in sarcastic tones. "Have you found out who is trying to kill my only son?"

"Could we step into your office?"

"Try and avoid it."

Walter strolled across the plush carpet of the senior partner's office. At some moment between slipping into his loafers and now he had made up his mind.

"I shall want a few others here before I speak."

"Oh, no you don't. No teasing. Who is it, you?" An evil smile crept over the piglike countenance of Mr. Cook.

"You say that because my car was seen in a lover's lane above your property."

"Aha. The state police have contacted you."

"Not at all. They are as anxious as I to keep the name of my companion out of this."

"You were with someone!"

Walter dropped his eyes.

"Who was she?"

"Mr. Cook, I could never command your respect again if I divulged her name." He had crossed his fingers and did not conceal the fact, but Cook did not notice. He was obviously impressed by such chivalry.

"I'm sorry, Walter."

"I shall want your son and Miss Kelso here when I reveal the assassin's name."

"You know who it is?"

Walter showed a palm as sign of his adamantine resolve to say nothing until there was an appropriate gathering for the revelation. Cook lit a filthy cigar and picked up the phone, into which he barked a series of peremptory orders.

"Do you have another of those?"

"I didn't know you smoked, Walter."

"I am thinking of having a baby."

A few seconds passed before the remark drew a senior partner type of chuckle. Cook handed Walter two of the massive cigars, and he slipped them into his pocket.

It was not twenty minutes before Lorraine and Howard arrived in the battle grey stretch limousine Cook had sent to fetch them. Lorraine coughed because of the smoke, and tears ran from her eyes. Walter found it pleasant to fancy that she wept for him.

"Walter Map has discovered who has been trying to kill you, Howard. I have called you here to hear him reveal the culprit's name."

"Walter, you mustn't!" Lorraine started toward him, but Cook senior stopped her. Walter smiled at her. She need not worry. If she did not yet know the depths of his love, she would learn them now.

"Who did it?" Howard asked with more a sneer than a smile.

Walter stood. "You did."

Howard laughed. His father shouted a word he should not have shouted with Lorraine present. It was doubtful that she heard it. With a fluttering cry, she sank into a chair.

"Get serious, Map," Howard said.

"I am quite serious."

Cook senior went behind his great desk, sat, and laid his fat hands on the blotter. "Clear out your desk, Walter."

"Hear me out. I realize this startles you. All of you but Howard, I mean. Actually, the solution is quite simple. Three attempts were made on Howard's life. We are all agreed on that. The presumption is that all three attempts were made by the same person. Very well. This entails that the killer be on the premises on each of the three occasions. There is only one person who fits that description. Howard Cook."

Cook senior hit his head with a popping sound. "Of course the victim has to be at the scene of the crime, you idiot. That doesn't make him guilty."

"Good point," Walter conceded. "But only if someone else fills the necessary requirement of being there."

"I do," Lorraine said in a small voice.

"No!" Walter cried. "You don't."

"She was always there at that," Cook senior said, getting to his feet and glowering at Lorraine.

"So was I!" Walter shouted. This was not going as he had planned.

Lorraine leapt to her feet, came to him, and began to beat on his chest with her little fists. "I did it, Walter. I did."

"There is only one flaw in that, my dear. You love Howard."

The last named emitted a strange sound. Walter turned to see the son of the senior partner sink into a chair. He looked at his father, he looked at Lorraine, he looked at Walter, and there was despair in his face. Where was the insolent young puppy who had stolen Lorraine from him?

"I did it. It was the only thing that worked," the young man said in abject tones.

"What in blazes are you saying?" his father demanded.

"I told her I would kill myself if she did not return my love. For weeks the threat alone worked, but she was beginning to doubt me. I had to make her think I was serious. So I pretended to have an accident."

"You destroyed your own car!"

"Dad, it had twelve thousand miles on it. In the hospital, we talked about it, and Lorraine knew too much about cars for comfort. I made another attempt with the needle, making sure I would be rescued. The plastic bag was meant to seal it. Then she would know I would destroy myself if she would not have me."

Lorraine had stood and was gazing at Walter. Their eyes locked and they were drawn together like two wraiths in Dante. She came into his arms, and Walter found her eminently embraceable.

"These past weeks have been hellish, Walter, but I just could not have his blood on my hands."

"That is where we differ," Walter murmured.

Behind them a loud quarrel went on between father and son. It seemed a good time to leave. Arm in arm they went to Walter's office where he began to clean out his desk. Cook senior came in five minutes later and put a stop to it.

"Nonsense," he cried. "I spoke in passion. Of course you will stay. It is Howard who is going. And there will be another bonus for your detective work. Is this the girl you intend to marry?"

Walter turned to Lorraine. She nodded vigorously.

"Oh, yes," she cried. "Yes."

The Victim
by P. D. James

You know Princess Ilsa Mancelli, of course. I mean by that that you must have seen her on the cinema screen; on television; pictured in newspapers arriving at airports with her latest husband; relaxing on their yacht; bejeweled at first nights, gala nights, at any night and in any place where it is obligatory for the rich and successful to show themselves. Even if, like me, you have nothing but bored contempt for what I believe is called an international jet set, you can hardly live in the modern world and not know Ilsa Mancelli. And you can't fail to have picked up some scraps about her past. The brief and not particularly successful screen career, when even her heart-stopping beauty couldn't quite compensate for the paucity of talent; the succession of marriages, first to the producer who made her first film and who broke a twenty-year-old marriage to get her; then to a Texan millionaire; lastly to a prince.

About two months ago I saw a nauseatingly sentimental picture of her with her two-day-old son in a Rome nursing home. So it looks as if this marriage, sanctified as it is by wealth, a title, and maternity may be intended as her final adventure.

The husband before the film producer is, I notice, no longer mentioned. Perhaps her publicity agent fears that a violent death in the family, particularly an un-

solved violent death, might tarnish her bright image.
Blood and beauty. In the early stages of her career they
hadn't been able to resist that cheap, vicarious thrill.
But not now. Nowadays her early history, before she
married the film producer, has become a little obscure,
although there is a suggestion of poor but decent par-
entage and early struggles suitably rewarded. I am the
most obscure part of that obscurity. Whatever you
know, or think you know, of Ilsa Mancelli you won't
have heard about me. The publicity machine has de-
creed that I be nameless, faceless, unremembered, that
I no longer exist. Ironically, the machine is right; in any
real sense, I don't.

I married her when she was Elsie Bowman, aged sev-
enteen. I was assistant librarian at our local branch library and fifteen years older, a thirty-two-year-old
virgin, a scholar manqué, thin-faced, a little stooping,
my meager hair already thinning. She worked on the
cosmetic counter of our High Street store. She was
beautiful then, but with a delicate, tentative, unsophisti-
cated loveliness which gave little promise of the polished mature beauty which is hers today. Our story was
very ordinary. She returned a book to the library one
evening when I was on counter duty. We chatted. She
asked my advice about novels for her mother. I spent
as long as I dared finding suitable romances for her on
the shelves. I tried to interest her in the books I liked.
I asked her about herself, her life, her ambitions. She
was the only woman I had been able to talk to. I was
enchanted by her, totally and completely besotted.

I used to take my lunch early and make surreptitious
visits to the store, watching her from the shadow of a
neighboring pillar. There is one picture which even now
seems to stop my heart. She had dabbed her wrist with
scent and was holding out a bare arm over the counter
so that a prospective customer could smell the perfume.

She was totally absorbed, her young face gravely preoccupied. I watched her, silently, and felt the tears
smarting my eyes.

It was a miracle when she agreed to marry me. Her
mother (she had no father) was reconciled if not enthu-
siastic about the match. She didn't, as she made it abun-
dantly plain, consider me much of a catch. But I had a
good job, with prospects; I was educated; I was steady
and reliable; I spoke with a grammar-school accent
which, while she affected to deride it, raised my status
in her eyes. Besides, any marriage for Elsie was better
than none. I was dimly aware when I bothered to think
about Elsie in relation to anyone but myself that she
and her mother didn't get on.

Mrs. Bowman made, as she described it, a splash.
There was a full choir and a peal of bells. The church
hall was hired and a sit-down meal, ostentatiously un-
suitable and badly cooked, was served to eighty guests.
Between the pangs of nervousness and indigestion, I
was conscious of smirking waiters in short white jackets,
a couple of giggling bridesmaids from the store, their
freckled arms bulging from pink taffeta sleeves, hearty
male relatives, red-faced and with buttonholes of carna-
tion and waving fern, who made indelicate jokes and
clapped me painfully between the shoulders. There
were speeches and warm champagne. And, in the middle of it all, Elsie, my Elsie, like a white rose.

I suppose it was stupid of me to imagine that I could
hold her. The mere sight of our morning faces, smiling
at each other's reflection in the bedroom mirror, should
have warned me it couldn't last. But, poor deluded fool,
I never dreamed that I might lose her except by death.
Her death I dared not contemplate, and I was afraid for
the first time of my own. Happiness had made a coward
of me. We moved into a new bungalow, chosen by

Elsie, sat in new chairs chosen by Elsie, slept in a be-frilled bed chosen by Elsie. I was so happy that it was like passing into a new phase of existence, breathing a different air, seeing the most ordinary things as if they were newly created. One isn't necessarily humble when greatly in love. Is it so unreasonable to recognize the value of a love like mine, to believe that the beloved is equally sustained and transformed by it?

She said that she wasn't ready to start a baby and, without her job, she was easily bored. She took a brief training in shorthand and typing at our local Technical College and found herself a position as shorthand typist at the firm of Collingford and Major. That, at least, was how the job started. Shorthand typist, then secretary to Mr. Rodney Collingford, then personal secretary, then confidential personal secretary. In my bemused state of uxorious bliss, I only half registered her progress from occasionally taking his dictation when his then secretary was absent to flaunting his gifts of jewelry and sharing his bed.

He was everything I wasn't. Rich (his father had made a fortune from plastics shortly after the war and had left the factory to his only son), coarsely handsome in a swarthy fashion, big-muscled, confident, attractive to women. He prided himself on taking what he wanted. Elsie must have been one of his easiest pickings.

Why, I still wonder, did he want to marry her? I thought at the time that he couldn't resist depriving a pathetic, underprivileged, unattractive husband of a prize which neither looks nor talent had qualified him to deserve. I've noticed that about the rich and success-ful. They can't bear to see the undeserving prosper. I thought that half the satisfaction for him was in taking her away from me. That was partly why I knew I had to kill him. But now I'm not so sure. I may have done him an injustice. It may have been both simpler and more complicated that that. She was, you see—she still is—so very beautiful.

I understand her better now. She was capable of kindness, good humor, generosity even, provided she was getting what she wanted. At the time we married, and perhaps eighteen months afterwards, she wanted me. Neither her egotism nor her curiosity had been able to resist such a flattering, overwhelming love. But for her, marriage wasn't permanency. It was the first and necessary step towards the kind of life she wanted and meant to have. She was kind to me, in bed and out, while I was what she wanted. But when she wanted someone else, then my need of her, my jealousy, my bitterness, she saw as a cruel and wilful denial of her basic right, the right to have what she wanted. After all, I'd had her for nearly three years. It was two years more than I had any right to expect. She thought so. Her darling Rodney thought so. When my acquaintances at the library learnt of the divorce, I could see in their eyes that they thought so, too.

And she couldn't see what I was so bitter about. Rodney was perfectly happy to be the guilty party; they weren't, she pointed out caustically, expecting me to behave like a gentleman. I wouldn't have to pay for the divorce. Rodney would see to that. I wasn't being asked to provide her with alimony. Rodney had more than enough. At one point she came close to bribing me with Rodney's money to let her go without fuss. And yet— was it really as simple as that? She had loved me, or at least needed me, for a time. Had she perhaps seen in me the father that she had lost at five years old?

During the divorce, through which I was, as it were, gently processed by highly paid legal experts as if I were an embarrassing but expendable nuisance to be got rid of with decent speed, I was only able to keep sane by the knowledge that I was going to kill Collingford. I

knew that I couldn't go on living in a world where he
breathed the same air. My mind fed voraciously on the
thought of his death, savored it, began systematically
and with dreadful pleasure to plan it.

A successful murder depends on knowing your victim,
his character, his daily routine, his weaknesses, those
unalterable and betraying habits which make up the
core of his personality. I knew quite a lot about Rodney
Collingford. I knew facts which Elsie had let fall in her
first weeks with the firm—typing-pool gossip. I knew
the fuller and rather more intimate facts which she had
disclosed in those early days of her enchantment with
him, when neither prudence nor kindness had been able
to conceal her obsessive preoccupation with her new
boss. I should have been warned then. I knew, none
better, the need to talk about the absent lover.

What did I know about him? I knew the facts that
were common knowledge, of course. That he was
wealthy, aged thirty, a notable amateur golfer; that he
lived in an ostentatious mock Georgian house on the
banks of the Thames looked after by overpaid but non-
resident staff; that he owned a cabin cruiser; that he
was just over six feet tall; that he was a good businessman but reputedly close-fisted; that he was methodical
in his habits. I knew a miscellaneous and unrelated set
of facts about him, some of which would be useful,
some important, some of which I couldn't use.

I knew—and this was rather surprising—that he was
good with his hands and liked making things in metal
and wood. He had built an expensively equipped and
large workroom in the grounds of his house and spent
every Thursday evening working there alone. He was a
man addicted to routine. This creativity, however mundane and trivial, I found intriguing, but I didn't let
myself dwell on it. I was interested in him only so far
as his personality and habits were relevant to his death.

I never thought of him as a human being. He had no existence for me apart from my hate. He was Rodney Collingford, my victim ...

First I decided on the weapon. A gun would have been the most certain, I supposed, but I didn't know how to get one and was only too well aware I wouldn't know how to load or use it if I did. Besides, I was reading a number of books about murder at the time and I realized that guns, however cunningly obtained, were easy to trace.

And there was another thing. A gun was too impersonal, too remote. I wanted to make physical contact at the moment of death. I wanted to get close enough to see that final look of incredulity and horror as he recognized, simultaneously, me and his death. I wanted to drive a knife into his throat.

I bought it two days after the divorce. I was in no hurry to kill Collingford. I knew that I must take my time, must be patient, if I were to act in safety. One day, perhaps when we were old, I might tell Elsie. But I didn't intend to be found out. This was to be the perfect murder. And that meant taking my time. He would be allowed to live for a full year. But I knew that the earlier I bought the knife the more difficult it would be, twelve months later, to trace the purchase. I didn't buy it locally. I went one Saturday morning by train and bus to a northeast suburb and found a busy ironmongers and general store just off the High Street. There was a variety of knives on display.

The blade of the one I selected was about six inches long and was made of strong steel screwed into a plain wooden handle. I think it was probably meant for cutting lino. In the shop its razor-sharp edge was protected by a strong cardboard sheath. It felt good and right in my hand. I stood in a small queue at the pay desk and the cashier didn't even glance up as he took my notes and pushed the change towards me.

But the most satisfying part of my planning was the second stage. I wanted Collingford to suffer. I wanted him to know that he was going to die. It wasn't enough that he should realize it in a last second before I drove in the knife or in that final second before he ceased to know anything forever. Two seconds of agony, however horrible, weren't an adequate return for what he had done to me. I wanted him to know that he was a condemned man, to know it with increasing certainty, to wonder every morning whether this might be his last day. What if this knowledge did make him cautious, put him on his guard? In this country, he couldn't go armed. He couldn't carry on his business with a hired protector always at his side. He couldn't bribe the police to watch him every second of the day. Besides, he wouldn't want to be thought a coward. I guessed that he would carry on, ostentatiously normal, as if the threats were unreal or derisory, something to laugh about with his drinking cronies. He was the sort to laugh at danger. But he would never be sure. And, by the end, his nerve and confidence would be broken. Elsie wouldn't know him for the man she had married.

I would have liked to have telephoned him, but that, I knew, was impracticable. Calls could be traced; he might refuse to talk to me; I wasn't confident that I could disguise my voice. So the sentence of death would have to be sent by post. Obviously, I couldn't write the notes or the envelopes myself. My studies in murder had shown me how difficult it was to disguise handwriting, and the method of cutting out and sticking together letters from a newspaper seemed messy—very time-consuming and difficult to manage wearing gloves. I knew, too, that it would be fatal to use my own small portable typewriter or one of the machines at the library. The forensic experts could identify a machine.

And then I hit on my plan. I began to spend my Saturdays and occasional half days journeying round London and visiting shops where they sold secondhand typewriters. I expect you know the kind of shop; a variety of machines of different ages, some practically obsolete, others comparatively new, arranged on tables where the prospective purchaser may try them out.

There were new machines, too, and the proprietor was usually employed in demonstrating their merits or discussing rental terms. The customers wandered desultorily around, inspecting the machines, stopping occasionally to type out an exploratory passage. There were little pads of rough paper stacked ready for use. I didn't, of course, use the scrap paper provided. I came supplied with my own writing materials, a well known brand sold in every stationers and on every railway bookstall. I bought a small supply of paper and envelopes once every two months and never from the same shop. Always, when handling them, I wore a thin pair of gloves, slipping them on as soon as my typing was complete. If someone were near, I would tap out the usual drivel about the sharp brown fox or all good men coming to the aid of the party. But if I were quite alone I would type something very different.

"This is the first comunication, Collingford. You'll be getting them regularly from now on. They're just to let you know that I'm going to kill you."

"You can't escape me, Collingford. Don't bother to inform the police. They can't help you."

"I'm getting nearer, Collingford. Have you made your will?"

"Not long now, Collingford. What does it feel like to be under sentence of death?"

The warnings weren't particularly elegant. As a li-

brarian, I could think of a number of apt quotations
which would have added a touch of individuality or
style, perhaps even of sardonic humour, to the bald sentence of death. But I dared not risk originality. The
notes had to be ordinary, the kind of threat which any
one of his enemies—a worker, a competitor, a cuck-
olded husband—might have sent.

Sometimes I had a lucky day. The shop would be
large, well supplied, nearly empty. I would be able to
move from typewriter to typewriter and leave with perhaps a dozen or so notes and addressed envelopes ready
to send. I always carried a folded newspaper in which I
could conceal my writing pad and envelopes and into
which I could quickly slip my little stock of typed
messages.

It was quite a job to keep myself supplied with notes
and I discovered interesting parts of London and fasci-
nating shops. I particularly enjoyed this part of my plan.
I wanted Collingford to get two notes a week, one
posted on Sunday and one on Thursday. I wanted him
to come to dread Friday and Monday mornings when
the familiar typed envelope would drop on his mat. I
wanted him to believe the threat was real. And why
should he not believe it? How could the force of my
hate and resolution not transmit itself through paper
and typescript to his gradually comprehending brain?

I wanted to keep an eye on my victim. It shouldn't
have been difficult—we lived in the same town—but
our lives were worlds apart. He was a hard and sociable
drinker. I never went inside a public house and would
have been particularly ill at ease in the kind of public
house he frequented. But from time to time I would
see him in the town. Usually he would be parking his
Jaguar, and I would watch his quick, almost furtive look
to left and right before he turned to lock the door. Was

it my imagination that he looked older, that some of the confidence had drained out of him?

Once, when walking by the river on a Sunday in early spring, I saw him maneuvering his boat through Teddington Lock. Ilsa—she had, I knew, changed her name after her marriage—was with him. She was wearing a white trouser suit, her flowing hair was bound by a red scarf. There was a party. I could see two more men and a couple of girls and hear high female squeals of laughter. I turned quickly and slouched away as if I were the guilty one. But not before I had seen Collingford's face. This time I couldn't be mistaken. It wasn't, surely, the tedious job of getting his boat unscratched through the lock that made his face look so grey and strained.

The third phase of my planning meant moving house. I wasn't sorry to go. The bungalow, feminine, chintzy, smelling of fresh paint and the new shoddy furniture she had chosen, was Elsie's home, not mine. Her scent still lingered in cupboards and on pillows. In these inappropriate surroundings I had known greater happiness than I was ever to know again. But now I paced restlessly from room to empty room fretting to be gone.

It took me four months to find the house I wanted. It had to be on or very near the river within two or three miles upstream of Collingford's house. It had to be small and reasonably cheap. Money wasn't too much of a difficulty. It was a time of rising house prices and the modern bungalow sold at three hundred pounds more than I had paid for it. I could get another mortgage without difficulty if I didn't ask too much, but I thought it likely that, for what I wanted, I should have to pay cash.

The house agents perfectly understood that a man on his own found a three-bedroom bungalow too large for him and, even if they found me rather vague about my new requirements and irritatingly imprecise about the reasons for rejecting their offerings, they still sent me orders to view. And then, suddenly on an afternoon in April, I found exactly what I was looking for. It actually stood on the river, separated from it only by a narrow tow path. It was a one-bedroom shacklike wooden bungalow with a tiled roof, set in a small neglected plot of sodden grass and overgrown flower beds. There had once been a wooden landing stage but now the two remaining planks, festooned with weeds and tags of rotted rope, were half submerged beneath the slime of the river.

The paint on the small veranda had long ago flaked away. The wallpaper of twined roses in the sitting-room was blotched and faded. The previous owner had left two old cane chairs and a ramshackle table. The kitchen was pokey and ill-equipped. Everywhere there hung a damp miasma of depression and decay. In summer, when the neighboring shacks and bungalows were occupied by holidaymakers and week-enders it would, no doubt, be cheerful enough. But in October, when I planned to kill Collingford, it would be as deserted and isolated as a disused morgue. I bought it and paid cash. I was even able to knock two hundred pounds off the asking price.

My life that summer was almost happy. I did my job at the library adequately. I lived alone in the shack, looking after myself as I had before my marriage. I spent my evenings watching television. The images flickered in front of my eyes almost unregarded, a monochrome background to my bloody and obsessive thoughts.

I practised with the knife until it was as familiar in my hand as an eating utensil. Collingford was taller than I by six inches. The thrust then would have to be upward. It made a difference to the way I held the knife and I experimented to find the most comfortable and effective grip. I hung a bolster on a hook in the bedroom door and lunged at a marked spot for hours at a time. Of course, I didn't actually insert the knife; nothing must dull the sharpness of its blade. Once a week, a special treat, I sharpened it to an even keener edge.

Two days after moving into the bungalow, I bought a dark-blue untrimmed track suit and a pair of light running shoes. Throughout the summer I spent an occasional evening running on the tow path. The people who owned the neighboring chalets—when they were there, which was infrequently—got used to the sound of my television through the closed curtains and the sight of my figure jogging past their windows. I kept apart from them and from everyone and summer passed into autumn. The shutters were put up on all the chalets except mine. The tow path became mushy with falling leaves. Dusk fell early, and the summer sights and sounds died on the river. And it was October.

He was due to die on Thursday, October 17th, the anniversary of the final decree of divorce. It had to be a Thursday, the evening he spent by custom alone in his workshop, and it was a particularly happy augury that the anniversary should fall on a Thursday. I knew he would be there. Every Thursday for nearly a year I had padded along the two and a half miles of the footpath in the evening dusk and had stood briefly watching the squares of light from his windows and the dark bulk of the house behind.

It was a warm evening. There had been a light drizzle for most of the day but by dusk the skies had cleared. There was a thin white sliver of moon and it cast a trembling ribbon of light across the river. I left the library at my usual time, said my usual goodnights. I knew that I had been my normal self during the day, solitary, occasionally a little sarcastic, conscientious, betraying no hint of the inner tumult.

I wasn't hungry when I got home but I made myself eat an omelette and drink two cups of coffee. I put on my swimming trunks and hung around my neck a plastic bag containing my knife. Over the trunks I put on my track suit, slipping a pair of thin rubber gloves into the pocket. Then, at about quarter past seven, I left the shack and began my customary gentle trot along the tow path.

When I got to the chosen spot opposite Collingford's house, I could see at once that all was well. The house was in darkness but there were the customary lighted windows of his workshop. I saw that the cabin cruiser was moored against the boathouse. I stood very still and listened. There was no sound. Even the light breeze had died and the yellowing leaves on the riverside elms hung motionless. The tow path was completely deserted. I slipped into the shadow of the hedge where the trees grew thickest and found the place I had already selected. I put on the rubber gloves, slipped out of the track suit, and left it folded around my running shoes in the shadow of the hedge. Then, still watching carefully to left and right, I made my way to the river.

I knew just where I must enter and leave the water. I had selected a place where the bank curved gently, where the water was shallow and the bottom was firm and comparatively free of mud. The water struck very cold, but I expected that. Every night during that autumn I had bathed in cold water to accustom my body to the shock. I swam across the river with my methodical but quiet breast stroke, hardly disturbing the dark surface of the water. I tried to keep out of the path of moonlight, but from time to time I swam into its silver gleam and saw my red-gloved hands parting in front of me as if they were already stained with blood.

I used Collingford's landing stage to clamber out the other side. Again I stood still and listened. There was no sound except for the constant moaning of the river and the solitary cry of a night bird.

I made my way silently over the grass. Outside the door of his workroom, I paused again. I could hear the noise of some kind of machinery. I wondered whether the door would be locked, but it opened easily when I turned the handle. I moved into a blaze of light.

I knew exactly what I had to do. I was perfectly calm. It was over in about four seconds. I don't think he really had a chance. He was absorbed in what he had been doing, bending over a lathe, and the sight of an almost naked man, walking purposely towards him, left him literally impotent with surprise. But, after that first paralyzing second, he knew me. Oh, yes, he knew me!

I drew my right hand from behind my back and struck. The knife went in as sweetly as if the flesh had been butter. He staggered and fell. I had expected that and I let myself go loose and fell on top of him. His eyes were glazed, his mouth opened, and there was a gush of dark-red blood. I twisted the knife viciously in the wound, relishing the sound of tearing sinews. Then I waited. I counted five deliberately, then raised myself from his prone figure and crouched behind him before withdrawing the knife. When I withdrew it there was a fountain of sweet-smelling blood which curved from his throat like an arch. There is one thing I shall never forget. The blood must have been red, what other color could it have been? But at the time and forever afterwards I saw it as a golden stream.

I checked my body for bloodstains before I left the workshop and rinsed my arms under the cold tap of his sink. My bare feet made no marks on the wooden block flooring. I closed the door quietly after me and, once again, stood listening. Still no sound. The house was dark and empty.

The return journey was more exhausting than I had thought possible. The river seemed to have widened and I thought I'd never reach my home shore. I was glad I'd chosen a shallow part of the stream and that the bank was firm. I doubt whether I could have drawn myself up through a welter of mud and slime.

I was shivering violently as I zipped up my track suit and it took me precious seconds to get on my running shoes. After I had run about a mile down the tow path, I weighted the bag containing the knife with stones from the path and hurled it into the middle of the river.

I guessed that they would drag part of the Thames for the weapon, but they could hardly search the whole stream. And even if they did, the plastic bag was one like thousands of others and I was confident that the knife could never be traced to me.

Half an hour later I was back in my shack. I had left the television on and the news was just ending. I made myself a cup of hot cocoa and sat to watch it. I felt drained of thought and energy as if I had just made love. I was conscious of nothing but my tiredness, my body's coldness gradually returning to life in the warmth of the electric fire, and a great peace . . .

He must have had quite a lot of enemies. It was nearly a fortnight before the police got round to interviewing me. Two officers came, a Detective Inspector and a Sergeant, both in plain clothes. The Sergeant did most of the talking; the other just sat, looking round at the sitting-room, glancing out at the river, looking at the two of us from time to time from cold grey eyes as if the whole investigation were a necessary bore.

The Sergeant said the usual reassuring platitudes about just a few questions. I was nervous, but that didn't worry me. They would expect me to be nervous. I told myself that whatever I did, I mustn't try to be clever. I mustn't talk too much. I had decided to tell them that I spent the whole evening watching television, confident that no one would be able to refute this. I knew that no friends would have called on me. I doubted whether my colleagues at the library even knew where I lived. And I had no telephone, so I needn't fear that a caller's ring had gone unanswered during that crucial hour and a half.

On the whole it was easier than I expected. Only once did I feel myself at risk. That was when the Inspector suddenly intervened. He said in a harsh voice:

"He married your wife didn't he? Took her away from you some people might say. Nice piece of goods, too, by the look of her. Didn't you feel any grievance? Or was it all nice and friendly? You take her, old chap, no ill feelings. That kind of thing?"

It was hard to accept the contempt in his voice but if he hoped to provoke me he didn't succeed. I had been expecting this question. I was prepared. I looked down at my hands and waited a few seconds before I spoke. I knew exactly what I would say.

"I could have killed Collingford myself when she first told me about him. But I had to come to terms with it. She went for the money, you see. And if that's the kind of wife you have, well, she's going to leave you sooner or later. Better sooner than when you have a family. You tell yourself 'good riddance.' I don't mean I felt that at first, of course. But I did feel it in the end. Sooner than I expected, really."

That was all I said about Elsie then or ever. They came back three times. They asked if they could look round my shack. They looked round it. They took away two of my suits and the track suit for examination. Two weeks later they returned them without comment. I never knew what they suspected, or even if they did

suspect. Each time they came I said less, not more. I
never varied my story. I never allowed them to provoke
me into discussing my marriage or speculating about
the crime. I just sat there, telling them the same thing
over and over again. I never felt in any real danger. I
knew that they had dragged some length of the river
but that they hadn't found the weapon. In the end they
gave up. I always had the feeling that I was pretty low
on their list of suspects and that, by the end, their visits
were merely a matter of form.

It was three months before Elsie came to me. I was
glad it wasn't earlier. It might have looked suspicious if
she had arrived at the shack when the police were with
me. After Collingford's death I hadn't seen her. There
were pictures of her in the national and local newspapers, fragile in somber furs and black hat at the inquest,
bravely controlled at the crematorium, sitting in her
drawing-room in afternoon dress and pearls with her
husband's dog at her feet, the personfication of loneliness and grief.

"I can't think who could have done it. He must have
been a madman. Rodney hadn't an enemy in the
world."

That statement caused some ribald comment at the
library. One of the assistants said:

"He's left her a fortune, I hear. Lucky for her she
had an alibi. She was at a London theater all the evening, watching *Macbeth*. Otherwise, from what I've
heard of our Rodney Collingford, people might have
started to get ideas about his fetching little widow."

Then he gave me a sudden embarrassed glance, remembering who the widow was.

And so one Friday evening, she came. She drove herself and was alone. The dark-green Saab drove up at
my ramshackle gate. She came into the sitting-room

and looked around in a kind of puzzled contempt. After a moment, still not speaking, she sat in one of the fireside chairs and crossed her legs, moving one caressingly against the other. I hadn't seen her sitting like that before. She looked up at me. I was standing stiffly in front of her chair, my lips dry. When I spoke I couldn't recognize my own voice.

"So you've come back?" I said.

She stared at me, incredulous, and then she laughed: "To you? Back for keeps? Don't be silly, darling! I've just come to pay a visit. Besides, I wouldn't dare to come back, would I? I might be frightened that you'd stick a knife into my throat."

I couldn't speak. I stared at her, feeling the blood drain from my face. Then I heard her high, rather childish voice. It sounded almost kind. "Don't worry, I shan't tell. You were right about him, darling, you really were. He wasn't at all nice really. And mean! I didn't care so much about your meanness. After all, you don't earn so very much, do you? But he had half a million! Think of it, darling. I've been left half a million! And he was so mean that he expected me to go on working as his secretary even after we were married. I typed all his letters! I really did! All that he sent from home, anyway. And I had to open post every morning unless the envelopes had a secret little sign on them he'd told his friends about to show that they were private."

I said through bloodless lips, "So all my notes—"

"He never saw them, darling. Well, I didn't want to worry him, did I? And I knew they were from you. I knew when the first one arrived. You never could spell communication could you? I noticed that when you used to write to the house agents and the solicitor before we were married. It made me laugh, considering that you're an educated librarian and I was only a shop assistant."

"So you knew all the time. You knew that it was going to happen."

"Well, I thought that it might. But he really was horrible, darling. You can't imagine. And now I've got half a million! Isn't it lucky that I have an alibi? I thought you might come on that Thursday. And Rodney never did enjoy a serious play."

After that brief visit I never saw or spoke to her again. I stayed in the shack, but life became pointless after Collingford's death. Planning his murder had been an interest, after all. Without Elsie and without my victim, there seemed little point in living. And about a year after his death, I began to dream.

I still dream, always on a Monday and Friday. I live through it all again; the noiseless run along the tow path over the mush of damp leaves; the quiet swim across the river; the silent opening of his door; the upward thrust of the knife; the vicious turn in the wound; the animal sound of tearing tissues; the curving stream of golden blood. Only the homeward swim is different. In my dream the river is no longer a cleansing stream, luminous under the sickle moon, but a cloying, inpenetrable, slow moving bog of viscous blood through which I struggle in impotent panic towards a steadily receding shore.

I know about the significance of the dream. I've read all about the psychology of guilt. Since I lost Elsie I've done all my living through books. But it doesn't help. And I no longer know who I am. I know who I used to be, our local Assistant Librarian, gentle, scholarly, timid, Elsie's husband. But then I killed Collingford. The man I was couldn't have done that. He wasn't that kind of person. So who am I? It isn't really surprising, I suppose, that the Library Committee suggested so tactfully that I ought to look for a less exacting job. A less exacting job than the post of Assistant Librarian? But you can't blame them. No one can be efficient and keep his mind on the job when he doesn't know who he is.

Sometimes, when I'm in a public house—and I seem to spend most of my time there nowadays since I've been out of work—I'll look over someone's shoulder at a newspaper photograph of Elsie and say:

"That's the beautiful Ilsa Mancelli. I was her first husband."

I've got used to the way people sidle away from me, the ubiquitous pub bore, their eyes averted, their voices suddenly hearty. But sometimes, perhaps because they've been lucky with the horses and feel a spasm of pity for a poor deluded sod, they push a few coins over the counter to the barman before making their way to the door and buy me a drink.

The Brothers
by Lawrence Treat

He was a loner and I first saw him sitting in a corner of the community center recreation room. He was fiddling with the pieces of a chess set, and from the very beginning I was struck by his face, narrow and gaunt, with hooded eyes and high cheekbones under which the flesh was pulled taut, leaving a kind of cicatrix. I wondered why nobody came over to him and I almost asked, but instead I walked over to his corner and said, "Care to play?"

Without answering, he held out his two fists with a pawn in each. White and black. I made my choice and sat down.

He did not smile and did not speak, except at the end of the game, which he won. He merely said, "Mate." And that was that.

In all the years during which we played almost every Tuesday at seven forty-five, he never smiled or laughed, and he seemed always to be thinking about some impending tragedy, although the tragedy had happened twenty years ago and had no further consequences, except in his own distorted mind.

I say distorted, but it was far from that. His life was organized down to the smallest detail. Chess with me every Tuesday at quarter to eight. Dinner at the community center on Friday. As I later found out, he bought chicken every Saturday, pork on Monday, and fish on Wednesday. Lemon sole, always. I suppose he got up at the same time every morning and ate exactly the same breakfast at the same time. And regularly, on the fourth day of every month, he went to the cemetery and put flowers on her grave.

He must have had a small income, besides a social security check, and he owned the house in which he lived. He'd been a painter, good enough to have a dealer in New York and make an occasional sale, but far from the big time. He still worked, judging by the paints and rolls of canvas he brought back from New York twice a year, but nobody had ever seen him leave his house with a painting under his arm. Not after it had happened.

People still talk about the trio, the brothers Victor and Bruce, and Evelyn, pronounced with a long *E*. They were inseparable and everybody expected her to marry one of them, but which? Victor was a painter, serious about his career, and Bruce sold insurance to practically everybody in town. He was well-liked, as easygoing as a puff of smoke, and the odds were five to three in his favor. And then one evening, sweet and clear, Evelyn's body was found lying in the grass in the small memorial park near their house. Supposedly she'd been walking her dog, a fluffy white poodle that stayed with her body and barked at everybody who came near. Investigation indicated that she'd been strangled somewhere else and carried there, but the police got no further than that.

Victor had been in nearby Fayetteville that evening, some kind of family celebration, and Bruce was away. Nobody knew where, but he'd been away. And never came back.

At first, nobody believed that Bruce could possibly have been implicated, and yet, how explain his disappearance? As for Victor, he said nothing, saw no one, and locked himself up to mourn.

After I'd settled down and come to be accepted in the town, I got various versions of the story and various points of view about the brothers. Arthur, at the filling station, smiled when I mentioned Bruce.

"One of the nicest guys I ever knew," Arthur said. "He'd do anything for you and pass it off as if it was nothing. I wonder what happened to him. A sweet guy like that."

Linda, at the Hamburger House, had a minority view. "Bruce? I dated him before Evie ever came along, and mister, I'm glad she did."

"Why? Why so bitter?"

"Behind that easygoing guy was one tough son of a bitch, so don't ask me about him or I'll get mad all over again."

I was between books and I decided to find out as much as I could about Evie. Maybe for an article, maybe just to satisfy my own curiosity, but word got around that I was interested. Incidents began to pop up like seeds long dormant and suddenly sprouting up. People would stop to ask me if I'd discovered anything new.

As far as I could tell, the town had been about evenly divided between those who thought Bruce must have killed her (why else would he have gone away?) and those who couldn't believe Bruce was capable of crime. The two sides compromised on the theory that some bum, some transient hobo, must have happened to see Evie walking her dog in the park that night and assaulted her. But if that was the case, I asked why Bruce had disappeared. People shrugged their shoulders and said, "Chief Posner ought to know everything there is. Ask him."

I did.

It was one of those drab, depressing days when it won't rain and won't clear up, and when I came into the chief's office, he was drawing circles on the back of a sheet of pink paper labeled Form B. He had one more intersecting circle to finish before he looked up and asked me what my business was. When I stated it, his big body rocked with suppressed laughter. He slurred his answer, muffling the words the way some fat people do, too much flesh hugging the jaw muscles to enunciate clearly.

"Not my job," he said, "and not yours, either."

"Think Bruce killed her?" I said. "Because from what I hear, it would be completely out of character. He just wasn't that kind."

"Everybody's that kind," Posner said, "when they get worked up."

Logical, I suppose, but more to the point, it saved the chief and his eight-man force a lot of work. Which he readily admitted.

"This here's a small town," he said, "and we don't have the equipment to handle major crimes, so why would anybody here go out and ask a lot of questions when all they'd do is stir things up?"

"For instance?" I said. "What kinds of things?"

He took a deep, snuffling breath and he looked at me as if he was going to accuse me of larceny and homicide and every other crime in the book. Except, of course, suicide. Nobody can accuse me of that.

"Things?" he said, sloshing the word around. "Gossip, neighbor against neighbor. I like to have friendly people around me, the kind that like to sit down and play pinochle with a fat man. Do you play?"

He was evading the point, but I kept pushing. "Are you telling me that you're holding back evidence because you don't feel like investigating?"

That was strong stuff to say to a cop, but it didn't seem to bother him. "Mister," he said, "if I had Bruce Cardigan's fingerprints, I'd send them on to Washington. But I don't."

"Okay, but tell me about Evie. What kind of person was she?"

"Like everybody else, there were two sides to her, and maybe a lot more. Which side do you want?"

"The side you don't want to tell me about," I said.

He leaned back and let his belly quiver. "I guess you heard a lot of talk about how she could have been Miss America if she'd only tried," he said. "Well, I'm telling you she tried, only they turned her down on moral grounds."

"What kind of moral grounds?"

"Ask her," he said.

End of interview.

But word gets out. In a small town the grapevine is a better source of information than the radio, TV, and the newspapers combined, and at Sol's Bar & Grill several people asked me why I'd gone to the police and whether it had anything to do with Evie.

I gave a straightforward answer. "Yes," I said, "and all I found out is, he likes pinochle."

I thought that settled the matter until a couple of days later when I was sitting by myself and nursing a drink and Jake Bohack came and sat down opposite me. I'd seen him at the supermarket a couple of times but had never said more than hello or what kind of day it was, and I wondered why he chose now to single me out. "Kind of quiet tonight," he remarked.

"You mean nobody's talking about Evie? After twenty years, why should they?"

"I got nothing against her and nothing against the chief except he weighs too much," Jake said, "but there never was much of an investigation and I wondered why. It looked like nobody wanted to bother. Including him."

"Standard police procedure," I said. "Cops don't do any more work than they have to, and it's too late now for any real investigation, but I keep wondering, for instance, why Evie decided to walk her dog in the park that evening. First time she ever did. The question is, was she alone?"

"If she'd been alone, nobody'd be there to kill her."

"Who do you think she was with?"

"With Popo. Her dog."

"You know? You were there?"

It was a shot in the dark but it made his hand bounce up hard enough to spill some of his beer. He studied the froth carefully, as if it were the Delphic oracle about to give him all the answers. "Walt," he said to me, putting the glass down slowly, "my sister was Evie's best friend and Evie told her things she wouldn't tell anybody else."

"For instance?"

"How do I know? My sister's dead and all I can tell you is this: Evie got fed up with waiting around for a couple of brothers to make up their minds. She couldn't stand it and she was ready to bust loose, so suppose it was just that. She went haywire with some guy and it got out of hand and he killed her."

"And she'd brought her pooch with her so it could share in the fun?"

Jake scratched his head. "Beats me," he said.

But it occurred to me that he knew much more than his sister was likely to have told him. If she was such a good friend of Evie, why tell her brother and hope he wouldn't spread the news all over town?

Sol, however, had apparently been listening to my conversation with Jake, because the next night Sol had a funny expression on his face every time he looked at me. I was sitting at one end of the bar and I figured that by and by Sol would come over and tell me what was on his mind. Therefore it was no surprise when he sidled down to where I was sitting and took a glance around the room to make sure nobody'd be yelling for another drink. Satisfied that he'd have a few minutes for himself, he leaned forward and said, as if it was something confidential, "I'm wondering what Jake said the other night."

"Not much. His sister knew Evie and Evie told her she was worried because neither Bruce nor Victor had proposed."

"Is that all? Jake's told that story to half the people in town and he changes it every week. But let me tell you this—Evie was a tough cookie and she never confided to anybody. She knew what she wanted, and she kept it strictly to herself."

"I wish I'd known her."

"You see Vic pretty regular," Sol said. "He ever talk about Evie?"

"Never. Never mentions anything personal. About all we ever do is play chess. One game, which he usually wins, and then he goes home. Or at least, I guess that's where he goes. Why?"

"I knew him pretty well before it all happened. And sometimes after a drink or two, people say more than they want to."

"So?"

"Well, one night Vic came here, he'd had a few, at first I wasn't sure whether I ought to serve him, but he could hold his liquor and about the only effect it ever had on him was he opened up. Always been kind of close-mouthed, but he couldn't hold back the big news. He was riding high, because he was going to make a lot of money, he was going to be rich and famous."

"How come?"

"A big mural for some bank in New York."

"But it didn't come through, did it?"

"Not that I know of, but that was only part of what

he told me. The big news was that Evie was going to marry him."

"He told you that? How come you never mentioned it before? Or did you?"

"Well, you see—that is, the three of them had been going steady, and everybody was sure she'd pick one or the other of them and there were some pretty big bets on who. We called it the Evie Sweepstakes and I was in pretty deep, I'd bet a half year's salary on Bruce. Think I was going to make a loser out of myself by giving out the news? I was trying to find a way of switching my bet and I'd hedged on some of it, and if folks found out—you see, mister, I was in trouble." And Sol turned and walked back to the beer spigot where a couple of customers were calling for him, but I'd learnt a lot in these last few minutes. I had the clue I'd been looking for, and it was pretty clear to me that Vic must have told Bruce the news. The brothers must have talked it over and Bruce, bereft of the only woman he could ever love, had accepted the inevitable and left to start a new career in some other part of the world.

It was a sad, sweet story, with Vic losing her on the very day he'd won her. As a result, he'd become a recluse, living with only that forever-lost memory.

The story bothered me. I kept seeing Vic's gaunt face, the hunted look in his eyes, and the next time we played chess I saw him in a different light, someone more tragic than pathetic, needing some shred of friendship to pierce the black night in which he lived, and I wondered how I could get through to him.

That would have to wait, however, because I had business with my publisher and was away for a few days. I'd left a message for Vic to the effect that I couldn't play that Tuesday but would be back the following week. When I returned from my trip I was greeted with the news that Vic had sat in his regular corner and started a game with himself, playing both sides. Suddenly he'd uttered a cry of pain, clutched at his side, and collapsed. By the time a doctor arrived, he was dead.

To my surprise, I was appointed executor of his estate, with half of it going to charity and the other half to me. A lawyer handed me a key to the house and told me to take a look, but not to disturb anything. The lawyer was pretty sure there was nothing in the estate except the house and a few dollars in securities. Plus a lot of worthless paintings that presumably you couldn't even sell.

Worthless? That was a premise I refused to accept. I thought of all the years Vic had been working, producing masterpieces nobody had ever seen. Why couldn't Vic be an undiscovered genius, recognized only posthumously? And there I was sitting on potential millions!

Despite my fantasy, I approached the house more in fear than in hope. I can't tell you why, except that this was the first time in twenty years that anybody except Victor Cardigan had crossed the threshold. I think the idea unnerved me, and I stood for perhaps a minute in front of the door.

I was thinking of what the trio must have been like. Three kids in their twenties, bubbling with life. A pair of brothers in love with the same girl and she trying to decide. On the one hand money, a pleasant and comfortable life in a small town, with all the security of the wife of a prominent citizen, and on the other hand a painter, maybe a life of poverty or maybe a husband with a career that was just beginning, with fame and fortune ahead. But had she really decided, as Sol had said, or was there more to the story, some facet that no one had even considered? And did this house have a clue to the tragedy and the answer as to why Evie had been in the park that night?

Suddenly angry at her, I rammed my key into the lock, turned the key, and took two long, quick strides inside. Then I stopped.

Nothing. What had I been expecting? A ghost? A stranger confronting me? Or a pet, perhaps a vicious dog waiting to attack? Ridiculous. This was merely an empty house, whose owner had died.

The first thing that impressed me was the almost hygienic cleanliness of the place, as if every item of furniture had just been polished, every inch of rug newly vacuumed. A housewife's delight, with the living room furnished in stark and yet tasteful simplicity.

I began to breathe more easily. I'd been concocting stories that had no foundation. Here was a perfectly ordinary room in a perfectly ordinary house, except for the studio. Most houses in this town not only had no studio, but their owners probably didn't even know what a studio looked like.

On entering it, the first thing I saw was the picture on the easel, unfinished and still smelling of paint. I'd never seen Evie, and yet I was certain that this was she. I knew she'd been beautiful, but the face on the easel had barely been sketched. This was a work in progress, too fragmentary to be judged.

I turned away from it and studied the long racks that lined three sides of the room. This was Vic's storehouse where he kept all the paintings he'd done during the past twenty years. They were probably in chronological order, for Vic had always been neat and well-organized. I'd noticed his wallet in which he kept his money in order, big bills at the back, the singles in front. Even the way he played chess, every move had to be calculated, with nothing left to chance. Protect the king before daring to plan an attack. That was the way he played and the way he conducted his life.

I bent down and slid the nearest painting from its slot. It was the portrait of a girl, a young girl in a red dress. She was radiant with youthfulness, ripe with promise. She was wearing a medallion as a necklace and her hair had a coronet of flowers. This was Evie, but which one? Art's or Linda's or Posner's or Sol's, or all of them brought together in the mind of one man. I put the picture back in its place and picked up another one.

This, too, was a portrait of Evie, but in a green dress and without the coronet. Thoughtfully, I pulled out a few more canvases. Always the same girl, painted over and over again. A different dress, a different pose, a different hair-do. Was this all I was going to find, the same picture replicated ad infinitum? Had Vic had no more imagination than the compulsion to repeat over and over again?

I moved on a few feet and pulled out another canvas. Evie of course, but this time she seemed older, some of her vibrancy and excitement had gone. This was Evie in her thirties, as Victor had imagined her.

I went further along the line and examined the paintings at random. Evie, always Evie, but now she changed. There were lines in her face, the mouth was thinner and tighter, and wrinkles had begun to expose layers hitherto hidden by the flesh of her cheeks.

I thought of Oscar Wilde's *The Picture of Dorian Gray*, the story of a painting that became old and mean and ugly with the dissipation of the actual man, while the man himself remained unchanged. But for Evie, the change came about through a series of paintings in which the inner eye of the artist drew what the mind was unable to see. And there she was, the Evie she might have been had she lived another twenty years.

Reluctantly I left the studio, not sure of what I felt, but anxious to analyze and collect my thoughts, to make some judgment of compassion or empathy or reach some cold, rational conclusion.

I went upstairs slowly. There were two rooms at the landing, one door partly open, the other one shut. I walked into the room with the door ajar.

The large double bed was covered with a white, embroidered coverlet, and on it lay a white silk nightgown. The slippers alongside the bed were white satin, and the entire room was dainty and unmistakably feminine. I stepped over to the bureau and counted the bottles of perfume and the various cosmetics. There were eleven items, all of them unopened. Evie would never have bought these. Evie, whom I was sure had never slept here or even been here. A woman Vic had invented, and worshiped for twenty years.

I leaned down and touched the nightgown, fingering the lace and feeling as if I was committing a sacrilege, for here, in this room, Evie was to have spent her wedding night, and in this room she would have borne children, grown older, and eventually died. Since it had never happened, Victor saw it in dreams, dreamt their life together, and painted her as his imagination directed him to.

And what about his brother? Had Victor believed that Bruce was the killer? And if Victor had admitted the likelihood or even the possibility, what had he done about it? Had he tried to forgive, or had he dried up inside, twisted with hate and reliving his tragedy every single day of his life?

After a few moments I straightened up, swung around slowly, and left the room. For some reason I decided to have a look at the cellar, a merely perfunctory glance, to check out the furnace and any other major piece of equipment.

The cellar had a concrete floor, swept clean. Washing machine and dryer stood against one wall, a long work-bench on the other, with every tool neatly in place. It was then I noticed that the concrete had been broken up at the far end of the cellar. An area about six feet by four had been cut out and filled with dirt. Approximately, I thought, the proper size for a grave.

The next day the authorities ordered the body exhumed. It lay in a simple, homemade coffin, and the coroner examining the withered remains reported that the cause of death had been a bullet, still lodged in the withered skeleton of Bruce Cardigan.

Breakfast Television

by Robert Barnard

The coming of breakfast television has been a great boon to the British.

Caroline Worsley thought so anyway, as she sat in bed eating toast and sipping tea, the flesh of her arm companionably warm against the flesh of Michael's arm. Soon they would make love again, perhaps while the consumer lady had her spot about dangerous toys, or during the review of the papers, or the resident doctor's phone-in on acne. They would do it when and how the fancy took them—or as Michael's fancy took him, for he was very imperative at times—and this implied no dislike or disrespect for the breakfast-time performer concerned. For Caroline liked them all, and could lie there quite happily watching any one of them—David, the doctor; Jason, the pop-chart commentator; Selma, the fashion expert; Jemima, the problems expert; Reg, the sports-roundup man; and Maria, the linkup lady. And of course Ben, the linkup man.

Ben—her husband.

It had all worked out very nicely indeed. Ben was called for by the studio at four-thirty. Michael always waited for half an hour after that, in case Ben had forgotten something and made a sudden dash back to the flat for it. Michael was a serious, slightly gauche young man, who would hate to be caught out in a situation both compromising and ridiculous. Michael was that rare thing, a studious student—though very well built, too, Caroline told herself appreciatively. His interests were work, athletics, and sex.

It was Caroline who had initiated him into the pleasures of regular sex. At five o'clock, his alarm clock went off—though, as he told Caroline, it was rarely necessary. His parents were away in Africa, dispensing aid, know-how, and Oxfam beatitudes in some Godforsaken part of Africa, so he was alone in their flat. He put his clothes on so that in the unlikely event of his being seen in the corridor he could pretend to be going out. But he never had been. By five past, he was in Caroline's flat, and in the bedroom she shared with Ben. They had almost an hour and a half of sleeping and lovemaking before breakfast television began.

Not that Michael watched it with the enthusiasm of Caroline. Sometimes he took a book along and read it while Caroline was drawing in her breath of horror at combustible toys, or tut-tutting at some defaulting businessman who had left his customers in the lurch.

He would lie there immersed in *The Mechanics of the Money Supply* or *Some Problems of Exchange-Rate Theory*—something reasonably straightforward, anyway, because he had to read against the voice from the set, and from time to time he was conscious of Ben looking directly at him. He never quite got used to that.

It didn't bother Caroline at all.

"Oh, look, his tie's gone askew," she would say, or, "You know, Ben's much balder than he was twelve months ago—I've never noticed it in the flesh." Michael seldom managed to assent to such propositions with any easy grace. He was much too conscious of balding, genial, avuncular Ben grinning out from the television screen as he tried to wring from some graceless pop-star three words strung together consecutively that actually made sense. "I think he's getting fatter in the face," said Caroline, licking marmalade off her fingers ...

"I am not getting fatter in the face!" shouted Ben. "Balder, yes, fatter in the face definitely not!" He added in a voice soaked in vitriol: "Bitch."

He was watching a video of yesterday's lovemaking on a set in his dressing-room, after the morning's television session had ended. His friend Frank, from the technical staff, had rigged up the camera in the cupboard of his study, next door to the bedroom. The small hole that was necessary in the wall had been expertly disguised. Luckily, Caroline was a deplorable housewife. Eventually she might have discovered the sound apparatus under the double bed, but even then she would probably have assumed it was some junk of Ben's that he had shoved there out of harm's way.

"Hypocritical swine!" yelled Ben, as he heard Caroline laughing with Michael that the Shadow Foreign Secretary had really wiped the floor with him in that interview. "She told me when I got home yesterday how well I'd handled it!"

As the shadowy figures on the screen turned to each other again, their bare flesh glistening dully in the dim light, Ben growled. "Whore!"

The makeup girl concentrated on removing the traces of powder from his neck and shirt-collar, and studiously avoided comment.

"I suppose you think this is sick, don't you?" demanded Ben.

"It's none of my business," she said, but added: "If she is carrying on, it's not surprising, is it? Not with the hours we work."

"Not surprising? I tell you, I was bloody surprised! Just think how you'd feel if your husband, or bloke, was two-timing you while you were at the studio."

"He is," said the girl. But Ben hadn't heard. He frequently didn't hear other people when he was off camera. His comfortable, sympathetic-daddy image was something that seldom spilled over into his private life. Indeed, at his worst, he could slip up even on camera: he could be leaned forward, listening to his interviewees with every appearance of the warmest interest, then reveal by his next question that he hadn't heard a word they were saying. But that happened very infrequently, and only when he was extremely preoccupied. Ben was very good at his job.

"Now they'll have tea," he said. "Everyone needs a tea-break in their working morning."

Tea—

Shortly after this, there was a break in Caroline's delicious early-morning routine: her son Malcolm came home for a long weekend from school. Michael became no more than the neighbor's son at whom she smiled in the corridor. She and Malcolm had breakfast round the kitchen table. It was on Tuesday morning, when Malcolm was due to depart later in the day, that Ben made one of his little slips.

He was interviewing Cassy Le Beau from the long-running pop group The Crunch, and as he leaned forward to introduce a clip from the video of their latest musical crime he said:

"Now, this is going to interest Caroline and Michael, watching at home—"

"Why did he say Michael?" asked Caroline aloud, before she could stop herself.

"He meant Malcolm," said their son. "Anyway, it's bloody insulting, him thinking I'd be interested in The Crunch."

Because Malcolm was currently rehearsing Elgar's Second with the London Youth Orchestra. Ben was about two years out of date with his interests.

* * *

"Did you see that yesterday morning?" Caroline asked Michael the next day.

"What?"

"Ben's slip on *Wake Up, Britain* yesterday."

"I don't watch breakfast telly when I'm not with you."

"Well, he did one of those 'little messages home' that he does. You probably don't remember, but there was all this focus about families when *Wake Up, Britain* started, and Ben got into the habit of putting little messages to Malcolm and me into the program. Ever so cosy and ever so bogus. Anyway, he did one yesterday, as Malcolm was home—only he said 'Caroline and Michael.' Not Malcolm, but Michael."

Michael shrugged.

"Just a slip of the tongue."

"But his own *son*! And for the slip to come out as *Michael*!"

"These things happen," said Michael, putting his arm around her and pushing her head back onto the pillow. "Was there a Michael on the show yesterday?"

"There was Michael Heseltine on, as usual."

"There you are, you see."

"But Heseltine's an ex-cabinet minister. He would *never* call him Michael."

"But the name was in his head. These things happen. Remember, Ben's getting old."

"True," said Caroline, who was two years younger than her husband.

"Old!" shouted Ben, dabbing at his artificially darkened eyebrows, one eye on the screen. "You think I'm old? I'll show you I've still got some bolts left in my locker!"

He had dispensed with the services of the makeup

girl. He had been the only regular on *Wake Up, Britain* to demand one anyway, and the studio was surprised but pleased when Ben decided she was no longer required. Now he could watch the previous evening's cavortings without the damper of her adolescent disapproval from behind his shoulder.

And now he could plan.

One of the factors that just had to be turned to his advantage was Caroline's deplorable housekeeping. All the table tops of their kitchen were littered with bits of this and that—herbs, spices, sauces, old margarine-tubs, bits of jam on dishes. The fridge was like the basement of the Victoria and Albert Museum, and the freezer was a record of their married life. And on the window-ledge in the kitchen were the things he used to do his little bit of gardening—

Ben and Caroline inhabited one of twenty modern service flats in a block. Most of the gardening was done by employees of the landlords, yet some little patches were alloted to tenants who expressed an interest. Ben had always kept up his patch, though—as was the way of such things—it was more productive of self-satisfaction than of fruit or veg. "From our own garden," he would say as he served his guests horrid little bowls of red currants.

Already on the window-ledge in the kitchen there was a little bottle of paraquat.

That afternoon, he pottered around in his moldly little patch. By the time he had finished and washed his hands under the kitchen tap, the paraquat had found its way next to the box of teabags standing by the kettle. The top of the paraquat was loose, having been screwed only about halfway round.

"Does you good to get out on your own patch of earth," Ben observed to Caroline as he went through to his study.

*   *   *

The next question that presented itself was: when?

There were all sorts of possibilities—including that the police would immediately arrest him for murder, he was reconciled to that—but he thought that on the whole it would be best to do it on the morning when he was latest home. Paraquat could be a long time in taking effect, he knew, but there was always a chance that they would not decide to call medical help until it was too late. If he was to come home to a poisoned wife and lover in the flat, he wanted them to be well and truly dead. Wednesday was the day when all the breakfast-TV team met in committee to hear what was planned for the next week—which aging star would be plugging her memoirs, which singer plugging his forth-coming British tour. Wednesdays Ben often didn't get home till early afternoon.

Wednesday it was.

Tentatively in his mental engagements-book he pen-cilled in Wednesday the fifteenth of May.

Whether the paraquat would be in the teapot of the Teasmade, or in the teabag, or how it would be admin-istered was a minor matter that he could settle long before the crucial Tuesday night when the tea things for the morning had to be got ready. The main thing was that everything was decided.

The fifteenth of May—undoubtedly a turning-point in her life—began badly for Caroline. First of all, Ben kissed her goodbye before he set off for the studio, something he hadn't done since the early days of his engagement on breakfast television. Michael had come in at five o'clock as usual, but his lovemaking was forced, lacking in tenderness. Caroline lay for an hour in his arms afterwards, wondering if something was worrying him. He didn't say anything for some time—

not till the television was switched on. Probably he relied on the bromides and the plugs to distract Caroline's
attention from what he was going to say.

He had taken up his textbook and the kettle of the
Teasmade was beginning to hum when he said, in his
gruff, teenage way:

"Won't be much more of this."

Caroline was watching clips from a Frank Bruno fight
and not giving him her full attention. When it was over,
she turned to him.

"Sorry—what did you say?"

"I said there won't be much more of this."

A dagger went to her heart, which seemed to stop
beating for minutes. When she could speak, the words
came out terribly middle-class-matron.

"I don't quite understand. Much more of what?"

"This. You and me together in the mornings."

"You don't mean your parents are coming home
early?"

"No. I've—got a flat. Nearer college. So there's not
so much traveling in the mornings and evenings."

"You're just *moving out?*"

"Pretty much so. I can't live with my parents
forever."

Caroline's voice grew louder and higher.

"You're not living with your parents. It's six months
before they come home. You're moving out *on me*. Do
you have the impression that I'm the sort of person you
can just move in with when it suits you and then flit
away from when it doesn't suit you any longer?"

"Well—yes, actually. I'm a free agent."

"You *bas*tard! You *bas*tard!"

She would have liked to take him by the shoulders
and shake him till the teeth rattled in his head. Instead,
she sat there on the bed, coldly furious. It was 7:15.

The kettle whistled and poured boiling water onto the teabags in the teapot.

"Have some tea or coffee," said Ben on the screen to his politician guest, with a smile that came out as a death's-head grin. "It's about early-morning teatime."

"It's someone else, isn't it?" said Caroline, her voice kept steady with difficulty. "A new girl friend."

"All right, it's a new girl friend," agreed Michael.

"Someone younger."

"Of course someone younger," said Michael, taking up his book again and sinking into monetarist theory.

Silently Caroline screamed: Of course someone younger! What the hell's that supposed to mean? They don't come any older than you? Of course I was just passing the time with a crone like you until someone my own age came along?

"You're moving in with a girl," she said, the desolation throbbing in her voice.

"Yeah," said Michael from within his Hayek.

"Tea all right?" Ben asked his guest.

Caroline sat there, watching the flickering images on the screen, while the tea in the pot turned from hot to warm. The future spread before her like a desert—a future as wife and mother. What kind of life was that, for God's sake? For some odd reason, a future as *lover* had seemed, when she had thought about it at all, fulfilling, traditional, and dignified. Now any picture she might have of the years to come was turned into a hideous, mocking, negative image, just as the body beside her in the bed had turned from a glamorous sex object into a boorish, ungrateful teenager.

They were having trouble in the *Wake Up, Britain* studio, where the two link-up people had got mixed up as to who was introducing what. Caroline focused on the screen—she always enjoyed it when Ben muffed something.

"Sorry," said Ben, smiling his kindly uncle smile. "I thought it was Maria, but in fact it's me. Let's see—I know it's David, our resident medico, but actually I don't know what your subject is today, David."

"Poison," said David.

But the camera had not switched to him, and the instant he dropped the word into the ambient atmosphere Caroline—and one million other viewers—saw Ben's jaw drop and an expression of panic flash like lightning through his eyes.

"I've had a lot of letters from parents of small children," said David, in his calm, everything-will-be-all-right voice, "about what to do if the kids get hold of poison. Old medicines, household detergents, gardening stuff—they can all be dangerous, and some can be deadly." Caroline saw Ben, the camera still agonizingly on him, swallow hard and put his hand up to his throat. Then, mercifully, the director changed the shot at last to the doctor, leaning forward and doing his thing. "So here are a few rules about what to do in that sort of emergency—"

Caroline's was not a quick mind, but suddenly a succession of images came together. Ben's kiss that morning, his smile as he offered his guest early-morning tea, a bottle of paraquat standing next to the box of teabags in the kitchen, Ben's dropping jaw at the sudden mention of poison.

"Michael," she said.

"What?" he asked, hardly bothering to take his head out of his book.

She looked at the self-absorbed, casually cruel body and her blood boiled.

"Oh, nothing," she said. "Let's have tea. It'll be practically cold by now."

She poured two cups, and handed him his. He put aside his book, which he had hardly been reading, his

mind congratulating himself on having got out of this
lightly. He took the cup and sat on the bed watching
the screen, where the sports man was now introducing
highlights of last night's athletics meeting from Oslo.

"Boy!" said Michael appreciatively, sipping his tea.
"That was a great run!"

He took a gulp, then two or three more to finish the
cup, then handed it back to Caroline.

Caroline did not take up her tea, but sat there looking
at the graceless youth. Round her lips there played a
smile of triumphal revenge—a smile the camera whir-
ring away in the secrecy of the study cupboard perfectly caught for Ben, for the criminal courts, and for
posterity.

A Letter Too Late
by Henry Slesar

"I insulted a nun this morning," Penny said to the ceiling of Dr. Winterich's office. Then she laughed, one of her sharp dry laughs that always made the doctor stab his pad with the point of his pen. "I wonder if it's bad luck, to insult a nun."

He waited for details. Winterich was a strict Freudian, who believed in the sanctity of free association. Eventually, he found out that the nun had been collecting money for some religious charity, and in Penny's depressed mood she had literally slammed the door in her face. The doctor scribbled a parenthetical note. *"Temp. outb. incr. freq."*

Penny was already aware of the recent escalation of her angry moods, but she had no trouble determining its cause.

"Why shouldn't I be upset?" she demanded. "This damned cruise is for *eight weeks*! Mike's never been gone more than three or four. He told me himself he hates the long ones. The passengers are much more trouble—"

"Why is that?" Winterich said, with genuine curiosity.

"Because they're older. Ancient, some of them. Only older people can afford the time and money for these long cruises. Do you know they actually bring *coffins* aboard? They're kept in the hold, just in case anyone dies on the voyage. Doesn't that make your flesh creep?"

"Has he left yet?"

"No. The ship sails this evening." She giggled suddenly. "Maybe I ought to do what I did the last time. The South Pacific cruise." She turned her head, but Winterich always stationed himself out of her line of sight.

"What did you do then?"

"I thought you knew." Then she remembered— Mamie Vogel had been her doctor at the time. Obviously, she hadn't turned over her notes to Winterich when Penny switched analysts. "I cut up his uniform, with scissors. Of course it was a childish thing to do." But she smiled at the recollection. Mike's face floated down from the ceiling, wearing an expression of fury and petulance.

"And what happened when you did?"

"He missed the sailing. He had to get a new purser's uniform fitted, so he flew down to Fiji and picked up the ship there. Of course we had a major, major fight about it. But that's one good thing about having a sailor for a husband, he's away so long we have plenty of time for our tempers to cool down."

"And your temper right now?"

Penny was amused. Winterich was getting positively loquacious.

"I'm glad he's going. I mean it. I've been thinking about it ever since he told me. Eight weeks! I couldn't be happier. I'm going to have the whole damned apartment painted. My friend Nan is going to Europe for a month, so I'll be able to stay at her place during the worst part of it. . . . I might even have the furniture upholstered. I know what you're going to say. Does Mike know about all the money I'm going to spend?

No, I want that to be a fun surprise for him when he gets back."

Winterich said nothing, disappointing her.

"Do you think I'm wrong? Do you think I'm just being spiteful? Oh, I know. You won't make any judgments. That's fine with me. I left Dr. Vogel because she made too many judgments."

"Was that really the reason?"

"What do you mean?"

"Dr. Vogel suggested that you and she reached some sort of impasse. That you came to a bridge that you refused to cross."

"So she *did* turn over her notes!"

"We had a brief professional consultation," Winterich said easily. "It was in your best interest. She seems to think that you ended your therapy when a certain subject surfaced. A man called Gordon."

Penny tried hard not to react to Winterich's thrust by remaining perfectly still. But the act of immobilizing herself was in itself a giveaway. She shot a look at her watch and then sat up.

"I know it's ten minutes early," she said. "But I want to get home before Mike leaves." She tried to twinkle at him. "I have to wish him Bon Voyage, don't I?"

There was no trace of the twinkle by the time she reached the parking lot behind Winterich's building. It was replaced by a bothersome twitch in her left eye, a symptom so familiar that she simply ignored it. But she couldn't ignore the trembling in both hands when she placed them on the wheel. She tried to steady them by tightening her grip, but the effort failed. She decided to sit quietly and wait until the tremors passed, until she was in control again. "Control" was an important word to Penny, possibly because she was always balanced on its thin edge, looking down into a swirling chaos.

Why did he have to mention Gordon?

She leaned back and closed her eyes, expecting memory to develop a photographic image of Gordon Cates. But she saw only darkness. She would have to delineate the face for herself, feature by feature. The deep-set eyes, sea-glass green. The patrician nose. The thin wide mouth, the twisty little smile he used a bit too deliberately. The straight blue-black hair, grown too long. She had tried to cut it once while he slept. Samson and Delilah. He hadn't laughed. He had torn the scissors from her hand and flung them across the room. Scissors again. She had to plead for his forgiveness, and he bestowed it like a Roman Emperor. He was almost preposterous in his haughty indignation, but Penny loved him all the more for it.

Dear God, she thought, how long ago that seemed! But it was only a year and a half. With a little effort, she could probably name the exact date. All she would have to do is count backwards from the night Mike Wharton asked her to marry him. The chronology of pain. She visualized a calendar, pages falling off like an old movie sequence. Her hands began to steady on the wheel. She turned on the ignition.

They had been a threesome. That was the word everyone used. Nan, not long on originality, had called them the "gleesome threesome." At the beginning, of course, they were four, the fourth being Nan herself. She was Mike's cousin, distant in more ways than one she used to say. Nan had a sisterly interest in seeing Mike happily paired off, and her friend Penny seemed like a logical candidate, even if she deplored Penny's occasional lapses into moodiness. Mike was easygoing enough for both of them. She described Mike as "breezy," and the word suited him. You could always picture Mike on an open boat, his thin blond hair lifting in the wind, smiling with small perfect teeth at an unseen horizon.

Penny had liked Mike from the first, and liked him even more when he introduced her to his best friend. The very fact that Mike could have a friend like Gordon Cates impressed her. Gordon seemed so remote, so impervious to friendship; she equated these qualities with superior standards. Gordon was an assistant editor in a publishing house, and he exuded an intellectual aura that Penny found stimulating even though she hadn't read a book all the way through since leaving college. That changed when she met Gordon, who always remembered to bring a purloined novel from his office when the gleesome threesome met—by this time, Nan had detached herself from the group.

To anyone seeing them together, it was quickly apparent which way the sexual current was flowing. Penny tried to divide her attention equally, but the quality of the attention was different. She flirted more openly with Mike, teased and tantalized him. But when she turned to Gordon, her large brown eyes seemed to melt like heated chocolate. If he touched her arm, it would quiver like the withers of a horse. Penny was passably pretty, but when she looked at Gordon Cates her complexion would become luminescent, highlights would glisten in her hair, her very features would alter into something approaching an Athenian ideal. She seemed to make herself over each time, in her desire to please him.

The trouble was, her transformation seemed to affect Mike more than it did his friend. Fortunately, he never objected when Penny suggested that Gordon be included in their twice-weekly dates. He seemed to enjoy the chase even more because Gordon was its spectator. He never realized that the glow she radiated on those Wednesday and Saturday evenings wasn't meant for him alone. Poor Mike! His innocence was touching.

Remembering those days, Penny felt sorry for him all over again, and almost lost the hard edge of the anger she had been feeling for the past week.

She had thought it was going to be Gordon who would finally put an end to the gleesome threesome. She had seen the signs of his discontent when Penny became a weekend visitor to the beach house the two friends shared every summer. She had arrived with her arms laden with cookbooks and copper frying pans and cleansing powder. She knew Mike and Gordon were both helpless in the kitchen and indifferent to domestic hygiene. She cooked and scrubbed and sewed all weekend, and reveled in it. At night, with linked arms, they would stride down the beach towards somebody's cookout or cocktail party. Both Mike and Gordon would drink copious amounts of alcohol, but only Mike seemed to get drunk, and she and Gordon would have to put him to bed, giggling like dormitory conspirators. One night, after a party, they had looked down at his comatose form like parents fondly regarding a wayward child. Gordon had turned to her and gathered her into his arms. She had known a dozen of Mike's kisses to that point, but this one, almost solemn and ceremonial, meant more to her than the total of them all.

Gordon didn't mention the event the next day. But it had changed the barometric pressure at the beach house. His mood was sullen, faintly hostile. He seemed to resent his role as designated spectator to Mike's romance. He looked on at Mike's clowny, clumsy flirtations with Penny with open resentment. It made her heart race, her blood accelerate through her veins. She found herself stoking the furnace of his jealousy. She was more than usually amorous with Mike. She sat on his lap at the breakfast table and gave him an overheated kiss, and it lasted too long for Gordon's patience. He slammed down his cup and declared that he was going for a swim. Mike would have been a block of wood not to recognize his distaste, and he went running after him. Penny sat alone, in simmering satisfaction.

Then came the *Laguna Queen*. It was a berth Mike had been wanting for almost a year, ever since he had been discharged from the navy. Mike had fallen in love with the ocean; he wanted to continue his career on the water, but he didn't want to be an ordinary deck hand on a commercial vessel. He was a college graduate, he had been a petty officer, and he loved handsome uniforms. On the *Laguna Queen*, he could wear gleaming whites and gold braid, and there was no way he could turn down the offer, not even if it meant a three-week intermission in his courtship.

In the rear-view mirror, Penny saw her own unconscious smile. She was thinking about the night of the sailing. She was hearing Mike's voice, telling Gordon to "take good care of Penny" in his absence. She had watched Gordon's face, wondering if he was pitying Mike's naiveté. She had been afraid that her own expression would reveal her excited anticipation so she had begged off early, claiming a cooking class, leaving Mike and Gordon to their bon voyages.

It had taken three days for Gordon to call her, and Penny had to be the one to suggest dinner. They went to their favorite Italian restaurant in the Village, and their favorite Italian waiter, who was actually Dominican, was surprised to seat them at a table for two. They drank their initial toast to Admiral Mike. There were three other toasts after that, and Penny was drunk for the first time since the formation of the gleesome threesome. Gordon had to take her home, and had to extricate himself from her drunken embrace. She remembered dragging him towards her bed, and how firmly he had resisted, and how scrambled her feelings had been, mixed resentment of his rejection and admiration for his chivalry.

Gordon didn't call for a week after that, and Penny had to instigate the next encounter herself. She did it brazenly, reminding him of his promise to Mike. He took her to dinner, and she had a chaste glass of white wine, and afterward they went to a movie and sat stiffly side by side, until her hand "accidentally" brushed his, and then their fingers locked. . . .

The day before the *Laguna Queen* was due back in port, Penny received her first postcard, from St. Croix. She crammed it into her purse without even bothering to decipher Mike's scrawl and went to Gordon's apartment. He was in his shirtsleeves, immersed in the galleys of a book; she had never seen him wear reading glasses before, and the sight of them perched on his patrician nose made her heart quicken. She showed him the postcard, and he promptly showed her the one he had just received himself, equally illegible. They smiled at each other, once more like indulgent parents. Then she sank to her knees in front of his desk chair and put her arms around him. Her kiss began as solemnly as their first, but it turned into a hungry exploration. They were off balance and slid from the chair to the carpet, and the length of their bodies met. His glasses were askew. She lifted them off and kissed him again.

Penny had been surprised when Gordon didn't show up at the pier the next morning to greet the arriving cruise ship. It made her all the more anxious about seeing Mike again. Then he was on the gangplank, a dashing figure in his white uniform, waving his braided cap. She ran to meet him, and he kissed her loudly, laughing for no particular reason. When he asked for Gordon, she could only claim mystification at his absence, and Mike's tanned face momentarily clouded. "Maybe it was the postcard," he said. When she confessed to an inability to read his message, Mike said: "I've signed on for another cruise—the Mediterranean. Isn't that terrific?"

That was how the threesome ended. Mike's decision to pursue a career at sea created a rift between him and his landlocked, desk-locked friend. She thought it might affect her own relationship (ship's officers were notoriously catnip to vacationing females) but Mike had no intention of letting that happen. On the night before he embarked on his third cruise, he took her to dinner (that same Italian restaurant, the same Dominican waiter) and proposed marriage. The linguine turned cold and pasty on her plate as she stared at it, not knowing what to say, thinking of Gordon. Mike didn't rush her decision. Cheerfully, he said the cruise was a short one; her answer could wait for his return.

She called Gordon the next day, at his office. Her heart constricted when she learned that he was at the Book Fair in Frankfurt, and wouldn't return for another six days.

She cajoled a secretary into giving her the travel schedule and drove out to the airport to meet Gordon's plane. Later, she would blame herself for being overanxious, for demonstrating too much concern. It was an aggressiveness that would have delighted Mike, but Gordon wasn't Mike (and wasn't that the reason she loved him?). He was not only surprised to see her at the terminal, he was openly disgruntled. He accepted the lift back into the city, but his mood didn't permit her to come to the point of her mission.

Gordon's disposition improved by the time they reached the city. He apologized. He admitted that he was still feeling the aches and pains of his amputated friendship, and seeing "Mike's girl" was an unhappy reminder. It was then that she told him that she wasn't "Mike's girl" if he didn't want her to be. She could be

"Gordon's girl" if he asked her to be. It came out so coquettishly, so charmlessly, that Penny regretted it the moment the words escaped her lips. She wished she could recapture the sentence, play it back in a different key, but it was too late. Gordon thanked her for the offer with an irony that was like the cold blade of a knife twisting in her body. She should have laughed. She should have left. She should have done anything but what she did. She told him about Mike's proposal. She warned him that she was tempted to accept it. When he failed to make a conciliatory reply, she raised her voice in anger and said that she had just made up her mind to say yes. Then she walked out and drove away, barely able to see the road. She got home safely, living proof that God protects sleepwalkers, drunkards, and the disappointed.

Mike's ship docked two days later, and he had somehow managed (radiogram?) to have a lavish bouquet of red and yellow roses delivered before his arrival. The enclosed card bore a simple question mark. She felt the onset of panic, and without thinking, dialed Gordon's office number. He was in a meeting. His secretary would take a message. "No message," Penny had answered. Her doorbell rang, and she hung up.

Mike had brought a bottle of champagne, pilfered from the ship. Penny wasn't used to champagne. She didn't object as Mike filled glass after glass. After a while, his face began to float towards her. His small white teeth were bared in a smile. His breath was on her neck, and he was whispering in her ear. She whispered something, too, and woke up the next morning with the realization that she had agreed to marry him.

When she saw her eyes in the bathroom mirror, she knew she couldn't confront Gordon that day. But she managed to reach him by phone, and she told him, casually, that she and Mike were engaged. He didn't pause very long before replying.

"Congratulations," he said. "I hope you're both very happy."

She didn't remember who disconnected first.

Penny didn't marry Mike until almost two months later. There were four more cruise jobs in between; he was traveling so much that he had given up his small Village apartment. He moved into Penny's even smaller quarters, where they played house until fall. Gordon went to the beach cottage alone. When Penny and Mike finally married, in a civil ceremony, the best man was Mike's brother-in-law. Gordon, invited, never showed up.

There was a garment bag hanging on the front door-knob. She had begged the building super not to expose her dry cleaning to the world, but he never listened. She brought the bag inside, and its weight told her that the contents belonged to her husband. She parted the zipper, and saw the gleam of gold braid against cottony white. She flung the bag over an armchair, but then relented. She slipped off the black plastic bag, and hung the uniform on the hall closet door.

There was a business card on the dining table, a rainbow arching out of a paint can. She put the card into her purse. She hadn't told Mike about her appointment with the painter tomorrow morning.

The living room was going to be celadon green. The kitchen would be white with yellow trim. The bedroom—but she hadn't decided on the bedroom color. The den, the room Mike considered "his," was going to be a pale shade of mauve to go with the carpet. Mike wouldn't have approved any of her choices. He liked either white or blue, navy colors, but Mike wasn't going to be there, and he would have to get used to her choices. If he didn't—too bad! She was the one who stayed home.

Penny went from room to room, imagining them transformed by their new colors.

She was about to leave the den when she observed something different about Mike's desk. At first, she wasn't sure what the difference was. It was the same well-polished walnut cube Mike had brought to the marriage from the first apartment they shared together. Mike relished its neat drawers and the perfect trim of its files. He was also scrupulous about locking every drawer. The fact had never made her curious. Her husband wasn't a man she expected to have secrets.

Then she realized what it was. The bottom left-hand drawer was out of alignment. Mike had forgotten to lock it. If she was in a prying mood, the opportunity had arrived. What the hell, Penny thought.

She opened the drawer and saw a neat array of folders. Each was labeled in block letters. BANK. LAUNDRY. GROCERIES. AUTO. Half a dozen more. For a moment, she thought about labeling a blank folder WIFE. She found one in the rear of the drawer, but decided Mike wouldn't be amused. Then she realized the blank folder wasn't empty. There was a letter in it, without an envelope. There was also something familiar about the stationery. It bore the antique imprint of a large letter "G" with a tiny elf sitting on the crossbar. Penny always thought it was a bit too coy for Gordon's personality, but he seemed to like it.

She opened the letter. It was undated, it was handwritten, and from the first words, she knew why Mike had hidden it from her.

My darling, it read.

My darling, when you told me about your engagement I know I must have seemed completely indifferent. The truth is I was in so much pain that I couldn't speak—I couldn't find words. Now I know how those poor authors I'm always maligning must feel—I know this isn't what you want—I know you'll regret it. That's why I'm asking you, begging you, not to go through with this marriage. If it's still not too late, please come to me—call me—I'll be waiting to hear from you—

It was signed: *Gordon.*

Penny had never screamed in her life. Even as a child, she had sulked away her rages. If her throat hadn't constricted, she would have screamed now. If she could have made her paralyzed muscles move, she would have broken things, smashed dishes, shattered glass. But there was no release. She sat down, she buried her head in her lap, she tried to think. The letter had come to her old apartment, of course. Maybe only a few days after she spoke to Gordon, maybe even a week later. Whenever it was, Mike had seen it first. Mike had seen the elf-ridden monogram Gordon used even on his envelopes. Mike had opened her letter and read Gordon's words. Maybe they didn't surprise him. Maybe he had always known there was something between Penny and his best friend. . . . Yes, of course he had! She was sure of it now. Mike was naive, but he wasn't blind! He must have seen it, he may even have relished it; wasn't there some special secret pleasure in outdoing your best friend? But he hadn't taken the risk of letting Penny see it. He had hidden the truth of Gordon's feelings from her. And then he had stored away this delicious souvenir, this trophy of his victory. . . .

And what had Gordon done? When there had been no answer? No phone call, no visit, no response of any kind? He had done nothing, of course. He had swallowed the bitterness he must have felt; he had shuttered up his resentment. They had seen him only once since, and that encounter had been a chance meeting in a restaurant. Gordon had nodded at them with a cool pretense of cordiality, but Penny thought there was another message in his green eyes. She looked at the letter again and knew what that message must have been. She was an expert in sulking rage.

But then her own fury took another form. She looked up and saw the nautical uniform hanging on the closet door. It was as if Mike was in front of her, looking down at her anguish with breezy amusement. She stood up quickly and scurried into the bedroom. She scrambled along a welter of objects on her dressing table until she found the sewing scissors she rarely used. She returned to the living room and with a strangled cry attacked the white and gold uniform by stabbing at the breast pocket as if Mike's heart had been underneath. Despite the strength of her anger, the crisp material resisted the thrust. She opened the scissors and went to work on the lining, shredding it rapidly. She managed to cut through the threads of the pockets and used her fingers to rip them into hanging flaps. She was slitting one of the trouser legs when the front door opened and Mike walked in, gripping a paper bag by twine handles. When he saw her, he dropped the bag and a pair of newly resoled shoes bounced on the floor.

"Stop it, Penny! For God's sake—"

He tried to seize her wrist, to halt the mayhem, but she pulled away, fighting him off with her free hand. She heard herself shouting words in a disjointed sentence, but Mike wasn't listening; he was desperately trying to save his precious uniform. She swung at it again with the closed scissors, not expecting him to defend it with his body. The points penetrated his blue cotton shirt, embedded themselves so effortlessly into the upper part of his chest that Penny barely felt the impact. He gave her a questioning look. She released the scissors, but they didn't fall, they remained incongruously in place. There was no blood. Mike didn't even cry out.

He coughed, putting his fist to his mouth, and his legs buckled. He lifted his right hand to touch the chrome handles and sank to his knees, like a man in prayer. Penny was going to help him up, when she realized that all she really wanted to do was get out of the apartment, into the street, into as much noise and bustle as possible. She didn't rush out. She had the presence of mind to take her purse and carefully put Gordon's letter inside.

She didn't remember entering the phone booth. For a moment, she considered dialing the police emergency number, but when she lifted the receiver the three digits she actually dialed were for directory assistance. Her voice was calm when she asked the operator for Gordon's number. She was surprised when she recognized it. She had assumed Gordon had moved in the past two years, since everything else about her life had changed. But the number was the same, and presumably so was the address. She hailed a cab and recited it to the driver. Then she leaned against the back seat cushion and waited for the next event.

Gordon lived in a brownstone next door to a small grocery with a massive outdoor fruit stand. She pushed the button next to his nameplate and there was an answering buzz that unlocked the heavy front door. It was as if Gordon was expecting her. She climbed two flights of stairs that sagged in exactly the same old way, and she sniffed the same familiar cooking smells she had smelled two years ago.

She had no idea what she was going to say when Gordon answered his doorbell. He would be surprised, of course; his green eyes would change, and she would look for clues in their sea-glass depths. She wasn't sure she would tell him what happened between her and Mike, or seek his help. Her first priority was to tell Gordon the truth, for him to know that his letter reached her too late, to find out if there was still time to give the answer that should have reached him eighteen months ago.

He opened the door, and she couldn't read anything in his eyes. Gordon was wearing tinted glasses. But she knew he was stricken by the sight of her. He was immobilized. He seemed to be looking over her shoulder into the hallway. That was when she realized he must have been expecting someone else, someone who didn't require identification, someone who might even be living there. It was the first question, she asked, even before he invited her inside.

"Yes," Gordon said. "I was expecting someone. But it's all right."

He closed the door and waited.

"I came because of this," Penny said. When she opened her purse and extracted the folded sheet of his stationery, Gordon removed his glasses. His eyes looked tired.

"What is this, Penny?" he asked.

"A letter," Penny said. "Your letter." She suddenly discovered that she could smile. "The mail is really terrible in this town, isn't it? It took eighteen months to get to me."

Gordon was about to take the letter from her when the door buzzer sounded from below. The expected visitor had arrived, but Gordon hesitated before responding. When the delay became extended, the buzzer sounded again and a thin, toneless voice crackled out of the speaker.

"Don't play games, Gordon! I said I was sorry, didn't I?"

Penny looked at him, and Gordon's lips tightened. Then he pushed the button that would unlock the door once more.

"It's my roommate," he said.

Penny began watching the door, forgetting the letter still in her hand. There was no doorbell this time. The new arrival had a key. He walked in, but halted in the doorway, posing with one hand on his narrow hip. He wore blue jeans, a grey sports shirt with a red vest, and a diamond earring. He was holding a gift-wrapped box, balanced on his fingertips like a waiter bearing a tray.

"Chocolate nut clusters," he said. "If that won't make you kiss and make up, you can go to hell—bitch."

He smiled engagingly. Then he noticed Penny for the first time, and the smile wobbled.

"Who's your friend?" he asked.

"I was just leaving," Penny said, moving to the door. "I just dropped in to say hello," she told him. Then she was outside the door and racing down the stairs, ignoring the loose steps, stumbling over the tattered carpet in the front hallway. She was on the street before she remembered that she was still clutching Gordon's letter. She hurled it into a wire wastebasket, not caring that it wasn't her property to discard, that it had been Mike's letter all along.

The Betrayers

by Stanley Ellin

Between them was a wall. And since it was only a flimsy, jerry-built partition, a sounding board between apartments, Robert came to know the girl that way.

At first she was the sound of footsteps, the small firm rap of high heels moving in a pattern of activity around her room. She must be very young, he thought idly, because at the time he was deep in *Green Mansions*, pursuing the lustrous Rima through a labyrinth of Amazonian jungle. Later he came to know her voice, light and breathless when she spoke, warm and gay when she raised it in chorus to some popular song dinning from her radio. She must be very lovely, he thought then, and after that found himself listening deliberately, and falling more and more in love with her as he listened.

Her name was Amy, and there was a husband, too, a man called Vince who had a flat, unpleasant voice, and a sullen way about him. Occasionally there were quarrels which the man invariably ended by slamming the door of their room and thundering down the stairs as loud as he could. Then she would cry, a smothered whimpering, and Robert, standing close to the wall between them, would feel as if a hand had been thrust inside his chest and was twisting his heart. He would think wildly of the few steps that would take him to her door, the few words that would let her know he was her friend, was willing to do something—

anything—to help her. Perhaps, meeting face to face, she would recognize his love. Perhaps—

So the thoughts whirled around and around, but Robert only stood there, taut with helplessness.

And there was no one to confide in, which made it that much harder. The only acquaintances he numbered in the world were the other men in his office, and they would never have understood. He worked, prosaically enough, in the credit department of one of the city's largest department stores, and too many years there had ground the men around him to a fine edge of cynicism. The business of digging into people's records, of searching for the tax difficulties, the clandestine affairs with expensive women, the touch of larceny in every human being—all that was bound to have an effect, they told Robert, and if he stayed on the job much longer he'd find it out for himself.

What would they tell him now? *A pretty girl next door? Husband's away most of the time? Go on, make yourself at home!*

How could he make them understand that that wasn't what he was looking for? That what he wanted was someone to meet his love halfway, someone to put an end to the cold loneliness that settled in him like a stone during the dark hours each night.

So he said nothing about it to anyone, but stayed close to the wall, drawing from it what he could. And knowing the girl as he had come to, he was not surprised when he finally saw her. The mail for all the apartments was left on a table in the downstairs hallway, and as he walked down the stairs to go to work that morning, he saw her take a letter from the table and start up the stairway toward him.

There was never any question in his mind that this was the girl. She was small and fragile and dark-haired, and all the loveliness he had imagined in her from the other side of the wall was there in her face. She was wearing a loose robe, and as she passed him on the stairway she pulled the robe closer to her breast and slipped by almost as if she were afraid of him. He realized with a start that he had been staring unashamedly, and with his face red he turned down the stairs to the street. But he walked the rest of his way in a haze of wonderment.

He saw her a few times after that, always under the same conditions, but it took weeks before he mustered enough courage to stop at the foot of the stairs and turn to watch her retreating form above: the lovely fine line of ankle, the roundness of calf, the curve of body pressing against the robe. And then as she reached the head of the stairs, as if aware he was watching her, she looked down at him and their eyes met.

For a heart-stopping moment Robert tried to understand what he read in her face, and then her husband's voice came flat and belligerent from the room. "Amy," it said, "what's holdin' you up!"—and she was gone, and the moment with her.

When he saw the husband he marveled that she had chosen someone like that. A small, dapper gamecock of a man, he was good-looking in a hard way, but with the skin drawn so tight over his face that the cheekbones jutted sharply and the lips were drawn into a thin menacing line. He glanced at Robert up and down out of the corners of blank eyes as they passed, and in that instant Robert understood part of what he had seen in the girl's face. This man was as dangerous as some half-tamed animal that would snap at any hand laid on him, no matter what its intent. Just being near him you could smell danger, as surely the girl did her every waking hour.

The violence in the man exploded one night with force enough to waken Robert from a deep sleep. It was not the pitch of the voice, Robert realized, sitting up half-dazed in bed, because the words were almost inaudible through the wall; it was the vicious intensity that was so frightening.

He slipped out of bed and laid his ear against the wall. Standing like that, his eyes closed while he strained to follow the choppy phrases, he could picture the couple facing each other as vividly as if the wall had dissolved before him.

"So you know," the man said. *"So what?"*

". . . getting out!" the girl said.

"And then tell everybody? Tell the whole world?"

"I won't!" The girl was crying now. *"I swear I won't!"*

"Think I'd take a chance?" the man said, and then his voice turned soft and derisive. *"Ten thousand dollars,"* he said. *"Where else could I get it? Digging ditches?"*

"Better that way! This way . . . I'm getting out!"

His answer was not delivered in words. It came in the form of a blow so hard that when she reeled back and struck the wall, the impact stung Robert's face. *"Vince!"* she screamed, the sound high and quavering with terror. *"Don't, Vince!"*

Every nerve in Robert was alive now with her pain as the next blow was struck. His fingernails dug into the wall at the hard-breathing noises of scuffling behind it as she was pulled away.

"Ahh, no!" she cried out, and then there was the sound of a breath being drawn hoarsely and agonizingly into lungs no longer responsive to it, the thud of a flaccid weight striking the floor, and suddenly silence. A terrible silence.

As if the wall itself were her cold, dead flesh Robert recoiled from it, then stood staring at it in horror. His thoughts twisted and turned on themselves insanely, but out of them loomed one larger and larger so that he had to face it and recognize it.

She had been murdered, and as surely as though he had been standing there beside her he was a witness to it! He had been so close that if the wall were not there he could have reached out his hand and touched her. Done something to help her. Instead, he had waited like a fool until it was too late.

But there was still something to be done, he told himself wildly. And long as this madman in the next room had no idea there was a witness he could still be taken red-handed. A call to the police, and in five minutes . . .

But before he could take the first nerveless step Robert heard the room next door stealthily come to life again. There was a sound of surreptitious motion, of things being shifted from their place, then, clearly defined, a lifeless weight being pulled along the floor, and the cautious creaking of a door opened wide. It was that last sound which struck Robert with a sick comprehension of what was happening.

The murderer was a monster, but he was no fool. If he could safely dispose of the body now during these silent hours of the night he was, to all intents and purposes, a man who had committed no crime at all!

At his door Robert stopped short. From the hallway came the deliberate thump of feet finding their way down the stairs with the weight dragging behind them. The man had killed once. He was reckless enough in this crisis to risk being seen with his victim. What would such a man do to anyone who confronted him at such a time?

Robert leaned back against his door, his eyes closed tight, a choking constriction in his throat as if the man's hands were already around it. He was a coward, there was no way around it. Faced with the need to show some courage he had discovered he was a rank coward, and he saw the girl's face before him now, not with fear in it, but contempt.

But—and the thought gave him a quick sense of triumph—he could still go to the police. He saw himself doing it, and the sense of triumph faded away. He had heard some noises, and from that had constructed a murder. The body? There would be none. The murderer? None. Only a man whose wife had left him because he had quarreled with her. The accuser? A young man who had wild dreams. A perfect fool. In short, Robert himself.

It was only when he heard the click of the door downstairs that he stepped out into the hallway and started down, step by careful step. Halfway down he saw it, a handkerchief, small and crumpled and blotched with an ugly stain. He picked it up gingerly, and holding it up toward the dim light overhead let it fall open. The stain was bright sticky red almost obscuring in one corner the word *Amy* carefully embroidered there. Blood. *Her* blood. Wouldn't that be evidence enough for anyone?

Sure, he could hear the policeman answer him jeeringly, *evidence of a nose-bleed, all right*, and he could feel the despair churn in him.

It was the noise of the car that roused him, and then he flew down the rest of the stairs, but too late. As he pressed his face to the curtain of the front door the car roared away from the curb, its tail-lights gleaming like malevolent eyes, its license plate impossible to read in the dark. If he had only been an instant quicker, he raged at himself, only had sense enough to understand that the killer must use a car for his purpose, he could easily have identified it. Now, even that chance was gone. Every chance was gone.

He was in his room pacing the floor feverishly when within a half hour he heard the furtive sounds of the murderer's return. And why not, Robert thought; *he's gotten rid of her, he's safe now, he can go on as if nothing at all had happened.*

If I were only someone who could go into that room and beat the truth out of him, the thought boiled on, *or someone with such wealth or position that I would be listened to . . .*

But all that was as unreal and vaporous as his passion for the girl had been. What weapon of vengeance could he possibly have at his command, a nobody working in a . . .

Robert felt the sudden realization wash over him in a cold wave. His eyes narrowed on the wall as if, word by word, the idea were being written on it in a minute hand.

Everyone has a touch of larceny in him—wasn't that what the old hands in his department were always saying? Everyone was suspect. Certainly the man next door, with his bent for violence, his talk of ten thousand dollars come by in some unlikely way, must have black marks on his record that the authorities, blind as they might be, could recognize and act on. If someone skilled in investigation were to strip the man's past down, layer by layer, justice would have to be done. That was the weapon: the dark past itself, stored away in the man, waiting only to be ignited!

Slowly and thoughtfully Robert slipped the girl's crumpled handkerchief into an envelope and sealed it. Then, straining to remember the exact words, he wrote down on paper the last violent duologue between murderer and victim. Paper and envelope both went into a drawer of his dresser, and the first step had been taken.

But then, Robert asked himself, what did he know about the man? His name was Vince, and that was all. Hardly information which could serve as the starting point of a search through the dark corridors of some-

one's past. There must be something more than that,
something to serve as a lead.

It took Robert the rest of a sleepless night to hit on
the idea of the landlady. A stout and sleepy-eyed woman
whose only interest in life seemed to lie in the prompt
collection of her rent, she still must have some information about the man. She occupied the rear apartment
on the ground floor, and as early in the morning as he
dared Robert knocked on her door.

She looked more sleepy-eyed than ever as she pon-
dered his question. "Them?" she said at last. "That's
the Sniders. Nice people, all right." She blinked at Robert. "Not having any trouble with them, are you?"

"No. Not at all. But is that all you can tell me about
them? I mean, don't you know where they're from, or
anything like that?"

The landlady shrugged. "I'm sure it's none of my
business," she said loftily. "All I know is they pay on
the first of the month right on the dot, and they're nice
respectable people."

He turned away from her heavily, and as he did so
saw the street door close behind the postman. It was as
if a miracle had been passed for him. The landlady was
gone, he was all alone with that little heap of mail on
the table, and there staring up at him was an envelope
neatly addressed to Mrs. Vincent Snider.

All the way to his office he kept that envelope hidden
away in an inside pocket, and it was only when he was
locked in the seclusion of his cubicle that he carefully
slit it open and studied its contents. A single page with
only a few lines on it, a noncommittal message about
the family's well-being, and the signature: *Your sister*,
Celia. Not much to go on—but wait, there was a return
address on the stationery, an address in a small upstate
town.

Robert hesitated only a moment, then thrust letter

and envelope into his pocket, straightened his jacket, and walked into the office of his superior. Mr. Sprague, in charge of the department and consequently the most ulcerated and cynical member of it, regarded him dourly.

"Yes?" he said.

"I'm sorry, sir," said Robert, "but I'll need a few days off. You see, there's been a sudden death."

Mr. Sprague sighed at this pebble cast into the smooth pool of his department's routine, but his face fell into the proper sympathetic lines.

"Somebody close?"

"Very close," said Robert.

The walk from the railroad station to the house was a short one. The house itself had a severe and forbidding air about it, as did the young woman who opened the door in answer to Robert's knock.

"Yes," she said, "my sister's name is Amy Snider. Her married name, that is. I'm Celia Thompson."

"What I'm looking for," Robert said, "is some information about her. About your sister."

The woman looked stricken. "Something's happened to her?"

"In a way," Robert said. He cleared his throat hard. "You see, she's disappeared from her apartment, and I'm looking into it. Now, if you . . ."

"You're from the police?"

"I'm acting for them," Robert said, and prayed that this ambiguity would serve in place of identification. The prayer was answered, the woman gestured him into the house, and sat down facing him in the bare and uninviting living room.

"I knew," the woman said, "I knew something would happen," and she rocked piteously from side to side in her chair.

Robert reached forward and touched her hand gently. "How did you know?"

"How? What else could you expect when you drive a child out of her home and slam the door in her face! When you throw her out into the world not even knowing how to take care of herself!"

Robert withdrew his hand abruptly. "You did *that*?"

"My father did it. *Her* father."

"But why?"

"If you knew him," the woman said. "A man who thinks anything pretty is sinful. A man who's so scared of hellfire and brimstone that he's kept us in it all our lives!

"When she started to get so pretty, and the boys pestering her all the time, he turned against her just like that. And when she had her trouble with that man he threw her out of the house, bag and baggage. And if he knew I was writing letters to her," the woman said fearfully, "he'd throw me out, too. I can't even say her name in front of him, the way he is."

"Look," Robert said eagerly, "that man she had trouble with. Was that the one she married? That Vincent Snider?"

"I don't know," the woman said vaguely. "I just don't know. Nobody knows except Amy and my father, the way it was kept such a secret. I didn't even know she was married until all of a sudden she wrote me a letter about it from the city."

"But if your father knows, I can talk to him about it."

"No! You can't! If he even knew I told you as much as I did . . ."

"But I can't let it go at that," he pleaded. "I have to find out about this man, and then maybe we can straighten everything out."

"All right," the woman said wearily, "there is somebody. But not my father, you've got to keep away from him for my sake. There's this teacher over at the high school, this Miss Benson. She's the one to see. And she liked Amy; she's the one Amy mails my letters to, so my father won't know. Maybe she'll tell you, even if she won't tell anybody else. I'll write you a note to her, and you go see her."

At the door he thanked her, and she regarded him with a hard, straight look. "You have to be pretty to get yourself in trouble," she said, "so it's something that'll never bother me. But you find Amy, and you make sure she's all right."

"Yes," Robert said. "I'll try."

At the school he was told that Miss Benson was the typewriting teacher, that she had classes until 3, and that if he wished to speak to her alone he would have to wait until then. So for hours he fretfully walked the few main streets of the town, oblivious of the curious glances of passers-by, and thinking of Amy. These were the streets she had known. These shop windows had mirrored her image. And, he thought with a sharp jealousy, not always alone. There had been boys. Attracted to her, as boys would be, but careless of her, never realizing the prize they had. But if he had known her then, if he could have been one of them . . .

At 3 o'clock he waited outside the school building until it had emptied, and then went in eagerly. Miss Benson was a small woman, gray-haired and fluttering, almost lost among the grim ranks of hooded typewriters in the room. After Robert had explained himself, and she had read Celia Thompson's note she seemed ready to burst into tears.

"It's wrong of her!" she said. "It's dreadfully wrong of her to send you to me. She must have known that."

"But why is it wrong?"

"Why? Because she knows I don't want to talk about

it to anyone. She knows what it would cost me if I did, that's why!"

"Look," Robert said patiently, "I'm not trying to find out what happened. I'm only trying to find out about this man Amy had trouble with, what his name is, where he comes from, where I can get more information about him."

"No," Miss Benson quavered, "I'm sorry."

"Sorry," Robert said angrily. "A girl disappears, this man may be at the bottom of it, and all you can do is say you're sorry!"

Miss Benson's jaw went slack. "You mean that he—that he *did* something to her?"

"Yes," Robert said, "he did," and had to quickly catch her arm as she swayed unsteadily, apparently on the verge of fainting.

"I should have known," she said lifelessly. "I should have known when it happened that it might come to this. But at the time . . ."

At the time the girl had been one of her students. A good student—not brilliant, mind you—but a nice girl always trying to do her best. And well brought-up, too, not like so many of the young snips you get nowadays.

That very afternoon when it all happened the girl herself had told Miss Benson she was going to the Principal's office after school hours to get her program straightened out. Certainly if she meant to do anything wicked she wouldn't have mentioned that, would she? Wasn't that all the evidence anyone needed?

"Evidence?" Robert said in bewilderment.

Yes, evidence. There had been that screaming in the Principal's office, and Miss Benson had been the only one left in the whole school. She had run to the office, flung open the door, and that was how she found them. The girl sobbing hysterically, her dress torn halfway down; Mr. Price standing behind her, glaring at the open door, at the incredulous Miss Benson.

"Mr. Price?" Robert said. He had the sense of swimming numbly through some gelatinous depths, unable to see anything clearly.

Mr. Price, the Principal, of course. He stood glaring at her, his face ashen. Then the girl had fled through the door and Mr. Price had taken one step after her, but had stopped short. He had pulled Miss Benson into the office, and closed the door, and then he had talked to her.

The long and the short of what he told her was that the girl was a wanton. She had waltzed into his office, threatened him with blackmail, and when he had put her into her place she had artfully acted out her little scene. But he would be merciful, very merciful. Rather than call in the authorities and blacken the name of the school and of her decent, respectable father he would simply expel her and advise her father to get her out of town promptly.

And, Mr. Price had remarked meaningfully, it was a lucky thing indeed that Miss Benson had walked in just in time to be his witness. Although if Miss Benson failed him as a witness it could be highly unlucky for her.

"And he meant it," Miss Benson said bitterly. "It's his family runs the town and everything in it. If I said anything of what I really thought, if I dared open my mouth, I'd never get another job anywhere. But I should have talked up, I know I should have, especially after what happened next!"

She had managed to get back to her room at the far end of the corridor although she had no idea of where she got the strength. And as soon as she had entered the room she saw the girl there, lying on the floor beneath the bulletin board from which usually hung the sharp, cutting scissors. But the scissors were in the girl's clenched fist as she lay there, and blood over everything. All that blood over everything.

"She was like that," Miss Benson said dully. "If you reprimanded her for even the littlest thing she looked like she wanted to sink through the floor, to die on the spot. And after what she went through it must have been the first thing in her head: just to get rid of herself. It was a mercy of God that she didn't succeed then and there."

It was Miss Benson who got the doctor, a discreet man who asked no questions, and it was she who tended the girl after her father had barred his door to her.

"And when she could get around," Miss Benson said, "I placed her with this office over at the county seat. She wasn't graduated, of course, or really expert, but I gave her a letter explaining she had been in some trouble and needed a helping hand, and they gave her a job."

Miss Benson dug her fingers into her forehead. "If I had only talked up when I should have. I should have known he'd never feel safe, that he'd hound her and hound her until he . . ."

"But he isn't the one!" Robert said hoarsely. "He isn't the right man at all!"

She looked at him wonderingly. "But you said . . ."

"No," Robert said helplessly, "I'm looking for someone else. A different man altogether."

She shrank back. "You've been trying to fool me!"

"I swear I haven't."

"But it doesn't matter," she whispered. "If you say a word about this nobody'll believe you. I'll tell them you were lying, you made the whole thing up!"

"You won't have to," Robert said. "All you have to do is tell me where you sent her for that job. If you do that you can forget everything else."

She hesitated, studying his face with bright, frightened eyes. "All right," she said at last. "All right."

He was about to go when she placed her hand anxiously on his arm. "Please," she said. "You don't think unkindly of me because of all this, do you?"

"No," Robert said, "I don't have the right to."

The bus trip which filled the remainder of the day was a wearing one, the hotel bed that night was no great improvement over the bus seat, and Mr. Pardee of *Grace, Grace, & Pardee* seemed to Robert the hardest of all to take. He was a cheery man, too loud and florid to be properly contained by his small office.

He studied Robert's business card with interest. "Credit research, eh?" he said admiringly. "Wonderful how you fellas track 'em down wherever they are. Sort of a Northwest Mounted Police just working to keep business healthy, that's what it comes to, doesn't it? And anything I can do to help . . ."

Yes, he remembered the girl very well.

"Just about the prettiest little thing we ever had around here," he said pensively. "Didn't know much about her job, of course, but you got your money's worth just watching her walk around the office."

Robert managed to keep his teeth clenched. "Was there any man she seemed interested in? Someone around the office, maybe, who wouldn't be working here any more? Or even someone outside you could tell me about?"

Mr. Pardee studied the ceiling with narrowed eyes. "No," he said, "nobody I can think of. Must have been plenty of men after her, but you'd never get anything out of her about it. Not with the way she was so secretive and all. Matter of fact, her being that way was one of the things that made all the trouble."

"Trouble?"

"Oh, nothing serious. Somebody was picking the

petty cash box every so often, and what with all the rest of the office being so friendly except her it looked like she might be the one. And then that letter she brought saying she had already been in some trouble—well, we just had to let her go.

"Later on," continued Mr. Pardee pleasantly, "when we found out it wasn't her after all, it was too late. We didn't know where to get in touch with her." He snapped his fingers loudly. "Gone, just like that."

Robert drew a deep breath to steady himself. "But there must be somebody in the office who knew her," he pleaded. "Maybe some girl she talked to."

"Oh, that," said Mr. Pardee. "Well, as I said, she wasn't friendly, but now and then she did have her head together with Jenny Rizzo over at the switchboard. If you want to talk to Jenny go right ahead. Anything I can do to help . . ."

But it was Jenny Rizzo who helped him. A plain girl dressed in defiant bad taste, she studied him with impersonal interest and told him coolly that she had nothing to say about Amy. The kid had taken enough kicking around. It was about time they let her alone.

"I'm not interested in her," Robert said. "I'm trying to find out about the man she married. Someone named Vincent Snider. Did you know about him?"

From the stricken look on her face Robert realized exultantly that she did.

"Him!" she said. "So she went and married him, anyhow!"

"What about it?"

"What about it? I told her a hundred times he was no good. I told her just stay away from him."

"Why?"

"Because I know his kind. Sharp stuff hanging around with money in his pocket, you never knew where it came from. The kind of guy's always pulling fast deals, but he's too smart to get caught, that's why!"

"How well did you know him?"

"How well? I knew him from the time he was a kid around my neighborhood here. Look," Jenny dug into a desk drawer deep laden with personal possessions. She came out with a handful of snapshots which she thrust at Robert. "We even used to double-date together, Vince and Amy, and me and my boy friend. Plenty of times I told her right in front of Vince that he was no good, but he gave her such a line she wouldn't even listen. She was like a baby that way; anybody was nice to her she'd go overboard."

They were not good photographs, but there were Vince and Amy clearly recognizable.

"Could I have one of these?" Robert asked, his voice elaborately casual.

Jenny shrugged. "Just go ahead and help yourself," she said, and Robert did.

"Then what happened?" he said. "I mean, to Vince and Amy?"

"You got me there. After she got fired they both took off. She said something about Vince getting a job downstate a-ways, in Sutton, and that was the last I saw of them. I could just see him working at anything honest, but the way she said it she must have believed him. Anyhow, I never heard from her after that."

"Could you remember exactly when you saw her last? That time she told you they were going to Sutton?"

Jenny could and did. She might have remembered more, but Robert was out of the door by then, leaving her gaping after him, her mouth wide open in surprise.

The trip to Sutton was barely an hour by bus, but it took another hour before Robert was seated at a large table with the Sutton newspaper files laid out before him. The town's newspaper was a large and respectable one, its files orderly and well-kept. And two days after the date Jenny Rizzo had given him there was the news Robert had hoped to find. Headline news emblazoned all across the top of the first page.

Ten thousand dollars stolen, the news report said. A daring, lone bandit had walked into the Sutton Bank and Trust, had bearded the manager without a soul around knowing it, and had calmly walked out with a small valise containing ten thousand dollars in currency. The police were on the trail. An arrest was expected momentarily . . .

Robert traced through later dates with his hands shaking. The police had given up in their efforts. No arrest was ever made . . .

Robert had carefully scissored the photograph so that Vince now stood alone in the picture. The bank manager irritably looked at the picture, and then swallowed hard.

"It's him!" he told Robert incredulously. "That's the man! I'd know him anywhere. If I can get my hands on him . . ."

"There's something you'll have to do first," said Robert.

"I'm not making any deals," the manager protested. "I want him, and I want every penny of the money he's got left."

"I'm not talking about deals," Robert said. "All you have to do is put down on paper that you positively identify this man as the one who robbed the bank. If you do that the police'll have him for you tomorrow."

"That's all?" the man said suspiciously.

"That's all," Robert said.

He sat again in the familiar room, the papers, the evidence, arranged before him. His one remaining fear had been that in his absence the murderer had somehow taken alarm and fled. He had not breathed easy until the first small, surreptitious noises from next door made clear that things were as he had left them.

Now he carefully studied all the notes he had painstakingly prepared, all the reports of conversations held. It was all here, enough to see justice done, but it was more than that, he told himself bitterly. It was the portrait of a girl who, step by step, had been driven through a pattern of betrayal.

Every man she had dealt with had been an agent of betrayal. Father, school principal, employer, and finally her husband, each was guilty in his turn. Jenny Rizzo's words rang loud in Robert's ears.

Anybody was nice to her she'd go overboard. If he had spoken, if he had moved, he could have been the one. When she turned at the top of the stairs to look at him she might have been waiting for him to speak or move. Now it was too late, and there was no way of letting her know what these papers meant, what he had done for her . . .

The police were everything Robert had expected until they read the bank manager's statement. Then they read and reread the statement, they looked at the photograph, and they courteously passed Robert from hand to hand until finally there was a door marked *Lieutenant Kyserling*, and behind it a slender, soft-spoken man.

It was a long story—Robert had not realized until then how long it was or how many details there were to explain—but it was told from start to finish without interruption. At its conclusion Kyserling took the papers, the handkerchief, and the photograph, and pored over them. Then he looked at Robert curiously.

"It's all here," he said. "The only thing you left out is why you did it, why you went to all this trouble. What's your stake in this?"

It was not easy to have your most private dream exposed to a complete stranger. Robert choked on the words. "It's because of her. The way I felt about her."

"Oh." Kyserling nodded understandingly. "Making time with her?"

"No," Robert said angrily. "We never even spoke to each other!"

Kyserling tapped his fingers gently on the papers before him.

"Well," he said, "it's none of my business anyhow. But you've done a pretty job for us. Very pretty. Matter of fact, yesterday we turned up the body in a car parked a few blocks away from your place. The car was stolen a month ago, there wasn't a stitch of identification on the clothing or anything; all we got is a body with a big wound in it. This business could have stayed up in the air for a hundred years if it wasn't for you walking in with a perfect case made out from A to Z."

"I'm glad," Robert said. "That's the way I wanted it."

"Yeah," Kyserling said. "Any time you want a job on the force you just come and see me."

Then he was gone from the office for a long while, and when he returned it was in the company of a big, stolid plainclothesman who smiled grimly.

"We're going to wrap it up now," Kyserling told Robert, and gestured at the man.

They went softly up the stairs of the house and stood to the side of the door while Kyserling laid his ear against it for some assurance of sound. Then he briskly nodded to the plainclothesman and rapped hard.

"Open up!" he called. "It's the police."

There was an ear-ringing silence, and Robert's mouth went dry as he saw Kyserling and the plainclothesman slip the chill blue steel of revolvers from their shoulder holsters.

"I got no use for these cute little games," growled Kyserling, and suddenly raised his foot and smashed the heel of the door. The door burst open, Robert cowered back against the balustrade of the staircase—

And then he saw her.

She stood in the middle of the room facing him wildly, the same look on her face, he knew in that fantastic moment, that she must have worn each time she came face to face with a betrayer exposed. Then she took one backward step, and suddenly whirled toward the window.

"*Ahh, no!*" she cried, as Robert had heard her cry it out once before, and then was gone through the window in a sheet of broken glass. Her voice rose in a single despairing shriek, and then was suddenly and mercifully silent.

Robert stood there, the salt of sweat suddenly in his eyes, the salt of blood on his lips. It was an infinity of distance to the window, but he finally got there, and had to thrust Kyserling aside to look down.

She lay crumpled on the sidewalk, and the thick black hair in loose disorder around her face shrouded her from the eyes of the curious.

The plainclothesman was gone, but Kyserling was still there watching Robert with sympathetic eyes.

"I thought he had killed her," Robert whispered. "I could swear he had killed her!"

"It was his body we found," said Kyserling. "She was the one who did it."

"But why didn't you tell me then!" Robert begged. "Why didn't you let me know!"

Kyserling looked at him wisely. "Yeah?" he said. "And then what? You tip her off so that she gets away; then we really got troubles."

There could be no answer to that. None at all.

"She just cracked up," Kyserling said reasonably.

"Holed up here like she was, not knowing which way to turn, nobody she could trust ... It was in the cards. You had nothing to do with it."

He went downstairs then, and Robert was alone in her room. He looked around it slowly, at all the things that were left of her, and then very deliberately picked up a chair, held it high over his head, and with all his strength smashed it against the wall. . . .

The Perfect Alibi

by Patricia Highsmith

The crowd crept like a sightless, mindless monster toward the subway entrance. Feet slid forward a few inches, stopped, slid forward again. Howard hated crowds. They made him panicky. His finger was on the trigger, and for a few seconds he concentrated on not letting himself pull it, which he had an almost uncontrollable impulse to do.

He had ripped open the bottom of his overcoat pocket, and he now held the gun in that pocket in his gloved hand. George's broad, short back was less than two feet in front of him, but there were a couple of people in between. Howard turned his shoulders and squeezed through the space between a man and a woman, jostling the man slightly.

Now he was right behind George, the front of his unbuttoned overcoat brushing the back of George's coat. Howard leveled the gun in his pocket. A woman bumped against his right arm, but he kept his arm steady at the small of George's back, kept his eyes straight ahead over George's felt hat. A wisp of George's cigar smoke came to Howard's nostrils, familiar and nauseating. The subway entrance was only a couple of yards away. *Within the next five seconds,* Howard told himself, and at the same time his left hand moved to push the right side of his overcoat back, made an incomplete movement, and a split second later the gun fired.

A woman shrieked.

Howard dropped the gun through the open pocket.

The crowd had recoiled from the gun's explosion, sweeping Howard back with them. A few people lurched in front of him, but for an instant he saw George in a little clear spot on the sidewalk, lying on his side, the thin, half-smoked cigar still gripped in his teeth which Howard saw bared, then covered by his relaxing mouth.

"He's shot!" someone screamed.

"Who?"

"Where?"

Then the crowd surged forward with a roar of curiosity and Howard was carried almost to where George was sprawled.

"Stand back! You'll trample on him!'" a man's voice shouted.

Howard sidled free of the crowd and went down the subway steps. The roar of voices on the sidewalk was replaced suddenly by the droning roar of an incoming train. Howard mechanically got out some change and bought a token. No one around him seemed aware that a dead man was lying at the top of the stairs. Couldn't he use another exit and go up and get his car? He had parked his car hastily on Thirty-fifth Street, near Broadway. No, he just might run into someone who had seen him near George in the crowd. Howard was very tall. He felt conspicuous. He could pick up the car a little later. He looked at his watch. Exactly 5:54.

He crossed the station and got on an uptown train. His ears were sensitive to noise, and ordinarily the subway screech of steel on steel was an intolerable torture to him; but now, as he stood holding on to a strap, he was oblivious of the din and grateful for the unconcern of the newspaper-reading passengers around him. His right hand, still in his overcoat pocket, groped automatically for the bottom of the pocket. He must sew that up tonight, he reminded himself. He glanced down at the front of his coat and saw with a shock, almost like a pain, that the bullet had made a hole in the coat. Quickly he pulled out his right hand and placed it over the hole, all the while staring at the advertisement placard in front of him.

He frowned intently, going over the whole thing again, trying to see if he had made a mistake anywhere. He had left the store a little earlier than usual—at 5:15—in order to be at Thirty-fourth Street by 5:30, when George always left his shop. Mr. Luther, Howard's boss, had said, "Finished early today, eh, Howard?" But it had happened a few times before, and Mr. Luther wouldn't think anything about it. And he had wiped the gun inside and out, had even wiped the bullets. He had bought the gun about five weeks ago in Bennington, Vermont, and he had not had to give his name when he bought it. He had not been to Bennington before or since. He thought it was really impossible that the police could ever trace the gun. And nobody had seen him fire the shot—he was sure of that. He had glanced around before he went into the subway, and nobody had been looking at him.

Howard had meant to ride uptown for a few stations, then go back downtown and get his car; but now he thought he should dispose of the coat first. Too dangerous to try to get a hole like this rewoven. It didn't look like a cigarette burn—it looked just like what it was. He'd have to hurry. His car was within three blocks of where he had shot George. He'd be questioned tonight, probably, about George Frizell, because the police would certainly question Mary, and if she didn't mention his name, their landladies—hers and George's—would. George had so few friends.

He thought of pushing the coat into some wastepaper bin in a subway station. But too many people would notice that. In an ashcan on the street? That too seemed conspicuous—after all, it was a fairly new coat. No, he'd have to go home and get something to wrap it in before he could throw it away.

He got out at the Seventy-second Street station. He lived in a small ground-floor apartment in a brownstone building on West Seventy-first Street, near West End Avenue. Howard saw no one when he entered, which was good because he could say, if he were questioned about it, that he had come home at 5:30 or so instead of nearly 6:00. As soon as he entered his apartment and turned on the light, Howard knew what he would do with the coat: burn it in the fireplace. That was the safest thing to do.

He raked some change and a flattened pack of cigarettes out of the left pocket of the coat, took the coat off, and flung it on the sofa. Then he picked up his telephone and dialed Mary's number.

She answered on the third ring.

"Hello, Mary," he said. "Hello, darling. It's done."

A second's hesitation. "Done? *Really*, Howard? You're not—"

No, he wasn't joking. He didn't know what else to say to her, what else he dared say to her over the phone. "I love you. Take care of yourself, darling," he said, absently.

"Oh, Howard!" She was starting to cry.

"Mary, the police will probably talk to you. Maybe in just a few minutes." He squeezed the telephone, wanting to put his arms around her, to kiss her cheeks that would be wet with tears now. "Don't mention me, darling—just *don't*, whatever they ask you. I've got some things to do yet and I've got to hurry. If your landlady mentions me, don't worry about it, I can handle it—but don't you do it first. Understand?" He was aware that he was talking to her again as if she were a child, and that it wasn't good for her; but it wasn't the right time to be thinking of what was good for her and what wasn't. "Do you understand, Mary?"

"Yes," she said, her voice thin.

"Don't be crying when the police come in, Mary. Wash your face. You've got to pull yourself—" He stopped. "Go out to a movie, honey. Will you? Go out now before the police come!"

"All right."

"Promise me!"

"All right."

He hung up and strode to the fireplace. He crumpled some newspaper, laid some kindling across it, and struck a match. He was glad now that he had bought a supply of wood and kindling for Mary, glad that Mary liked fires, because he'd lived here for months before he met Mary and never thought of having a fire.

Mary lived directly across from George, on West Eighteenth Street. The police would logically go to George's house the first thing and question his landlady—because George had lived alone and there'd be nobody else there to question. George's landlady—Howard remembered his few glimpses of her as she leaned out the window last summer, thin, gray-haired, prying with a hideous intensity into what everybody in her house was doing ... undoubtedly she would tell the police that there was a girl across the street whom Mr. Frizell spent a lot of time with. Howard only hoped that the landlady wouldn't mention him right off, because she was bound to have guessed that the young man with the car who came to see Mary so often was her boy friend, bound to have suspected a jealousy between him and George. But maybe she wouldn't mention him. And maybe Mary would be out of the house by the time the police came.

For a moment he paused, tensely, in the act of putting more wood on the fire. He was trying to imagine exactly what Mary was feeling now, having just learned that George Frizell was dead. He was trying to feel it himself, so that he could predict her behavior, so that he would be better able to comfort her. *Comfort her!* He had freed her of a monster! She ought to be rejoicing. But he knew she would be shattered at first. She had known George since she was a child. George had been her father's best friend—and how differently George must have behaved with another man, Howard could guess; and when her father had died, George, a bachelor, had taken Mary over as if he had been her father. But with the difference that he controlled every move she made, convinced her that she couldn't do a thing without him, convinced her that she shouldn't marry anybody he disapproved of. Which was everybody. Howard, for instance. Mary had told him that there had been two other young men whom George had thrust out of her life.

But Howard hadn't been thrust out. He hadn't fallen for George's lies about Mary's being sick, Mary's being too tired to go out or to see anybody. George had actually called him up several times and tried to break their dates—but he had gone down to her house and gotten her, many evenings, in spite of her terror of George's anger. Mary was twenty-three, but George had kept her a child. Mary had to have George along even to buy a new dress. Howard had never seen anything like it in his life. It was like a bad dream, or something in a fantastic story that was too incredible to believe. Howard had supposed that George was in love with her in some strange way, and he had asked

Mary about this shortly after he had met her, and she had said, "Oh, no! Why he never even touches me!" And it was quite true that George never even touched her. Once, while they were saying goodbye, George had bumped her shoulder and had jumped back as if he had been burned, saying, "Excuse me!" It was very strange.

Yet it was as if George had locked Mary's mind away somehow—like a prisoner of his own mind, as if she had no mind of her own. Howard couldn't put it into words. Mary had soft, dark eyes that looked tragically, hopelessly sad, and it made him fighting mad to look at them sometimes, mad enough to fight back at the person who had done that to her. The person was George Frizell. Howard could never forget the look George had given him when Mary had introduced them, a superior, smiling, knowing look that had seemed to say, "You can try. I know what you're trying. But you won't get very far."

George Frizell had been a short, swarthy man with a heavy jaw and heavy black eyebrows. He had a little shop on West Thirty-sixth Street where he specialized in chair repairs, but it seemed to Howard that he had had no other interest in life but Mary. When he was with her, he concentrated on her alone, as if he were exerting some hypnotic power over her, and Mary behaved as if she were hypnotized. She wasn't herself around George. She was always looking at him, looking back over her shoulder at him to see if he approved of whatever she was doing, even if it were only getting some chops out of the oven.

Mary loved George and hated him at the same time. Howard had been able to make her hate George—up to a point, and then she would suddenly start defending him again. "But George was so kind to me after my father died, when I was all alone, Howard," Mary would protest. And so they had drifted for almost a year, Howard trying to outmaneuver George and see Mary a few times a week, Mary vacillating between continuing to see him and breaking it off because she felt she was hurting him too much. "I want to marry you!" Howard had said a dozen times when Mary had gone into her agonized fits of self-condemnation. He'd never been able to make her understand that he would go through anything for her. "I love you, too, Howard," Mary had said many times, but always with a tragic sadness that was like the sadness of a prisoner who cannot find a way to escape. But there had been a way to free her, a violent and final way. Howard had taken it . . .

He was on his knees in front of the fireplace now, trying to tear the coat into sections small enough to burn. He found the tweed extremely difficult to cut, and the seams almost equally difficult to tear. He tried burning it without cutting it up, starting at a bottom corner, but the flames crawled up the nap of the tweed toward his hands, while the material itself seemed as resistant to the fire as asbestos. He'd have to cut it up in small pieces, he realized. And the fire would have to be bigger and hotter.

Howard put more wood on. It was a mean little fireplace with a bellied-out iron grate and not much of a recess, so that the pieces of wood he had put on stuck out in front over the rim of the grate. He attacked the coat again with the scissors. It took him minutes simply to remove a sleeve. He opened a window to get some of the smell of burning cloth out of the room.

The whole coat took him nearly an hour because he couldn't put much on at a time without smothering the fire. He watched the last piece beginning to smoke in the center, watched the flames break through and lick a widening circle. He was thinking of Mary, seeing her white, fear-stricken face when the police arrived, when they told her for the second time about George's death.

He was trying to imagine the worst—that the police
had arrived just after he had spoken to her and that she
had made some blunder, revealed to the police that she
already knew about George's death, yet was not able to
say who had told her; he imagined that in her hysteria
she had blurted out his name, Howard Quinn, as the
man who might have done it.

Howard moistened his lips, terrified suddenly by the
realization that he couldn't depend on Mary. She loved
him—he was sure of that—but Mary couldn't depend
on herself.

For one wild, unthinking instant, Howard wanted to
rush down to West Eighteenth Street to be with her
when the police arrived. He saw himself defiantly facing
the police, his arm around Mary's shoulders, answering
every question, parrying every suspicion. But that was
insane. The mere fact that they would be there in her
apartment together—

He heard a knock at his door. A moment before, he
had been aware that some people had come in the front
door, but he had not thought that they were coming to
see him. Suddenly he was trembling.

"Who is it?" he asked.

"The police. We're looking for Howard Quinn. Is
this apartment One A?"

Howard glanced at the fire. The coat was all burned,
nothing but glowing wisps left of the last piece. And
they wouldn't be interested in the coat, he thought.
They had only come to question him, just as they had
questioned Mary. He opened the door and said, "I'm
Howard Quinn."

There were two policemen, one quite a bit taller than
the other. They came into the room. Howard saw them
both glance at the fireplace. The smell of burned cloth
was still in the room.

"I suppose you know why we're here," said the taller

officer. "You're wanted down at the station. You'd better come with us now." He looked at Howard. It was not a friendly look.

For a moment Howard thought he was going to faint. Mary must have told them everything, he thought, everything.

"All right," he said.

The shorter officer was looking into the fireplace. "What've you been burning? Cloth?"

"Just a few old—a few old clothes," Howard said.

The policemen exchanged a glance, a kind of amused glance, and said nothing. They were so sure of his guilt, Howard thought, that they didn't need to ask any questions. They had guessed he had burned his overcoat and why he had burnt it. Howard got his trenchcoat from the closet and put it on.

They walked out of the house and down the front steps to a Police Department car parked at the curb.

Howard wondered what was happening to Mary now? She hadn't meant to betray him, he was sure. Maybe it had been an accidental slip that the police had caught and questioned her about until she had broken down. Or maybe she had been so upset when they arrived that she had told them before she knew what she was doing. Howard cursed himself for not having taken more precautions about Mary, for not having sent her out of town. He had told Mary last night that he was going to do it today, just so it *wouldn't* come as a shock to her. How stupid he had been! How little he really understood her after all his efforts to understand! How much better if he had killed George and said nothing at all to her!

The car stopped and they got out. Howard had paid no attention to where they had been driving, and he did not try to see now. There was a big building in front of him, and he walked through the doorway with the two officers and then into a room that resembled a small courtroom where a police officer sat at a high desk, like a judge.

"Howard Quinn," one of the policemen announced.

The officer at the high desk looked down at him with interest. "Howard Quinn. The young man in a terrible hurry," he said with a sarcastic smile. "You're the Howard Quinn who knows Mary Purvis?"

"Yes."

"And George Frizell?"

"Yes," Howard murmured.

"I thought so. Your address tallies. I've just been talking to the homicide boys. They want to ask you some questions. You seem to be in trouble there, too. It's a busy evening for you, isn't it?"

Howard didn't quite understand. He looked around the room for Mary. There were two other policemen sitting on a bench against the wall and a man in a shabby suit dozing on another bench; but Mary was not in the room.

"Do you know why you're here tonight, Mr. Quinn?" the officer asked him in a hostile tone.

"Yes." Howard stared down at the base of the high desk. He felt that something within him was collapsing—a framework that had held him upright for the past several hours, but which had been imaginary all the time—his feeling that he had had a duty to perform in killing George Frizell, that he had been liberating the girl he loved and who loved him, that he had been ridding the world of an evil, hideous monster of a man. Now under the cold, professional eyes of the three policemen, Howard could see what he had done as they saw it—as the taking of a human life, nothing else. And the girl he had done it for had betrayed him! Whether Mary had wanted to or not, she had betrayed him. Howard covered his eyes with his hand.

"I can imagine you were upset by the murder of someone you knew, Mr. Quinn, but at a quarter to six you didn't know anything about that—or did you, by any chance? Was that why you were in such a hurry to get home or wherever you were going?"

Howard tried to figure out what the officer meant. His brain seemed paralyzed. He knew he had shot George at almost exactly 5:43. Was the officer still being sarcastic? Howard looked at him. He was a man of about forty with a chubby, alert face. His eyes were contemptuous.

"He was burning some clothes in his fireplace when we walked in on him, Captain," said the shorter policeman who was standing near Howard.

"Oh?" said the Captain. "*Why* were you burning clothes?"

He knew very well, Howard thought. He knew what he had burned and why, just as the two police officers knew.

"Whose clothes were you burning?" the Captain asked.

Howard still said nothing. The ironic questions infuriated him and shamed him at the same time.

"Mr. Quinn," the Captain said in a louder tone, "at a quarter to six this evening you knocked a man down in your car at the corner of Eighth Avenue and Sixty-eighth Street and drove on. Isn't that correct?"

Howard looked up at him, uncomprehending.

"*You were aware that you hit him, were you not?*" the Captain asked more loudly.

He was here for something else, Howard realized. Hit-and-run driving! "I—I don't—"

"Your victim isn't dead, if that'll make you more able to talk. But it's not your fault. He's in the hospital with a broken leg—an old man who can't afford a hospital!" The Captain scowled down at him. "I think you ought to be taken to see him. I think it would be good for you. You've committed one of the most shameful crimes a man can be guilty of—hit-and-run driving. If not for one woman who was quick enough to get your license number, we'd never have caught you."

Howard suddenly understood. The woman had made a mistake, maybe a mistake of only one figure in his license number—but it gave him an alibi. If he didn't take it, he was lost. There was too much against him, even if Mary had said nothing—the fact that he had left the store earlier than usual today, the hellish coincidence of the police walking in just as he was burning the coat. Howard looked up at the Captain's angry face. "I'm willing to go see the man," he said contritely.

"Take him to the hospital," the Captain said to the two policemen. "By the time you get back, the homicide boys'll be here. And incidentally, Mr. Quinn, you're being held on five thousand dollars' bail. If you don't want to spend the night here, you'd better get it. Do you want to try to raise it tonight?"

Mr. Luther, his boss, could get it for him tonight, Howard thought. "May I make a phone call?"

The Captain gestured toward a telephone on a table against the wall.

Howard looked up Mr. Luther's home number in the directory on the table and dialed it. Mrs. Luther answered. Howard knew her slightly, but without any police exchanges, he asked if he could speak to Mr. Luther. "Hello, Mr. Luther," he said. "I'd like to ask you a favor. I've had a bad accident. I need five thousand dollars for my bail ... No, I'm not hurt, but—could you write a check for me and send it over by a messenger?"

"I'll bring the check myself," Mr. Luther said. "Just sit tight. I'll get the company lawyer on it, if you need help. Don't take any lawyer they offer you, Howard. We've got Lyles, you know."

Howard thanked him. Mr. Luther's loyalty embarrassed him. Howard asked a police officer who was standing near him the address of the station, and gave it to Mr. Luther. Then he hung up and walked out with the two policemen who had been waiting for him.

They drove to a hospital in the West Seventies. One of the policemen inquired at the downstairs desk where Louis Rosasco was, and then they went up in an elevator.

The man was in a room by himself, propped up in bed with one leg in a cast that was suspended by cords from the ceiling. He was a gray man of about sixty-five or seventy with a long, seamed face and dark, deep-set eyes that looked extremely weary.

"Mr. Rosasco," said the taller police officer, "this is Howard Quinn, the man who knocked you down."

Mr. Rosasco nodded without much interest, though he kept his eyes on Howard.

"I'm very sorry," Howard said awkwardly. "I'll be glad to pay any bills you have, you can be sure of that." His car insurance would take care of the hospital bill, Howard thought. Then there'd be the matter of the court fine—at least a thousand dollars by the time he got through, but he'd manage it with some loans.

The man on the bed still said nothing to him. He looked groggy with sedatives.

The officer who had introduced them seemed dissatisfied because they had nothing else to say to each other. "Do you recognize the man, Mr. Rosasco?"

Mr. Rosasco shook his head. "I didn't see the driver. All I saw was a big black car coming down at me," he said slowly. "Hit the side of my leg—"

Howard set his teeth, waiting. His car was green, a light green. And it was not particularly big.

"It was a green car, Mr. Rosasco," the shorter police-man said, smiling. He was checking with a small yellow card he had taken from his pocket. "A green Pontiac sedan. You made a mistake."

"No, it was a black car," Mr. Rosasco said positively.

"Nope. Your car's green, isn't it, Quinn?"

Howard nodded once, stiffly.

"It was getting dark around six. You probably couldn't see very well," the cheerful officer said to Mr. Rosasco.

Howard watched Mr. Rosasco, holding his breath. For a moment Mr. Rosasco stared at the policemen, frowning, puzzled, and then his head fell back on the pillow. He was going to let it go. Howard relaxed a little.

"Guess you'd better get some sleep, Mr. Rosasco," the shorter officer said. "Don't worry about anything. Everything'll be taken care of."

The last thing Howard saw in the room was Mr. Rosasco's tired, rugged profile on the pillow, his eyes closed. The memory of his face stayed with Howard as he walked down the hall. His alibi . . .

When they got back to the station Mr. Luther had already arrived, and also a couple of men in civilian clothes—the men from homicide, Howard supposed. Mr. Luther came toward Howard, his round pink face troubled.

"What's this all about?" Mr. Luther asked. "Did you really hit somebody and drive on?"

Howard nodded, shamefacedly. "I wasn't quite sure I hit him. I should have stopped—but I didn't."

Mr. Luther looked at him reproachfully, but he was going to remain loyal, Howard thought.

"Well, I've given them the check for your bail," Mr. Luther said.

"Thank you, sir."

One of the men in civilian clothes walked up to Howard. He was a slender man with sharp blue eyes in a thin face. "I have some questions to ask you, Mr. Quinn. You're acquainted with Mary Purvis and George Frizell?"

"Yes."

"May I ask where you were tonight at twenty minutes to six?"

"I was—I was driving uptown. I was driving from the store where I work at Fifty-third and Seventh Avenue to my apartment on Seventy-first Street."

"And you hit a man at a quarter to six?"

"I did," Howard said.

The detective nodded. "You know that George Frizell was shot this evening at exactly eighteen minutes of six?"

The detective suspected him, Howard thought. What had Mary told them? If he only knew . . . But the Captain of police had not specifically said that George Frizell had been shot. Howard drew his brows together hard. "No," he said.

"He was. We talked to your girl friend. She says you did it."

Howard's heart stopped for a moment. He stared into the detective's questioning eyes. "That's just not true."

The detective shrugged. "She's plenty hysterical. But she's plenty positive, too."

"It just isn't true! I left the store—I have to report to the store I work for around five. I drove—" His voice broke. It was Mary who was shattering him—Mary.

"You're Mary Purvis's boy friend, aren't you?"

"Yes," Howard replied. "I can't—she must be—"

"Did you want Frizell out of the way?"

"I didn't kill him. I had nothing to do with it! I didn't even know he was dead!" Howard babbled.

"Frizell saw Mary quite a lot, didn't he? That's what I heard from both landladies. Did you ever think they might be in love with each other?"

"No. Of course not."

"You weren't jealous of George Frizell?"

"Of course not."

The detective's arched eyebrows had not once come down. His whole face was like a question mark. "No?" he asked sarcastically.

"Listen, Shaw," the police captain said, stepping down from his desk. "We know where Quinn was at a quarter of six. He might know who did it, but he didn't do it himself."

"Do you know who did it, Mr. Quinn?" the detective asked.

"No, I don't."

"Captain McCaffery tells me you were burning some clothes in your fireplace tonight. Were you burning a coat?"

Howard's head bobbed in a desperate nod. "I was burning a coat and a jacket, too. They were full of mothholes. I didn't want them in my closet any longer."

The detective put a foot on a straight chair and leaned closer to Howard. "It was a funny time to burn a coat, wasn't it? Just after you thought you might have knocked a man down in your car and maybe killed him? Whose coat were you burning? The murderer's? Maybe because there was a bullet hole in it?"

"No," Howard said.

"You didn't arrange with somebody to kill Frizell? Somebody who brought you his coat to get rid of?"

"No." Howard glanced at Mr. Luther, who was listening attentively. Howard stood up straighter.

"You didn't shoot Frizell, jump in your car, and rush home, knocking a man down on the way?"

"Shaw, that's impossible," Captain McCaffery put in. "We've got the exact times on this. You can't get from Thirty-fourth and Seventh to Sixty-eighth and Eighth in three minutes no matter how fast you drive! Face it!"

The detecitve kept his eyes on Howard. "Do you work for this man?" he asked, nodding toward Mr. Luther.

"Yes."

"What do you do?"

"I'm the Long Island salesman for William Luther Sporting Goods. I contact schools on Long Island and also place our goods in stores out there. I report to the Manhattan store at nine and at five." He recited it like a parrot. He felt weak in the knees. But his alibi was holding—like a stone wall.

"Okay," the detective said, taking his foot down from the chair and turning from Howard to the Captain. "We're still working on the case. It's still wide open for any news, any clues." He smiled at Howard, a cold smile of dismissal. Then he said, "By the way, have you ever seen this before?" He brought his hand out of his pocket with the little revolver from Bennington in his palm.

Howard frowned at it. "No, I haven't seen it before."

The man pocketed the gun. "We may want to talk to you again," he said with another faint smile.

Howard felt Mr. Luther's hand on his arm. They went out into the street.

"Who's George Frizell?" Mr. Luther asked.

Howard wet his lips. He felt very strange—as if he had just been hit over the head and his brain had gone numb. "A friend of a friend. A friend of a girl I know."

"And the girl? Mary Purvis, was it? Are you in love with her?"

Howard didn't answer. He looked down at the ground as he walked.

"Is she the one who accused you?"

"Yes," Howard said.

Mr. Luther's grip tightened on his arm. "You look like you could stand a drink ... Don't you want to go in?"

Howard saw that they were standing in front of a bar. He opened the door.

"She's probably very upset, you know," Mr. Luther said. "Women get like that. It was a friend of hers who was shot, wasn't it?"

Now it was Howard's tongue that was paralyzed, though his brain was spinning. He was thinking that he couldn't ever go back to work for Mr. Luther after this, that he couldn't trick a man like Mr. Luther. ... Mr. Luther was talking on and on. Howard picked up the little jigger glass and drank half of it. Mr. Luther was telling him that Lyles would get him off as easily as he could possibly be got off.

"You've got to be more careful, Howard. You're impulsive, I've always known that. It has its good and bad sides, of course. But tonight—I have a feeling you knew you might have hit that man."

"I've got to make a phone call," Howard said. "Excuse me for a minute." He hurried to the booth at the back of the bar. He had to hear it from her. She had to be home. If she weren't home, he'd drop dead, right there in the phone booth. He'd explode.

"Hello." It was Mary's voice, dull and lifeless.

"Hello, Mary, it's me. You didn't—what did you say to the police?"

"I told them," Mary said slowly, "that you killed my friend."

"Mary!"

"I hate you."

"Mary, you don't mean that!" he cried out. But she did mean it and he knew it.

"I loved him and I needed him and you killed him," she said. "I hate you."

He clenched his teeth, letting the words echo in his brain. The police weren't going to get him. She couldn't do that to him, anyway. He hung up.

Then he was standing at the bar, and Mr. Luther's calm voice was going on as if it had never stopped while Howard telephoned.

"People have to pay, that's all," Mr. Luther was saying. "People have to pay for their mistakes and not make them again. . . . You know I think a lot of you, Howard. You'll live through this all right." A pause. "Did you just talk to Miss Purvis?"

"I couldn't reach her," Howard said.

Ten minutes later he had left Mr. Luther and was riding downtown in a taxi. He had told the driver to stop at Thirty-seventh and Seventh, so that in case he was being followed by the police, he could just walk on from there and keep clear of his car.

He got out at Thirty-seventh Street, paid the driver, and glanced around him. He saw no car that seemed to be trailing him. He walked in the direction of Thirty-fifth Street. The two straight ryes with Mr. Luther had braced him. He walked quickly, with his head up, and yet in a curious, frightening way he felt utterly lost. His green Pontiac was standing at the curb where he had left it. He got out his keys and opened the door.

He had a ticket—he saw it as soon as he sat down behind the wheel. He reached around and pulled it from under the windshield wiper. A parking ticket. A small matter, he thought, so small that he smiled. Driving homeward, it occurred to him that the police had made a very silly slip in not relieving him of his driving license when they had him at the station, and he began to laugh at this. The ticket lay beside him on the seat. It looked so petty, so innocuous compared to what he had been through, that he laughed at the ticket, too.

Then just as suddenly, his eyes filled with tears. The wound that Mary's words had made in him was still wide open, had not yet begun to hurt, he knew. And before it began to hurt, he tried to fortify himself. If Mary persisted in accusing him, he'd demand that she be examined by a psychiatrist. She wasn't completely sane, he'd always known that. He'd tried to get her to go to a psychiatrist about George, but she'd always refused. She didn't have a chance with her accusations, because he had an alibi—a perfect alibi. But if she *did* persist—

Mary had really encouraged him to kill George—he was sure of that now. She had really put the idea into his head with a thousand things she had hinted. *There's no way out, Howard, unless he dies.* So he had killed him—for *her*—and Mary had turned on him. But the police weren't going to get him.

There was a stretch of about fifteen feet of parking space near his apartment house, and Howard slid in next to the curb. He locked the car, then went into his house.

The smell of burned cloth still lingered in his apartment, and it struck him as odd, because he felt that so much time had passed. He scanned the parking ticket again in the better light.

He saw suddenly that his alibi was gone.

The ticket had been written at 5:45—exactly.